CORRUPTED BY SIN

TOUCH OF EVIL - BOOK FIVE

KENNEDY LAYNE

KENNEDY LAYNE PUBLISHING, INC.

Copyright © 2022 by Kennedy Layne

Cover Designer: Sweet 'N Spicy Designs

ALL RIGHTS RESERVED: The unauthorized reproduction or distribution of this copyrighted work is illegal. Criminal copyright infringement is investigated by the FBI and is punishable by up to 5 years in federal prison and a fine of $250,000.

All characters and events in this book are fictitious. Any resemblance to actual persons living or dead is strictly coincidental.

Jeffrey — Break out the salted caramel candles and the pumpkin-spiced coffee...our favorite time of year is almost here!

Cole — You bring the popcorn, because it's almost time for our annual scary movie marathon!

About the Book

A chilling confession unleashes deadly secrets in the next riveting thriller by USA Today Bestselling Author Kennedy Layne...

In downtown D.C., an emergency surgery is performed on a prominent psychiatrist following a multi-car accident. The ICU nurse on duty has heard many interesting utterances from her groggy patients over the years. Unfortunately, nothing can prepare her for the disturbing revelation that surfaces from her current patient as he regains consciousness from a drug-induced state.

Former FBI consultant Brooklyn Sloane is well acquainted with how doubt and fear can ruin a person's life. It's that reason she takes on a case no one else wants to touch. A respected nurse believes that her patient is a serial killer. A doctor held in the highest esteem by his colleagues, admired by his friends, adored by his family, and who is now claiming his innocence.

As each layer of the investigation is pulled back, something sinister begins to emerge from the darkness. Brook and her team eventually find themselves on the brink of a terrifying discovery that will change the dynamics of the case. The dark and twisted truth will ultimately shake D.C.'s high society and shatter lives forever.

Contents

1. Chapter One — 1
2. Chapter Two — 8
3. Chapter Three — 22
4. Chapter Four — 31
5. Chapter Five — 41
6. Chapter Six — 53
7. Chapter Seven — 66
8. Chapter Eight — 75
9. Chapter Nine — 82
10. Chapter Ten — 96
11. Chapter Eleven — 103
12. Chapter Twelve — 110
13. Chapter Thirteen — 118
14. Chapter Fourteen — 123
15. Chapter Fifteen — 131
16. Chapter Sixteen — 136

17.	Chapter Seventeen	152
18.	Chapter Eighteen	161
19.	Chapter Nineteen	171
20.	Chapter Twenty	176
21.	Chapter Twenty-One	182
22.	Chapter Twenty-Two	187
23.	Chapter Twenty-Three	195
24.	Chapter Twenty-Four	200
25.	Chapter Twenty-Five	208
26.	Chapter Twenty-Six	217
27.	Chapter Twenty-Seven	224
28.	Chapter Twenty-Eight	231
29.	Chapter Twenty-Nine	240
30.	Chapter Thirty	248
31.	Chapter Thirty-One	253
32.	Chapter Thirty-Two	260
33.	Chapter Thirty-Three	266
34.	Chapter Thirty-Four	270
35.	Chapter Thirty-Five	281
36.	Chapter Thirty-Six	292
	Other Books By Kennedy Layne	296
	About the Author	302

Chapter One

Brooklyn Walsh
December 2005
Tuesday — 7:14am

"THIS IS CRAZY."

Brook couldn't agree more with her best friend.

They had done some foolish things over the course of their short lives, but this ranked right up there with the time that they had climbed down the tree right outside of her bedroom window.

Two stories high, in the rain.

Needless to say, neither one of them had made it to Nate Brimmer's keg party last year. They had both been grounded for a month, and that was *after* the emergency room visit for Sally's broken wrist.

"We technically aren't doing anything wrong," Brook tried to point out, but Sally wasn't buying a word of it. Her hands tightened on the steering wheel as the snow flurries turned into a huge white sheet in front of the vehicle. "You're a good driver,

Sally. Plus, you said yourself that your mom had new snow tires put on the car last week."

They had lied to Sally's mom about why they needed to borrow her car. If Mrs. Pearson ever found out that they had driven to Peoria in the snow, Sally wouldn't be driving anywhere for the rest of the school year. Brook needed to make sure that didn't happen.

"Once we see where Jacob is going, I promise you that we will drive straight back to Morton."

Brook decided to stop talking when a tractor trailer passed them on the highway. They didn't even have the radio tuned into their favorite station. For some reason, they had turned it off when they were waiting for her brother to leave the house. It was as if they thought that he could hear the music three houses down. Brook had Sally park in front of Mr. Mason's house just to be safe.

There was something wrong with Jacob.

Really wrong, although Brook hadn't told Sally the extent of what she believed Jacob had done.

How could a sister believe that her brother might have murdered someone? Saying something so horrendous out loud might give truth to the statement, and Brook couldn't bring herself to do it. She just couldn't, which was why Sally was only aware of half the story. She thought that they were out to prove that Jacob was stealing money from their parents, and not earning it at the so-called job that he claimed to have in Peoria.

Sally had no idea that Brook believed her brother had killed Pamela Murray, a young girl who had gone to their school. As a matter of fact, her body had been found five years ago, almost to the day.

"How sure are you that Jacob is stealing from your parents?" Sally asked once the tractor trailer had passed and given them some breathing room. She had even relaxed her grip on the steering wheel now that the white sheet of snow had cleared.

They were left with a clear view of Jacob's car. "I mean, don't you think they would have noticed that they were missing money?"

"Jacob is smart." Brook turned one of the vents toward her. The heat was finally at full strength. She'd been so cold lately. The stress over getting caught had made it hard to relax, so the warmth of the air was most welcome. "If Mom sends him to pick up milk, he'll add on ten dollars at the checkout counter. He'll bring home milk, and no one notices that it cost more than it should. If Dad asks Jacob to get cash out of the ATM, Jacob will add twenty dollars to the amount and then say that he forgot to get a receipt. I don't think that my dad ever checks the account against his withdrawals."

Jacob had chosen not to go to college. He claimed that he was working at a car dealership in Peoria, but Brook was pretty confident that her brother had no such job. If she could prove to her parents that her brother was lying, then there was a good chance they would believe her when she told them about the sketch book that she'd found in his desk drawer. More specifically, they would believe her about the drawing that depicted Pamela Murray's face being...

Brook quickly swallowed back the bile that hit the back of her throat as she recalled the memory of finding Jacob's sketchbook.

"Are you okay?" Sally asked as she quickly glanced in Brook's direction. "You don't look so good."

"Just getting a bit car sick," Brook said dismissively, lowering her arm. She hadn't even realized that she'd pressed the back of her hand to her mouth. "Thanks for doing this with me."

Brook had hatched the plan over a week ago. Since they were out of school for Christmas break, it had been easy to convince her mother to let her stay overnight at Sally's house.

"What are best friends for?" Sally asked as she turned her attention toward the road. "What's the plan, anyway? If Jacob pulls into the car dealership, do we keep driving?"

Brook had also turned her attention to the car that her parents had given to Jacob at his high school graduation last year. The four-door sedan wasn't new, by any means. The Ford Taurus was ten years old and had belonged to her father for as long as Brook could remember.

"Look." Brook pointed to the right blinker on Jacob's car. "Your brother is turning off the highway."

Sally sighed with relief as she flipped her own turn signal on so that the car behind them would know they were taking the exit. She preferred driving back roads at a lesser speed, which came in quite handy right now. She wasn't following Jacob too closely, and another car had swerved in front of them at the last second. When they came to the stoplight, the buffer prevented Jacob from spotting them in his rearview mirror.

"Shouldn't he have taken the next exit?" Sally asked as she sat a bit straighter in her seat. "Plus, he's making a right. I know this area, because my brother's math tutor lives out this way."

Brook didn't have to remind Sally to hang back, especially after the car in front of them had turned left. No one was between them and Jacob now, and he would probably recognize Mrs. Pearson's vehicle. While Sally might not have been happy about it, Brook's tension eased when the snow picked up a bit more.

"I knew that he didn't work for any car dealership." Brook rested her hand on the dashboard when she caught sight of Jacob's taillights. He was slowing down again, this time to make a lefthand turn. The road seemed to split two cornfields in half. "Don't turn, Sally. Keep going straight. We can make a U-turn at the next intersection and catch up that way."

Thankfully, Sally had been driving slow enough that Jacob had already been mid-turn when they passed him. Jacob would have been paying attention to the road instead of a passing car.

"Where do you think he's going?" Sally asked as she pressed the brake pedal. She turned on her left blinker as she maneuvered her mom's car into the far lefthand lane. The light was red, so they had no choice but to come to a full stop. "I don't like this, Brook."

Brook shifted in her seat so that she could look out the back window. Her hope of finding out where her brother went five days a week was dying with each passing second. She quickly shot a glance at the red light. Why was it taking so long to turn green?

"We aren't going to find him," Sally finally said a minute later. She drummed her fingers on the steering wheel. "Brook?"

Brook sighed in defeat.

It didn't matter that Sally was finally able to make a U-turn, because it was clear that the weather was turning worse. It was dangerous for them to be on the roads this far from home. Sally's mom believed that they'd remained in town. One of the boutiques was having a jewelry sale for the holidays, and the sale started today.

Sally had convinced her mom that she and Brook wanted matching bracelets, which was going to be their gifts to one another for Christmas. When Mrs. Pearson had asked why they wanted to leave so early, Sally had said that they had wanted to be the first customers so that no one else bought the jewelry.

To make the story even more believable, they had thrown into the discussion their desire to visit a friend who worked at Eli's Coffee Shop. That part had been true, and the two of them had eaten the blueberry muffins while waiting for Jacob to come out of the house.

"Just head back home, Sally. I shouldn't have talked you into doing this, anyway."

Brook leaned back against her seat and stared out the window.

She was left to wonder if she would ever be able to prove that her brother was a liar.

Worse, she believed that he was a cold-blooded murderer.

She'd been in denial for so long, but that had all changed when she figured out that Jacob had been stealing from their parents. Brook technically hadn't lied to Sally. There *had* been a bit of truth mixed in with her fib.

The more Brook thought back to Jacob's behavior when Pamela Murray's remains had been found, the greater her belief became that there was something really wrong with her brother.

Unfortunately, she had no proof.

"I'm going to talk to Mom and Dad," Brook stated as she reversed her mindset. Maybe her parents would believe her instead of Jacob. "I've decided to tell them, Sally."

"My brother would kill me if I ever ratted him out," Sally muttered as she slowed the car down so that they could take the onramp back to the highway. "What are you going to say to them?"

"I'm going to tell them to check their receipts." Brook was also going to call the car dealership when they got home. She would prove that Jacob was lying, and then maybe she would fill them in on the rest. She debated sharing her theories regarding Pamela Murray with Sally, but something was holding her back. She would come clean once she had more proof. "They'll have evidence that Jacob is stealing, and then they can figure out what to do."

"Like what? Jacob is twenty years old, Brook. Your parents won't call the police, because then your brother would be arrested," Sally pointed out as she once again straightened in her seat. The snow was coming down heavier than before, and the traffic was starting to slow down. "My parents would never do something like that, and I can't believe yours would, either. I guess they could kick him out of the house, though."

Brook shouldn't want something like to happen, but she couldn't deny being relieved at the possibility of not having to look over her shoulder all the time. It wasn't healthy to live in a house where she was constantly on edge. Didn't she deserve to spend the rest of her high school years without the stress of thinking her brother had killed someone?

If she was honest with herself, the reason that she wanted her parents to know about the money was so that they would look deeper into his life. Maybe then they would find the sketchbook.

Maybe then they would believe her that Jacob was capable of murder.

Chapter Two

Brooklyn Sloane
December 2022
Thursday — 5:34pm

The loud crowd nearly drowned out the holiday music that was spilling from the overhead speakers of the pub. Most of the patrons were glued to the televisions that had been strategically placed in specific corners, and every single one of them was tuned into the World Cup.

The world's largest fútbol tournament was being hosted in Qatar this time around, and the U.S. Men's National Soccer team had qualified to participate. Since more than one game was being played throughout the eight stadiums scattered along the eastern side of the country, it was easier to have the TVs muted while keeping everyone in the holiday spirit. Celebratory moods usually meant more alcohol consumption over the course of an evening.

A round of applause broke out just as Brook spotted her group sitting at a table in the back corner of the venue.

CHAPTER TWO

She hadn't even taken three steps toward them when someone sitting at the bar reached out and touched her arm. She'd thought it was simply a mistake, but then she'd heard her name being called out above the noise.

"Brooklyn Sloane?"

Brook refrained from answering the woman right away. If she was a member of the press or an investigative journalist wanting a comment from the sister of a notorious serial killer, there would be no point in prolonging their conversation. As a matter of fact, Brook came very close to walking away without saying a single word. She changed her mind after quickly scrutinizing the woman's unique uniform.

"And you are?"

Brook had to raise her voice to be heard, but she didn't want to be caught leaning in and potentially being made a mark. They *were* in downtown D.C., after all. Crime had risen lately, and she'd purposefully left her purse at the office located around the corner just to be safe. She'd recently bought a cute card holder that fit perfectly onto the back of her cell phone cover, which was currently in the left pocket of her dress coat.

Fortunately, the distinctive blue scrubs indicated that the woman wasn't looking to pickpocket anyone.

"My name is Millie Gwinn." Another round of sudden exclamations went through the pub, though this time the patrons weren't pleased with whatever outcome had occurred on one or more of the screens. "I've been trying to reach you at your office. I'm sorry. I know that I shouldn't be ambushing you right now, but I'm desperate."

Brook was jostled from behind, but she somehow managed to hold her own. The brief respite gave her time to weigh her options.

She was well-acquainted with Millie Gwinn, though not of a personal nature. Every day this week, the woman had phoned the offices of S&E Investigations, Inc. Millie had left numerous messages with the firm's administrative assistant, Kate Lin, in regard to having secondhand knowledge of a murder. In fact, Millie had been very insistent with her claims.

Brook had purposefully instructed Kate to refer Millie to the local police.

S&E Investigations, Inc. was a private firm that specialized in solving cold cases. While there had been a few active investigations over the course of the past year where certain state police departments had requested their assistance, such an undertaking hadn't been the primary goal when she'd established the business. Their current case involved the death of a young man who had been murdered sixteen years ago while attempting to hitchhike from the East Coast to the West Coast of the United States. The police had little to go on back then. The lonely stretch of highway where the body had been found had no cameras at the time, and the case had eventually been shelved to collect dust.

Brook had agreed a little over a year ago to partner up with a former Commanding General Marine Forces Special Operations Command (MARSOC) by the name of Graham Elliott. He was technically her silent partner in their freshly established business. However, he'd recently made known to her that he wouldn't mind if their personal relationship took a more intimate turn.

She wasn't so sure a change in their interpersonal status was the brightest of ideas.

Her life had changed drastically since she'd been a consultant for the FBI. That was technically an understatement, but the holidays were closing in. She'd found herself in a giving mood, which was why she'd hesitated to walk away from Ms. Gwinn.

In truth, Brook's life was nothing like it had been during her tenure with the Bureau. Sure, she still profiled unsubs, also known as unknown subjects, but there had only been a handful

CHAPTER TWO

of times that Brook had been in the field with the FBI. Such an occasion detailed by her supervisor had been rare.

As for her personal life, it had always been nonexistent.

She had spent almost every waking moment outside of work pursuing leads on her brother. Yet tonight, she was joining her newly assembled team for drinks at a local pub while contemplating talking to a client over an alcoholic beverage.

No, her life was nothing like it had been before.

"Ms. Gwinn, I—"

"Please, Ms. Sloane," Millie said with utter despair. She tightened her grip on the purse that was in her lap. "My employers don't believe me, my friends and family think that I'm making a big deal out of nothing, and the police have even suggested that I'm some type of lunatic seeking attention. All I'm asking is that you hear me out. Please."

By this time, the bartender had made his way down the long line of patrons. Over the past five weeks, Brook had joined her team for their Thursday night get-togethers. It was a bit out of character for her, but she'd found herself enjoying the downtime. Such a drastic change in her routine didn't mean she had forgone her somewhat overdeveloped sense of situational awareness.

Being the sister of a serial killer hadn't done her any favors in the trust department. At least, that was the initial reason that Brook had given herself while conducting several cursory background checks on the staff of the pub.

Hugh Steger had worked as a bartender for the establishment for the past three years while putting himself through law school. He still had another two years before graduation, but she was confident that he had the intellect and determination to finish his degree. He also hadn't blinked an eye when she and the team had chosen this particular pub as their regular Thursday night stress relief station.

Brook held up a hand and signaled that she would buy the next round for the table, catching Hugh's immediate nod of affirmation.

"This isn't how I usually conduct my professional business, Ms. Gwinn," Brook explained as she glanced toward the far corner of the pub. Her team wasn't expecting to engage in shoptalk tonight, but they were the ones who constantly reminded her that she was far too set in her ways. It wouldn't hurt to throw them a curveball. "My colleagues have a table in the corner. I can't promise you anything, but we will hear you out and help point you in the right direction."

Brook led the way through the crowded pub, not needing to wait to see if that scenario was agreeable with Millie. If the woman had gone to so much trouble to establish a face-to-face meeting with the owner of S&E Investigations, she wouldn't give up such an opportunity and simply leave.

While Brook understood what doubt could do to a person, whatever Millie believed she knew about a murder obviously hadn't been substantial enough for the police to open an investigation. Plus, it was unlikely that the woman would want to pay a high-end firm out of her own pocket when it didn't even sound as if the victim was a close relative. Kate had specifically asked that question in one of the previous phone calls.

"Is everything okay?"

The question had come from Theo Neville, a former FBI agent. He was focused on Brook's facial expression for any indication the situation was otherwise. She gave him a single nod in answer to alleviate his concern.

A severe injury in the field had resulted in the loss of his right eye. Notwithstanding, he'd almost certainly noticed her encounter with Ms. Gwinn at the bar moments before. If he had stayed with the Bureau, he would have been relegated to desk duty for the rest of his career. He'd opted to work for S&E

Investigations instead, and as far as she was aware, he hadn't regretted the change in jobs.

"Millie Gwinn, these are my colleagues—Theo Neville, Sylvie Deering, Bit Nowacki, and Kate Lin." Brook paused while her team all nodded their greetings. She also caught the way Kate's eyes had widened with recognition. "Kate was who you spoke with on numerous occasions this past week."

Theo had quickly vacated his chair and motioned for Millie to have a seat. He claimed the empty one at the end of the table while Brook removed her dress coat and draped it over the back of her own. She made sure to take out her cell phone with the leather card holder to place on the table in front of her. As a matter of fact, two tables had been pushed together so that they could all sit comfortably without knocking elbows.

Bit was to Brook's right, Kate was at the other end of the table, and Sylvie was sitting across from Bit. That meant their guest was seated directly in front of Brook, while Theo made himself comfortable to her left.

"If I may, how is it that you knew we would be here?" Brook asked as she spotted a waitress heading their way with two pitchers of beer. While Brook preferred a sparkling white wine, she usually opted to be more casual when drinking with the group. "Why didn't you simply come up to our offices?"

Millie Gwinn still hadn't bothered to take off her winter jacket, and she held onto her purse as if it was a lifeline. Her brown hair had been pulled back with a clip, though there was no hiding the natural curl of the strands. Her bangs were slightly lower than her thin eyebrows, enough so that her lashes hit them every time that she raised her eyes. She wore no makeup, her nails were neatly trimmed, and she wasn't wearing a wedding ring.

What Brook found most interesting was that she kept checking her surroundings, as if she believed that she was being followed by someone.

"I was about to open the door to your building when Ms. Deering stepped out with the rest of the group. I assumed that your offices had closed for the evening."

It didn't come as a shock that Millie had recognized Sylvie. A couple of months ago, Sylvie had been abducted by a serial killer who S&E Investigations had been investigating, and her face had been splashed across national news networks for close to a week. It was also no secret that the firm had been garnering the attention of the press for various other reasons over the past year. Truthfully, the past month had been a godsend with a cold case that had posed next to no danger to the team.

"I followed them here, hoping that you would join them at some point," Millie explained with a reluctant shrug. "I'm sorry. I truly am, but no one believes me. I'm hoping that you will be able to recognize that I'm being sincere."

By *you*, Millie meant everyone at the table.

Everyone fell silent as the waitress set two pitchers of draft beer down onto the table. Bit, who was the firm's technical guru, began to pour the malted beverage into several chilled glasses. The first of which he proffered to their guest.

He wore a pair of faded jeans with a long-sleeved t-shirt sporting one of the Marvel superheroes and a grey-knitted hat. Whereas Sylvie had blonde hair that was usually pulled back into a bun, Bit's strands were a bit darker and on the longer side.

"Ms. Gwinn?" Bit was still holding up one of the chilled glasses in her direction, but she quickly shook her head. "Are you sure? This is hands down my favorite beer that this pub has on tap."

"No, thank you," Millie murmured as her gaze darted toward the front of the pub. She then focused her attention on Brook. "Dr. David Kolsby is one of the hospital's top psychiatrists. He's a serial killer, and he needs to be stopped."

The crowd of the pub groaned in unison, their reaction to what had taken place on one of the televisions covering up Bit's mutter about how they were all going to need another pitcher or two. Theo ran a hand over his chin as he processed Millie's words, though his black eye patch didn't move from its secure position. As for Sylvie, her black-rimmed glasses had slipped down the bridge of her nose as her head had whipped in Millie's direction.

"I'm sorry. Are you talking about *the* Dr. David Kolsby?" Sylvie asked before adjusting her glasses and shifting in her chair so that she had a better view of Millie. "The one who made national headlines last year when he talked a man down from the ledge of the hospital?"

Brook vaguely recalled the news coverage of that event.

Unfortunately, such tragic occurrences were almost commonplace in cities such as Washington D.C.

"Yes," Millie replied, once more glancing over Brook's shoulder toward the front entrance of the pub. "*That* Dr. David Kolsby. He was in a very serious car accident a few weeks ago."

"The multi-car pileup on the Beltway?" Theo asked for clarification.

Millie nodded her response to his question.

"Dr. Kolsby had some very significant injuries that required immediate surgery. I won't go into specifics, other than to say that he was in an induced coma for nearly forty-eight hours. I was his ICU nurse when they began to gradually bring him out of anesthesia, and..." Millie visibly swallowed and glanced down at her hands. The grip on her purse had turned her knuckles white. "Dr. Kolsby repeatedly said that he had killed someone. At first, I thought that he was referring to the car accident. I continued to reassure him that no one had died from the collision, but nothing I said seemed to calm him down."

"I take it there is more to the story."

Brook didn't like having her back to the door. She almost always sat facing any entrance, but she'd been late joining the others for drinks. Seeing as Theo and Sylvie also shared her outlook when it came to situational awareness, they had been the ones to claim those specific chairs.

Fortunately, Sylvie had also taken notice with the way Millie kept glancing in the direction of the bar. The former FBI analyst had as close to an eidetic memory as one could get, which meant that she would likely notice if something was amiss.

"Dr. Kolsby continued to say how he liked to watch the life drain from the women's eyes, and that no one would ever find their bodies. Plural." Millie inhaled a rather shaky breath, and Brook didn't get the sense that the woman was lying. "His laugh finally faded, but it was a horrible sound that I will never forget. I didn't misunderstand what was being said during that time, and I don't believe for a second that Dr. Kolsby was dreaming or had an overactive imagination. For that matter, I have never been accused of having an overactive imagination. I also don't consider myself dramatic. Dr. Kolsby killed someone. Several someones, and I wouldn't be able to live with myself if I didn't warn people. You can help stop him."

It was apparent that Millie's family, friends, coworkers, and the police had all attempted to excuse away Dr. Kolsby's alleged confession as drug-addled nonsense. Someone in his position also carried the respect of his peers.

Brook was a firm believer that people should stay in their lanes of expertise. She wasn't familiar with the medical field, so she had no idea the reaction that patients had to anesthesia. To keep a patient in an induced coma was almost certainly a complicated process, and she couldn't imagine that every patient reacted to the medication in the same manner.

"My father works for the CDC," Kate said cautiously, as if she wasn't sure she should contribute to the conversation. She'd proven on a few occasions that she could be beneficial to an investigation, although she'd yet to be allowed in the field. Brook nodded for her to continue. "Anesthesia isn't a truth serum. It doesn't force someone to tell his or her darkest secret."

"I've been told that a lot recently, too," Millie replied wryly. "And while I do agree with you, this was different."

"How so?" Sylvie asked.

"I'm pretty sure that Dr. Kolsby thought that I was one of the women who he had killed. One of his victims." Millie shifted uncomfortably in her seat. "He was almost frightened when he first saw my face. As I've already told you, I originally believed he'd assumed someone had died during the car accident. It soon became very clear to me that he meant something else entirely different."

Brook noticed that Sylvie was subconsciously rubbing her right wrist. She still had physical scars from when she'd been abducted by an unstable male subject. He had truly believed that her soul had been possessed by another simply due to her having blonde hair and blue eyes. To hear that another individual might have been mistaken due to her physical features had to be difficult.

"I know who you are," Millie declared as she straightened her shoulders. She was speaking directly to Brook. "Your real name is Brooklyn Walsh."

On the plus side, Millie was no longer focused on the front entrance. She had tilted her chin slightly in an upward angle, as if she was ready to engage in battle. No one could say that she didn't have grit.

"I saw the interview that you gave at the beginning of the year," Millie disclosed with no chagrin. "Your brother is a serial killer, and he is the reason that you became a profiler. The reporter asked why you didn't say anything to your parents sooner, and your response was that you were afraid they would doubt you. It was your word against his. Well, it's my word against a prominent psychiatrist. Not to mention they have claimed that I'm in violation of my pledge as a nurse and probably a dozen different HIPAA violations. I'm not, by the way. I have been very careful with my words regarding Dr. Kolsby's medical care. The bottom line is that you were right. No one believes me."

Brook didn't respond to the bait.

Instead, she made the calculated decision to savor the malt beverage that Bit had poured for her earlier. She needed a moment to form her response.

Brook *had* given an interview at the beginning of the year, but that had solely been to draw her brother out of hiding. There had been drawbacks, of course. The surname that she'd chosen to take at the age of eighteen had been made public, her life had been placed under a microscope, and her face had been splashed across every television station in the nation. Her decision to grant such an interview had upended her life, but she didn't regret her choice. It had been her way of taking control of the narrative.

Millie Gwinn was attempting to do the same thing in her own way, but good intentions didn't always yield the desired results. There were several reasons why S&E Investigations wasn't the right avenue for Millie.

First and foremost, they were a private firm.

Their revenue usually came from personal clients who wanted to procure closure or law enforcement agencies who were seeking consultation for what was usually a high-profile case.

Second, the firm currently had a cold case that would no doubt spill over into the new year. They were being paid for their time and resources, and it wouldn't be fair to their client to drop everything in order to go on a fishing expedition.

"I *do* believe you heard your patient confess to murder, Ms. Gwinn." Brook carefully set her glass down on the table. She licked her lips to remove any excess foam. "My professional opinion remains the same, though. This is a police matter. You mentioned that you filed a report with them. Regardless that the officer who you spoke with indicated that you were simply trying to garner attention from such claims, it is still his or her duty to follow through with a thorough investigation."

Millie finally released her hold on the purse in her lap. She used the zipper to open the main area. In seconds, she had produced a single piece of paper and slapped it down on the table.

"Is this thorough enough in your opinion?" Millie asked, her opinion obviously disagreeing with such a premise. "Officer Hadley Soerig spoke with Dr. Kolsby, who in turn stated that he didn't recall confessing to such crimes. He then suggested that the stress of my job might have caused me to make such horrific allegations. The investigation has since been closed, and I am now required to attend weekly sessions with a therapist until my employers decide otherwise. Have I mentioned that I am no longer working in the ICU? I've been moved down to the rehabilitation unit."

Sylvie grimaced as she reached for the piece of paper. It didn't take her long to peruse the contents, and Brook didn't need to inquire about the authenticity of Millie's summation.

"Please tell me that the therapist isn't the psychiatrist in question," Theo said right after he had brought his chair closer to the table. "Talk about awkward."

"No," Millie replied as she shot him a relieved glance. "I have an appointment set up on Monday with a psychologist. It's not like I have a choice in the matter. I could very well lose my job over this if I don't follow their recommendations. I'm seriously considering handing in my resignation and working in a doctor's office."

"Does your appointment have to be with someone affiliated with your hospital?" Kate asked as she leaned forward on her elbows so that Millie could hear her. "As I mentioned before, my father works for the CDC. I know firsthand that they support one another. Usually, that's not a bad thing. In this case, I don't know if I would be comfortable speaking with one of Dr. Kolsby's colleagues."

Kate had a very valid point. If Millie had been their client, Brook would have suggested the same thing. Only Millie wasn't their client, and Brook could only continue to point the nurse in the right direction.

"I'm going to be brutally honest with you, Ms. Gwinn."

Brook sensed the weight of everyone's stares, and she regretted hearing Millie out in front of the team. The meeting shouldn't have taken place at all. It was evident that the team was breaking down under the nurse's story. So much so that Bit had been on his cell phone for the past few minutes. Brook didn't want to know if he'd found anything, because then it would be left up to her whether or not she shared those details with the police. It was best not to get involved in something that was beyond the scope of their mission statement.

"There isn't much that can be done right now. From what you've already shared with us, it's clear that you fulfilled your duties as Dr. Kolsby's nurse during his time in ICU. You've spoken to your employers and the police about your suspicions of ongoing criminal behavior. Your obligations have been met. Truthfully, there isn't much else that you can do that hasn't already been done."

Theo had been the one to follow Millie's stare, which had once again been diverted over Brook's shoulder toward the entrance of the pub.

"Unless, of course, there's something that you're not telling us."

All curious gazes landed on Millie.

Even Bit had lowered his cell phone in anticipation of additional details.

"Would you believe me?"

"Yes." Brook's affirmative reply had nothing to do with trust. She simply had a talent for reading people, and Millie Gwinn came across as a rational human being. That didn't mean Brook wouldn't tread with caution. "What is it that you are withholding from us?"

"I'm pretty sure that someone has been following me the last few days," Millie revealed, her eyes filling up with tears. She quickly got her emotions under control. "I can't prove it. I technically haven't seen anyone. And no, before you ask, I didn't inform Officer Soerig or anyone else of my suspicions. Everyone already believes that I've overreacted, and I won't have them thinking that I'm crying wolf. I know that you're a private firm. I also know that I most likely couldn't afford your fees. Ms. Sloane, I'm here because you are my last hope."

Chapter Three

Brooklyn Sloane
December 2022
Friday — 5:48am

The green light evenly scanned Brook's iris to trip the locks on the double glass door entrance of S&E Investigations, Inc. The biometric scanner was one measure of the multilayered security system that Bit had installed for the firm. Only those who had approval to enter the offices were in the system, and any other guest needed to be buzzed in by Kate. Basically, everyone on the team had the ability to unlock the main entrance from their electronic tablets.

The faint sound of the lock being disengaged allowed her to open one of the doors. Both her purse and the soft leather bag that served as her briefcase were strapped over her right shoulder. She also carried a large caramel macchiato in her left hand while a small tote bag that contained her black high heels hung from her right forearm. She probably should have driven into work, but walking two blocks from her condo wearing winter boots had been easier.

CHAPTER THREE

Ever since her brother had tried to brutally murder a reporter back in May, Brook hadn't needed to keep the same daily routine. She'd known that Jacob had been monitoring her comings and goings before then, and she'd intentionally been trying to draw him out. She was almost certain that her decision to do so had been having the desired effect, too. Unfortunately, certain events had unfolded that had been too much for Jacob to resist.

Her brother was no longer in Washington D.C.

Brook couldn't explain how she knew that detail, but he was somewhere out west searching for Sarah Evanston—the only victim to have ever survived one of his vicious attacks. She was currently in witness protection after having received multiple facial surgeries to try and restore what remained of her face. There hadn't been much left to work with, and Brook couldn't imagine the pain the woman had suffered during her recovery. More surgeries were no doubt on the horizon, which meant that Sarah Evanston would have to remain in one place for at least a couple of years.

Jacob would know that small piece of information, and he would use it to his advantage. Brook knew her brother better than anyone, and there wasn't a chance in hell that he would allow one of his victims to get the best of him.

She grimaced when the handle of her tote bag got caught by the silver handle.

"Do you need a hand?"

The male voice behind her wasn't unexpected, though she had found herself somewhat taken aback by Kyle Paulson's presence in the downstairs lobby. He was one of the portfolio managers for the hedge fund across the hall. The two businesses shared the floor, including a public restroom that was nestled into a hidden hallway right outside the heavy wooden doors of the financial firm.

Before Brook could respond, Kyle had stepped forward and helped to unhook the strap of her tote bag from the door handle. She usually went out of her way to avoid conversations or run-ins of any kind with the hedge fund's employees. She preferred to maintain a professional distance.

S&E Investigations had opened their doors at relatively the same time that she'd given an interview and all but bared her personal life to every household in the country. Their curiosity was expected, but that didn't mean she had to feed into their conspiracy theories.

"Thank you," Brook murmured as she was finally free to stand to her full height of five feet and five inches. Her winter boots didn't quite give her the additional height she was used to in her heels, but Kyle Paulson was maybe only five inches taller. Hoping to stave off further encounters, she probed for the reason that he was in the office at such an odd hour. "You're in earlier than usual."

"I have an important meeting today with a potential, high-net-worth investor." Kyle didn't seem to be in any hurry to go and prepare for his sales pitch. He carried a standard briefcase, unlike her bag with the soft leather. "I saw you last night. At the pub."

Brook almost asked if that had won him a prize that she hadn't been aware was up for grabs, but she remained silent. In the twelve months that they had worked in the same building and on the same floor, Kyle Paulson usually went out of his way to avoid her. She could count on one hand the times that he had even made direct eye contact.

"I was having drinks with some of my colleagues," Kyle said to fill in the awkward silence. He unfastened his dress coat before sliding his hand into the right pocket. He had a penchant for wearing expensive suits and jackets, but he'd yet to splurge on a worthwhile pair of quality shoes. The glaring omission in his appearance was either due to being prudent with his money or he wasn't that good at managing his personal funds. The latter didn't shine the brightest light on his firm. "I recognized the woman who was sitting at your table. Her first name is Millie, right?"

Brook was rarely caught off guard.

"I'm sorry, but I can't discuss potential clients." Brook's purse strap slipped a bit, and she used the excuse to extricate herself from the conversation. "Good luck with your presentation."

Brook had no idea if such a meeting was called a presentation in the financial industry, but it was the only description that she could come up with on short notice. Multiple questions were running through her mind, but what she really wanted to know was how Kyle Paulson knew Millie Gwinn.

"Thanks," Kyle responded with a small smile before he pulled out the keys that would obviously give him entrance into the hedge fund. "Have a good day."

Brook stepped back so that the glass door slowly closed behind her. It was in her nature to be suspicious, but no one could argue that such an obviously staged run-in wasn't highly questionable. She would have Bit find the connection between Millie and Kyle. If there was something more than curiosity that had Kyle approaching Brook, she wanted to know upfront.

In the meantime, she had a lot of groundwork to cover before meeting with the team at eight o'clock. While they had not technically taken the case, the decision to do so was definitely leaning in that direction. First, Brook needed to consult with the firm's accountant regarding the viability to conduct a pro bono investigation.

Brook crossed the marble tile through the large waiting area to her office. The Christmas tree that Kate had decorated in crystal-clear blinking lights with white and black ribbon at the beginning of the month had been positioned in the corner. The brilliant white lights had been set on a timer, and they weren't scheduled to start their preprogrammed blinking pattern for another hour or so. The team had made the decision to decorate while she'd been testifying in court on a previous case.

She should have known they'd take the idea to extremes. It was literally a color-coordinated black and white Christmas to match the modern décor of the office.

It wasn't that Brook was opposed to holidays.

She had simply never had reason to celebrate them before, and that technically hadn't changed. Come Christmas morning, the team would be with their families, and she would be at her condo staring at her dining room wall that served as a murder board dedicated to her brother's brutal crimes.

Work had become her life early on, and she'd accepted long ago that it was her responsibility to stop her brother and his sick desire to kill women who believed their lives were perfect. She wouldn't stop until he was behind bars or six feet under. Until then, she would continue her search while also attempting to give closure to other families of similar crimes.

Brook had purposefully chosen an executive office right off the open foyer due to its location. She wasn't one for surprises, which was why she preferred to observe the comings and goings of individuals from the elevator bank. The modern décor of their offices had been intentional. The glass structures allowed for the easy monitoring of others.

It didn't take her long to change out of her winter boots in exchange for her favorite pair of heels. She hung the straps of her purse and leather bag on the antique coatrack in the corner. She'd removed a couple of folders, her phone, and her electronic tablet before placing all the items on her desk.

Bit had set the overhead lights on a timer, so there was no need to walk the perimeter and flip numerous switches on the walls. She was able to settle in her chair and reach for the remote in record time.

The fifty-five-inch screen television came to life. It had already been tuned into her favorite national news channel, but she wasn't interested in those stories today.

She was more intrigued by the local news.

CHAPTER THREE

The ringing of her cell phone stopped her from perusing the four main local channels. Brook literally experienced her heart flutter at the sound, and she didn't appreciate the betrayal. There hadn't been one day in her adult life that she hadn't been in control of her emotions. She'd like to keep it that way, but General Graham Elliott wasn't making such an endeavor easy to achieve as of late.

"Good morning," Brook greeted after clearing her throat. She'd made sure to do so before answering, with the strict objective that he wouldn't hear the hitch in her voice. "You didn't have to call me back. I was just keeping you in the loop since this is almost certainly going to be our first pro bono case."

Brook had purposefully sent a text to Graham an hour ago, knowing full well that he was currently in California. It was technically in the middle of the night where he was staying, and she'd thought for sure that he would be asleep. While he'd retired after thirty years serving in the Marine Corps, the government hadn't been eager to cut ties completely.

Graham had been a senior Marine officer commanding the Marine Raider Battalions, the Corps' next-level contribution to the joint nature of Special Operations Command. A highly skilled group of Marines a cut above the regular Marine forces. A group that took the *Art of War* to be their operational center piece. They were an intelligent yet brutally efficient organization. Their reputation among other special operators was topnotch.

Of course, the sentiment to not cut ties went the other way, as well.

Graham currently worked as a government contractor. His travel itinerary of late had given her some breathing room after he'd made his personal intentions clear.

"Good morning." Graham's rich voice traveled across the line. It was way too early in the morning for her to be dealing with him. "I was just wondering where you'll be headed for this new case. Midwest? South?"

"Actually, right here in the city," Brook responded as she perused the line of captions across the television screen. "I won't bore you with the details, but it involves an ICU nurse at one of our local hospitals. We've talked before about taking pro bono cases, but that was before...well, before business dried up."

Brook didn't need to go into depth regarding the reason why potential clients hadn't been knocking on their door. Very few clients would understand her close, personal link to an active serial killer. It seemed no one wanted to invite that kind of trouble to their front door.

Thankfully, an investigation a couple of months ago had changed their trajectory. They now had enough funds to see them through the following year, and there were more prospective clients on the horizon.

As a matter of fact, Kate had been fielding quite a few calls recently for their services. It had certainly been a nice change of pace.

"Well, let me know if you need anything. I'm slated to return home on Monday if the weather cooperates."

Graham fell silent, allowing her to take the lead.

They'd had lunch twice where business wasn't discussed, and it had been quite an adjustment for her. They were both adults, but both of them were aware that any deviation away from the current status of their professional relationship could very well blow up in their faces. When she needed to scratch an itch, it was usually with someone who had the same agenda—no expectations and no commitments. She would have considered such an arrangement with Graham, but he'd made no secret that he desired more from her.

Brook wasn't sure she had anything else to give, but damn if the temptation to try wasn't there. It wasn't that he didn't know about her unhealthy baggage, her emotional scars, or the fact that she had a brother who was a psychotic serial killer. One of those should have been enough to clue Graham in on the fact that she could never compete with his dead wife. Maybe that was why she'd respected his patience.

"Dinner. Wednesday night. My place at eight."

Brook didn't bother to wait for his acceptance speech. She pulled the phone away from her ear. Before she was able to disconnect the line, she thought she'd heard him say his standard goodbye—*be safe*.

Again, the changes in their relationship weren't something that she was going to waste time analyzing to the Nth degree. If she gave it too much thought, she might find her fears had been realized in a way that could eventually break her.

Purposefully pushing the thought of dinner with Graham out of her mind as she set her phone down on her desk, she then picked up her caramel macchiato and savored the sweet flavor.

Her morning routine was one of the few vices that she didn't regret in the least.

Once the caffeine from her favorite beverage invaded her bloodstream, she would then be ready to dive into some research. She'd already conducted a quick search for any online articles related to Dr. David Kolsby. By all accounts, he was a renowned psychiatrist who had made headlines last year by preventing a suicide. There had been other articles and mentions in various medical journals and prestigious sites.

Nothing pointed to the man being a murderer, let alone a serial killer.

The ringing of her cell phone once again interrupted her morning routine.

Brook was tempted to let it go to voicemail, but a quick glance at the display had her taking the call.

"Theo? You're up early. Is everything okay?"

"No," Theo replied tersely. "I'm outside the front entrance of the building. We need to drive over to Millie Gwinn's apartment immediately. Her place was broken into last night, and the police are taking her statement now."

"Let me grab my coat," Brook said with a sigh of regret. So much for her morning routine. "I'll be down in a minute."

Chapter Four

Brooklyn Sloane
December 2022
Friday — 6:58am

THE FAINT SCENT OF pine hung in the air, but the pleasant aroma wasn't from the tree itself. Instead, holiday candles had been strategically placed around the small, two-bedroom apartment. The level of the green wax in the glass jars indicated that the wicks were burned quite frequently. There was also garland strung over the mantel of an electric fireplace that hadn't come with the apartment, and there were two red and white stockings attached to the laminate wood hearth.

Brook figured the Christmas decorations were more for show than use. Maybe an effort on Millie Gwinn's part to replicate what she once knew as the spirit of Christmas.

Brook empathized with the woman's desperate search for contentment.

Millie Gwinn might have decorated for the upcoming holiday, but her body language suggested she wasn't in a merry mood. No one could really blame her, especially given that the doorjamb to her apartment had been shattered into small fragments of kindling that were still strewn across a close-knit area of the floor.

"Nothing was taken?" Officer Soerig of the Metro Police Department asked for the fourth time. Brook didn't envy the woman her job. While a crime might have been committed, it would be impossible to charge someone with burglarizing Millie's apartment when not one thing was missing. "You checked everything before you called us?"

"Nothing is missing, but this can't be a coincidence," Millie exclaimed in frustration as she wrapped her arms around her midsection. "I'm telling you, someone has been following me ever since I reported Dr. Kolsby's drug-induced confession to the police…to you, Office Soerig."

Brook winced when she realized that Millie's plea had once again landed on deaf ears. Officer Soerig had been the initial officer to look into Millie's original claim, and nothing had come from the cursory investigation. Brook had an official copy of the original MPD Incident/Offense Report (form PD-251) that Officer Soerig had filed in her purse.

The officer had technically done her due diligence. She hadn't uncovered one shred of evidence to support Millie's accusation that Dr. David Kolsby was anything other than a well-respected psychiatrist with a spotless reputation.

Before Officer Soerig could reply to Millie, her partner had leaned in and whispered something in private. The way his gaze had darted to Brook spoke to the obvious subject.

She and Theo had arrived moments after the two officers. No introductions had been made as of yet, but Brook figured that small oversight was about to be corrected.

Theo had taken advantage of the brief distraction to conduct a short exchange with Millie. Brook suspected that he was instructing the nurse to remain cautious in her bid to make

CHAPTER FOUR 33

unsubstantiated claims by connecting the home invasion to her story about the psychiatrist.

Millie Gwinn lived in the heart of D.C.

Break-ins were quite common in this area, and there was no substantive evidence that someone had been following Millie, let alone having any of it tying back to Dr. Kolsby.

Oddly enough, Millie was wearing the same blue nursing scrubs that she'd had on last night. Brook had noticed the stain on the front shirt from what appeared to be some type of beverage from the long, vertical shape.

From what Theo had explained on the drive over to Millie's place, the nurse had stayed the night at her sister's house in Fairfax. Upon arriving back home to shower and change for another shift at the hospital, she'd discovered the damaged door to her apartment.

Millie had not only dialed 911, but she'd wisely called Theo, who had given her his cell phone number last night. The team hadn't had a chance to discuss whether or not they were officially taking the case, but their presence alone signified the likelihood of such an undertaking.

"Am I missing something here?" Officer Soerig asked warily as she clicked the end of her pen. She was wearing a thick jacket, a cuffed beanie, and an unofficial, non-department issued dark blue scarf that was tucked in behind the zipper. "Is it true? Are you Brooklyn Sloane?"

The fact that Officer Soerig had to ask such a question meant that she wasn't one to put too much stock in reputations, tarnished or otherwise. That was actually an advantage for the team, because it meant that Soerig didn't put bias before her duty to ascertain the facts.

"Yes," Brook replied truthfully, knowing exactly how her presence would be interpreted by both officers. She set her purse down on the coffee table. "This is my colleague, Theo Neville. Ms. Gwinn reached out to us yesterday with her concerns for her personal safety. She provided us a copy of your PD-251 report regarding her allegations against Dr. Kolsby. You conducted a thorough investigation, and we can see why you closed out the initial complaint."

"Yet here you are," Officer Soerig stated with a mixture of curiosity and derision. "Something has clearly caught your attention."

Officer Soerig wasn't being rude for the sake of being rude. She was only wondering if she'd missed something pertinent to the case.

Brook understood that her presence meant the officer's work ethic would most likely be put under a microscope by her immediate superiors at the precinct. Unfortunately, there was no good way to handle this situation. What was interesting was the officer's tone.

"May we please speak in private?"

At first, Brook thought that Officer Soerig was going to decline. She'd even taken the time to slide the small notebook and pen into the interior pocket of her jacket. It was after her brief nod of concession that Brook realized she'd made the right assumption about the officer. She led the way past Theo, Millie, and the other officer toward a small kitchen.

"Officer Soerig, you believe that Ms. Gwinn is telling the truth," Brook stated quietly as she slipped her hands into the pockets of her black dress coat. "Don't you?"

"Regardless of what I personally believe, the outcome of the investigation remains unchanged—there is no evidence linking Dr. David Kolsby to any reported crime in the District or any of the surrounding states."

Officer Hadley Soerig appeared to be in her early thirties. She came across as competent and observant. She wasn't a rookie. While she was biracial, the light green hue of her irises was rather prominent. Stunning, really. It was difficult to tell how long or short her hair was underneath her beanie. Her uniform was immaculate, she wore no jewelry, and she'd ensured from her position in the kitchen that she remained in full view of the occupants in the other room while speaking with Brook.

It was clear that Officer Soerig took pride in her work.

"Any personal opinions that I have concerning someone's character are immaterial. I remain impartial while I'm in uniform." Officer Soerig cleared her throat and nodded toward her partner. "Officer Hutchins has taken the appropriate photographs, and we'll speak to Ms. Gwinn's neighbors and landlord before vacating the premises. The cold temperatures contribute to busy shifts, as I'm sure you know from your time with the FBI. It's why I sometimes unwind with a beer around six o'clock after working the day shift. You know, without the uniform on and all."

Brook didn't need additional time to catch onto the not-so-subtle hint that Officer Soerig was dropping like a truckload of bricks.

"Really? What local bar do you usually go to after your shift?" Brook asked casually as she monitored the three others in the living room. Officer Hutchins had engaged in conversation with Theo, which had allowed Millie to somewhat relax. "My team and I like this quaint pub on..."

Brook continued to make small talk with Officer Soerig, eventually garnering specific details about the name and address of the establishment that she would be at this evening at approximately six o'clock. Brook would make sure she was there to hear what the officer had to say about her initial impression of Dr. Kolsby, and also of Millie's allegations.

"It was nice meeting you, Ms. Sloane."

Officer Soerig eventually joined her partner before explaining to Millie what she should expect over the coming hours and days. Brook didn't miss the way that Theo was monitoring the officer's movements. Was he doing so out of curiosity over her professionalism or was his interest of a more personal nature?

Brook mentally shrugged off the question.

It wasn't any of Brook's business what Theo did or didn't do on his own personal time.

He'd recently moved into her building, but his condo was located on the other side of the mirrored structure. Although they shared the same lobby, they didn't utilize the same elevator bank, which was probably for the best. While Brook didn't mind his close proximity, she also didn't want her personal life put under a microscope by a work colleague. Such a revelation made her second-guess the dinner invitation that she'd handed out to Graham earlier this morning.

Brook rarely second-guessed herself, and she didn't like that she was doing so now.

Her invite to Graham would stand.

She didn't need to justify her actions to anyone.

Brook waited patiently for Officer Soerig and her partner to vacate the apartment, leaving Theo to follow suit to close the door behind them. It wouldn't latch securely until the landlord was able to fix it sometime later today.

"Millie? Would you please walk us through what happened one more time?"

"I didn't feel comfortable coming back to my apartment after leaving the pub." Millie sighed before she took a seat on the couch. From the blemishes underneath her eyes, it was obvious that she hadn't slept well last night. "I stayed with my sister and her family. I drove back to the city this morning."

"Did you notice if anyone followed you out of the city?" Brook asked as she removed her dress coat. She laid it across her lap as she claimed a chair. "Did you see a vehicle close behind you? Maybe an unusual car parked near your sister's residence?"

"No," Millie responded with a shake of her head. "I would know, too. I've been keeping a close eye out for Dr. Kolsby."

"That's the problem," Brook pointed out as Theo joined them. He sat down on the other end of the couch. "You're so focused

CHAPTER FOUR

on Dr. Kolsby that you might be missing someone else. When you arrived home, where did you park? I noticed that this apartment building doesn't have an attached garage. Did you park on the street or in the parking lot next door?"

"In the parking lot, but we don't have designated spots. It's basically first come, first serve." Millie reached up and removed the hair tie that had kept her long strands in place. Her curls immediately sprang free from their restraint, surrounding her face. Now that her dark hair was against her cheeks, it was easier to notice her pallor. "No one was in or around the elevator, and no one was in my hallway. This proves that I was right, though."

"All this proves is that someone broke into your apartment," Brook countered, not wanting Millie to get ahead of herself. "Listen, Theo is going to stay behind and make sure that you arrive at the hospital for your shift. I want you to keep in sight of other people whenever possible during your shift. Do not make yourself an easy target. We have no idea what we are dealing with quite yet, and I would like to err on the side of caution."

"Does this mean that you'll take my case? I can't pay much, but I'll ask my sister if she can—"

"There's no need for that, Ms. Gwinn." Brook shared a knowing look with Theo. A decision had been made, and now it was time to get to work. "Yes, we are taking your case, though at no cost to you. It has always been our intention to work one or two investigations per year as pro-bono. A service to the community. Your case will be our first. Again, I'm not promising any particular result. There could be a chance that we investigate Dr. Kolsby and find him completely innocent. This is a very unusual investigation. I'm going to head back to the office while Theo remains with you until we can set up a protective detail. We will make sure that your apartment is secured prior to leaving the new keys with you during your shift. There will most likely be a security camera on your mantel when you get home. It will cover the front door and main room only.

Once your security detail is in place, we can reevaluate the need for the electronic surveillance inside your home. I know it's inconvenient, but we need to keep your safety our prime objective."

Millie had secured the hair tie around her wrist so that her hands were free to run through her hair in relief. Her sigh was audible, and her shoulders sank with immediate respite.

"Thank you. Thank you so much," Millie exclaimed with a short laugh, as if she couldn't believe her luck. "And please, call me Millie."

"Well, Millie," Brook said as she stood from the chair. She draped her coat over her arm before picking up her purse. There was no need to put it on when she could potentially be waiting awhile downstairs in the lobby for a ride back to the office. "I'd like for you to continue your routine. Don't stop working at the hospital, going out with your friends, or any other activities that you do on a daily basis. Speaking of work, what is your schedule usually like?"

"I work three, twelve hour shifts per day back-to-back, with four days off." Millie stood, followed by Theo. "Today is my third day."

"Good." Brook held out her arm. "Would you please stop by the office sometime tomorrow so that we can obtain a probative account of what transpired between you and Dr. Kolsby?"

"Of course," Millie replied as she shook Brook's hand. "Would ten o'clock work?"

"I'll see you then. In the meantime, I'd like for you to recheck your apartment. Look for anything you think might be out of place. Second, you should also go through your clothing, both clean and dirty, to determine if any articles might be missing. Theo will then escort you to the hospital. He will let you know when we have a protective detail in place, as well as make the introductions so you know who will be close by in case of an emergency." Brook glanced toward the splintered wood on the

CHAPTER FOUR   39

floor. "Theo, would you also make sure that the landlord fixes the door before the two of you leave? You know the drill. Have him contact a locksmith, and then explain that he can't have a key until the investigation is complete. Also make sure the locksmith installs a heavy strike plate reinforcer for the deadbolt and a matching ten-pin, anti-pick lock combo."

Once everything else had been verbally set, Theo followed Brook to the door.

"How is this protective detail going to work?" Theo asked quietly as he joined her in the hallway. S&E Investigations had never hired outside personal security teams, so they were wading into uncharted territory. "If you want to keep this in-house, I guess the team could split time running the surveillance. I heard Bit mention the other day that the van is up and operational."

The black 2022 Mercedes Sprinter technical van was nondescript, enough to pass as just another one of a hundred messenger service vans crisscrossing the city streets. Its purpose was created for exactly a case such as this one, but they simply didn't have the staff to operate a twenty-four-hour surveillance alongside an ongoing investigation. It was best to hire outside consultants for Ms. Gwinn's personal protective detail. The technical van could then be utilized for observing the suspect.

In this case, that would be one Dr. David Kolsby.

Expansion for the firm hadn't been something she'd ever considered, and she wasn't about to change course now. The future wasn't set in stone, though. She'd take things one client at a time, and this specific client needed personal protection immediately. A bodyguard, for lack of a better term.

"Give me the morning to get things fully in place," Brook responded, already having an independent firm in mind. "I've already texted Sylvie. She's picking me up in ten minutes. I've also messaged Bit and requested that he pull every security camera in the area to try and capture footage of everyone entering and exiting this apartment building. I couldn't locate any type of surveillance on this floor, but there was a camera in the front lobby. City Public Services with their Department of Public Transportation also has CCTV citywide, but the alley behind the building might have a blind spot. I'll have Bit check with you for details."

"Did Officer Soerig offer up anything that might aid in the investigation?"

"Maybe." Brook hadn't planned on spending so much time in the hallway. She set her purse on the floor and began to slip her arms into the sleeves of her dress coat, hoping that she wouldn't be waiting too long downstairs. "I like her. She's smart, observant, and not willing to compromise her ethics as an officer. She'll be unwinding at a bar after her shift tonight. If I happen to be there at six o'clock, there is a good chance that she'll give me her personal insight on Dr. David Kolsby and what she discovered during her investigation."

"That is certainly an interesting way to go about it," Theo surmised with a smile.

"I'll give you the specifics regarding Millie's protective detail once I have confirmation."

Brook positioned her purse strap over her shoulder before pulling her black leather gloves out from her pocket. The temperature outside was hovering in the low twenties, and snow flurries seemed to be a constant thing over the past few days. Such inclement weather would only prove to be a hindrance in their case, but they'd dealt with far worse.

"Let me guess," Theo said before he turned to push open the damaged door. "You have people in mind, and they all owe you favors. You know, Bit swears that you have a little black book with blackmail details on almost everyone in the city."

"Bit reads too many spy thrillers," Brook muttered as she started to walk down the long hallway toward the elevator bank. She made sure that Theo didn't catch her smile. After all, she had a reputation to uphold. "Time to get to work."

Chapter Five

Brooklyn Sloane
December 2022
Friday — 9:23am

"Are you sure this is how you want to use your chip?" Alex DeSilva held his tie against his starched dress shirt as he took a seat behind his desk. The coffee cup in his hand was full, and he carefully set it next to a small pile of manilla folders. While he was speaking directly to Brook, his dark gaze had settled on Sylvie with what appeared to be some measure of interest. Introductions had already been made, and Brook had heard through the grapevine that he was fresh off a divorce.

Brook sensed Sylvie's perceptive glance upon Alex's question.

While it was known amongst the team that Brook had cultivated many relationships during her time with the Bureau, those distinct favors had been acquired for the sole purpose of locating Jacob.

Alex misunderstood her visit, though.

She wouldn't be calling in any favors today.

"Who said anything about a quid pro quo?" Brook countered, crossing her legs. She made herself comfortable, knowing this meeting could take a while. "S&E Investigations would like to hire DeSilva Securities on behalf of a client for a protective detail. We'll pay your normal fee, of course."

Brook had met Alex a few years ago when the daughter of a prominent senator had garnered the attention of an admirer. The unsub hadn't been a serial killer in the way that the public viewed that particular term. The male subject had specifically targeted family members of government officials. Considering the nature of the case, Brook had personally delivered her profile to various agencies. Alex and some of his team members had been in attendance.

As for the favors that she'd managed to procure from Alex, there had been a handful of times that she'd garnered intelligence within her purview that had aided in certain protective details. She wasn't ready to call in any of those tokens that she'd collected with her time at the Bureau, so this visit would be kept strictly a business transaction.

"Just so we're being completely transparent, there is more than one chip on that pile," Brook reminded him.

Alex smiled as he leaned back in his chair.

He certainly was a charmer, but he was a businessman first. As for his former military connections, he'd been in the perfect position to build his company with experienced men and women whose qualifications were a step or two above the norm for personal protective details. She had no doubt that he'd crossed paths with Graham a time or two in the past. They were cut from the same bolt of cloth, and they no doubt ran in the same circles.

The offices of DeSilva Securities were located in downtown D.C., not far from the hospital where Millie Gwinn worked on the ICU floor. Alex had fostered a lot of relationships in the area, and his firm had a stellar reputation when it came to security, whether personal or technological. The business had recently branched out to cybersecurity, which would almost certainly turn into his bread and butter.

"I thought for sure that the private sector would have softened you up," Alex said with a shake of his head. His comment was enough to spur Sylvie into a small coughing fit, though she recovered quickly after Brook raised an eyebrow her way. "It's been a while. In all seriousness, are you doing okay? I happened to catch the interview that you gave earlier this year."

"I'm fine, thank you." Brook had always been cautious when appropriating favors. She'd purposefully never mentioned her brother, and she wouldn't do so now. When and how she utilized those contacts would be on her own terms and strictly on a need-to-know basis. "As you know, S&E Investigations prefer handling cold cases, but something local has landed in our lap that we can't ignore. A client's apartment was broken into last night, and she's convinced that she is being followed by someone. I'm hoping that you have a team available for twenty-four-hour surveillance until we can ascertain the validity of her concerns."

"Your partner has a regular contact over at Troughton & Associates."

Alex had narrowed his gaze, monitoring Brook's expressions as if there was a catch to her impromptu visit. He was also searching for any indication that the rumors regarding Troughton & Associates' bankruptcy were true.

There was a bit of truth to the speculation that Troughton & Associates would be closing their doors, but the reason had nothing to do with money. Eric Troughton had recently been diagnosed with Parkinson's Disease, and his partner had decided to finally retire. Until both were ready to release a statement regarding their firm, it wasn't Brook's place to add grist to the mill.

Brook *had* reached out to Graham, but she would have expected nothing less if the situation had been reversed. They both had a financial stake in S&E Investigations, and they had built relationships with outside firms when necessary. Graham had explained the situation with Troughton & Associates in confidence, and she wouldn't betray his trust.

"Why me?" Alex asked directly, still waiting for a response. He pulled his chair in and rested his forearms on his desk. "Why choose DeSilva Securities?"

"Alex, if you don't want S&E's business, all you have to do is politely decline."

While Brook had other options, both she and Graham had decided that Alex DeSilva and his firm were the wisest choices. She waited patiently for him to make a decision. He'd make the right choice, and he would do so for multiple reasons. First and foremost, he would want an inroad into Graham's government connections that Alex hadn't been able to procure himself.

"Here is our standard fee structure," Alex said as he lifted the top manilla folder off the pile. "If you're in agreement, I'll have Tricia draw up our usual private subcontractor contract. I take it you need a detail for your client by this afternoon?"

Brook already had Bit look into the expense of DeSilva Securities, and she already had a counteroffer in mind.

Sylvie remained silent, almost as if she was enjoying the back-and-forth banter.

"We'd like a ten percent discount," Brook replied as she casually perused the contents of the folder. She closed it before handing it back to him. "Your assistant can include an addendum that states S&E Investigations will solely utilize DeSilva Securities' protective details for the next three years, with the caveat that we reserve the right to use our own subcontracted hostage and rescue team if there is a need for special weapons and tactics."

CHAPTER FIVE 45

Alex clicked the end of his pen repeatedly as he mulled over her offer. He was obviously curious about Brook's provision for their own HRT group. It was a good business decision, and she'd purposefully left room to negotiate.

"Five percent. Five years."

"Eight percent, and I'm not budging on the three-year commitment."

"And HRT? Who did you have in mind? You do know that we have our own special weapons team, right?"

"You have no need to know that information. At least, for right now."

Alex shifted his gaze from Brook to Sylvie, who simply shrugged as if to say it was the best deal that he was going to get from S&E Investigations. Usually, Brook would have conducted such a meeting on her own. However, it would have been pointless to drive back to their office building when this appointment wouldn't take much time out of their morning.

"You drive a hard bargain, Sloane." Alex pressed a button on the intercom and instructed his assistant to draw up the necessary paperwork. "Alright. Let's get down to business. Name?"

"Millie Gwinn."

"Age?"

"Thirty-nine."

"Marital status?"

"Single."

Brook continued to answer Alex's questions, appreciating his thoroughness on the matter. In the middle of providing such details, the ringtone of her phone could be heard. She usually silenced her cell during meetings, but she wanted to be available should Theo run into any potential problems at the hospital.

She recognized the phone number on the display, and she weighed her decision on whether or not to answer.

Curiosity got the best of her, though.

"Sylvie, would you please take over answering Alex's questions? I need to take this call."

Brook didn't wait for an answer. Instead, she stood from the chair and quietly exited the office. There had been a small conference room down the hallway that hadn't been in use when she'd walked by it earlier, so she headed in that direction.

"Sloane."

"We believe there was a breach in the North Dakota branch office of the U.S. Marshals Service." Agent Russell Houser was the special agent in charge of Jacob's case within the FBI. They hadn't always seen eye to eye, neither trusting the other, which was why it was odd that he would be calling her over something that she shouldn't even be privy to. "The marshal in question swears he wasn't the one who accessed their system to try and ascertain information on Sarah Evanston. His password and credentials demonstrate otherwise."

Brook's heels were soundless on the carpet as she quietly closed the door to the conference room. She took her time walking over to a window that overlooked the city. Every now and then, snow flurries could be seen falling from the overcast sky. Traffic was basically at a crawl below on the city streets, though not due to the weather.

City congestion was a daily occurrence.

"Considering that no one appointed to the Evanston case can access information on the U.S. Marshals' database, her location should still be secure." Brook wasn't telling Agent Houser anything that he didn't already know. He was calling for another reason. Unfortunately, she didn't have a crystal ball. "I take it that you'll move her anyway?"

"As a precaution, yes." Agent Houser apparently needed a moment to compose his next statement. "You were right. Your brother purposefully wanted to be seen on camera at a gas station near Evanston's half-brother's home so that we would turn our focus to an area in Idaho."

CHAPTER FIVE

The U.S. Marshals Service might be moving Sarah Evanston to a new safehouse, but it wouldn't be far from where she was receiving medical care under the same plastic surgeon. The amount of damage done to her facial features would require several more surgeries over the course of the next one or two years. Switching surgeons wouldn't be an option due to the intricate nature of her injuries.

"I'm not sure how I can help you, Agent Houser."

"You mentioned a couple of months ago that your brother would focus on searching for plastic surgeons who had the expertise to handle Evanston's surgeries."

"Yes," Brook responded cautiously as she sensed the direction of this discussion. She wasn't opposed to a ploy of some sort. "Dr. John Roden, Dr. Crystal Shelley, or Dr. Timothy Ursitti. If I can narrow Evanston's surgeons down to three, so can Jacob."

The chances of the U.S. Marshals Service sharing the name of Sarah Evanston's plastic surgeon with Agent Houser was practically nonexistent. Brook respected the branch, their marshals, and the lengths they went to in order to protect those who needed safeguarding from outside sources. While Jacob might have attempted to utilize a marshal in North Dakota to garner confidential details on Evanston's whereabouts, only those assigned to her case had that privileged information.

What had Jacob *really* been doing while in North Dakota?

"I propose—"

"A sting," Brook interjected, her interest level relatively high. She would need to think over such a suggestion, especially since such a plan would be at the hands of Agent Houser. "I'm going to assume that the U.S. Marshals Service has already changed Sarah Evanston's handler and any other protective agents assigned to her while she's in recovery."

Jacob hadn't sought out a random agent in a remote state believing that he would instantly locate the reporter's location. He'd targeted a marshal to gain access to their computer system.

He was once again giving them crumbs to follow. He had to know that he would be cut off before he was anywhere near Sarah's location.

If her brother was well aware of such blockades, that meant he wanted something else entirely from the U.S. Marshals Service's software. Brook's brother was consistently one step ahead, whereas she was always one behind.

As for Agent Houser, he'd wondered off somewhere in the desert.

"You want to keep the original detail in place and use them as bait." Brook's earlier interest had all but deflated, but Agent Houser had a genuine idea that possessed merit. "Jacob wouldn't fall for it, and he intentionally wants us to believe that he was searching for Evanston."

"You said that your brother would be searching for the surgeon," Agent Houser pointed out as he continued to traipse across hot sand. "Either way, there is a way for us to use this breach to our advantage. I'd like you on board."

Brook couldn't imagine how many times Agent Houser had rehearsed such a request, and it had still fallen flat. He didn't want her on board. As a matter of fact, he wouldn't have her anywhere near the investigation if he had his way. The only reason that he'd been reaching out to her recently was due to his newfound revelation that Jacob was unlike the average serial killer. She had her thoughts on the reasons why, but she currently had a client whose life was in danger.

"One week," Brook requested as she finally turned away from the window. There were two men in deep conversation outside of the conference room. They hadn't even noticed her presence until she'd moved from her spot on the other side of the table. "I'll give you my answer in one week."

Brook disconnected the line before Agent Houser could get another word in edgewise. He meant well, and he was like a dog with a bone. The bone might have been twice the size of his

CHAPTER FIVE

head, but it would take someone with that type of determination to even get close to her brother.

"...client's trip to Iran. It's going to be a shitshow."

Brook nodded toward the man facing her after she'd exited the conference room. His dark gaze had been monitoring her progress, and she could sense that he was well aware of her identity.

"What if we bring in Caine and his group?"

Brook wasn't sure how she'd managed not to falter her steps toward Alex's office upon hearing the name. Granted, the gentlemen could have been talking about someone else, but the circles that ran through this type of industry tended to be rather small. The special training that required such a detailed area of study was quite limited.

Certain specialist long range snipers were limited to less than two dozen inside the United States. That was just one of many skillsets that a team must possess. Professional teams like the one Caine ran were fewer and much farther in between.

She'd recently become acquainted with a mysterious male subject named Caine. He and his team had literally saved her and Sylvie's lives on an investigation they had undertaken in Northern Illinois. After Sylvie had been abducted, Graham had called in reinforcements. He'd brought in a team that had been prepared for all types of situations. She began to wonder if Caine's team specialized in a very specific type of tactical outcome.

Fortunately, they'd succeeded in their mission.

Brook opened the door to Alex's office.

"...two of my men over to the hospital within the hour," Alex finished saying to Sylvie as he shifted his focus toward Brook. "Your colleague and I have gone over the specifics of the contract, she's given me what information you have so far, and I'll have a rotating detail on your client until we hear otherwise from your office."

"I'm glad to hear it." Brook leaned down and slid her phone back into the side pocket of her purse. She didn't bother to reclaim her seat. They had a lot of groundwork to cover today, and she trusted Sylvie's judgement when it came to the contract. The young analyst had as close to an eidetic memory as one could get, and she would alert Brook to any conflict of interest. "Sylvie? Is there anything that should concern me?"

"It's pretty standard, and Alex's assistant adjusted the price per the discount that the two of you negotiated, as well as stipulating the contract would be in effect for three years." Sylvie handed Brook the contract and a pen. "I did have a separate addendum added that this was a temporary contract until such time as the firm's lawyers had a chance to look over the fine print. Your caveat was included in the first addendum."

"Alex?" Brook asked, setting the contract on the desk as she hovered the pen over the designated line. "I take it you're fine with both addendums? I already have a call into our lawyer's office, and they're expecting a hardcopy to be messengered to them by end of day."

"Sylvie was quite thorough in her read-through," Alex replied without a hint of sarcasm. In fact, he seemed quite impressed with Sylvie's professionalism. "In reference to the first addendum, our agency reserves the right not to work with certain groups that we've designated as cowboys. That would include several groups currently in the employment of the Central Intelligence Agency. We would need prior notice before your mysterious special action group is employed on a case that we are also working. Other than that, I just have one question. Did you steal Sylvie away from the Bureau or another agency?"

"Sylvie, are you happy at S&E Investigations?" Brook asked as she finally signed on the line with the red X.

"Very much so," Sylvie stated before she stood from her seat.

"You are not poaching any of my colleagues, Alex." Brook handed Sylvie's pen back to her before she reached down to pick up her purse. She settled the strap over her shoulder. "It seems to be a common theme lately."

Sylvie was all smiles, and she was no doubt recalling how a good friend of Brook's would have bent over backward to get his hooks into Bit. Next, Alex would meet Theo and decide he would be a perfect fit for one of the protective detail teams.

Alex wouldn't be wrong, either.

"As always, Brook, it's been a pleasure," Alex said after he'd laughed at her statement. He stood and walked around the desk, holding his hand out to Sylvie. "Should you ever be in the market, you have my number."

Alex escorted them to the front reception area, where they had left their winter coats. The two gentlemen who had been in the short hallway were no longer in view. Tricia was currently typing on her keyboard, her attention solely on the screen in front of her.

"I overheard one of your associates talking about Caine and his team." Brook slipped her arms into the sleeves of her dress coat for the hundredth time this morning. It would be nice to spend more than an hour in one place. "Do they work for you?"

"You know Caine?"

The caution in Alex's tone alerted Brook to the fact that Caine and his former Marine Raiders weren't exclusive to one firm. It would also explain how Graham had been able to obtain their services for a single day.

"You could say that," Brook replied guardedly while readjusting her scarf.

She refrained from saying anything else that might cause Alex to remain silent on the subject.

"The men and women who work with me here at DeSilva & Associates are quite discreet during their assigned protective details. Let's just say that when a client needs a tool more like a sledgehammer, Caine and his team fit the bill."

That would explain why Caine had been brought up in the same conversation as a foreign country that the United States didn't consider a political ally.

"Alex, we appreciate the partnership on such short notice," Brook said as she shook his hand. "Sylvie will be your point of contact, and she'll share with you any background checks on those who we believe to be a threat to our client."

Before too long, Brook and Sylvie were inside the elevator and on the way down to the main floor of the building. They remained silent until they reached Sylvie's car that had been parked on the third level of the parking garage.

"Do I want to know who this Caine is or why you're so interested in him and his group?"

Sylvie had no idea that Caine and his team had been in the apple orchid the day that she'd avoided being a victim of a serial killer. Brook hadn't wanted their involvement to be a complication when they'd only become involved at the request of Graham.

"It's not important." Brook grimaced when piercing air blew from the car's vent. They'd been inside the building long enough that the engine had become cold. "I'll text Kate to have lunch brought into the office. We've got a busy day ahead of us."

Chapter Six

Brooklyn Sloane
December 2022
Friday — 3:09pm

"Kate, I want you to keep working on the Rastini case." Brook didn't look up from her electronic tablet. She waited until she'd finished inserting a few notes that would give Kate a couple of avenues to explore based on the initial profile that Brook had built of the unsub.

The victim who had been traveling from the East Coast to the West Coast had nothing to do with two open investigations at the Bureau involving interstate truckers. Brook had triple checked those profiles constructed by the BAU. There were known to be a handful of serial killers that combed specific interstates or highways for their victims while working fulltime as independent truckers. A few had been apprehended, while others were still active.

The BAU had full knowledge of them due to these truckers exchanging digital photographs of their victims. Considering the number of women who had gone missing, there had to be at least a half dozen more perpetrators hunting their prey using similar Modus Operandi (MO).

It was Brook's belief that the murder of Kyle Rastini had been personally motivated. She suspected that Kyle's killer was someone who he'd been well acquainted with during his short life.

Brook didn't believe that his death was connected to any other case, and that meant the investigation was about to take a more intimate turn. His parents wouldn't be pleased with the new direction, but she would inform them of her reasoning on their next scheduled update by conference call.

"I'll get right on it," Kate said as she picked up the approved expense reports that Brook had signed yesterday. The young woman did her best to contain her excitement, but Brook caught the eagerness in her tone. "Will Bit be working solely on the Gwinn case?"

"No," Brook replied as she pushed the chair back from her desk. "He'll have to pull double duty."

She collected her tablet and phone, leaving the small space heater turned on behind her. Everyone always complained that her office was too hot, but it was quite comfortable in her opinion. They probably thought she had some circulatory issue, which wasn't outside the realm of possibility. Her mother had been the same way.

Unfortunately, Brook had concluded long ago that it was almost assuredly a psychological response. She hadn't experienced true warmth since her childhood, well before she discovered her best friend's body in the middle of a cornfield all those years ago.

"If you need something from Bit, feel free to make a request. I see no reason why we can't run with multiple open investigations. You'll have to help him prioritize anything you send him—routine, urgent, and critical."

CHAPTER SIX

Brook had no current plans to expand the team. She would only ever work one active case at a time, but there were some cold cases that had no end in sight. Those types of investigations weren't time sensitive like ongoing cases, such as the one involving their new client.

As a matter of fact, Brook had been contemplating another client who had reached out to her last week in regard to a missing person who had been presumed dead for years. Two older cases were doable with their small team, but she would wait until after Millie Gwinn was satisfied with their results. Either Dr. Kolsby was guilty of murdering several women or his confession had simply been the result of the anesthesia cocktail used for his induced coma.

Kate led the way out of the office, though she detoured her path by going around the main desk in the reception area. She would prepare an envelope for the expense reports to be couriered over to the firm's accountant before joining the rest of the team in the conference room.

Brook had gotten to know the young woman's habits after working with her for the past six months or so. She would fit in well when she finally made the decision to apply for the FBI academy. The Bureau was built of rigid routine and lockstep procedures. Old-fashioned routine policework solved crime more often than most people suspected. Most detectives just referred to it as the daily grind.

Brook had known when she'd hired Kate that her employment had simply been that of a steppingstone. She would miss the dynamic nature of S&E's daily operations after she'd made the transition, but that was something that Kate would need to figure out on her own.

"Boss?"

"Yes?"

Brook came to a stop in the hallway as Bit walked out of his own area. To say it was an office didn't do the room justice. His desk consisted of a long table with several monitors, numerous keyboards, and too many specialty gizmos that she couldn't even pronounce. Racks of equipment had been strategically placed in corners with ventilation towers reaching the ceiling.

Honestly, the office was like something one would find in a basement with no windows at the NSA.

"You should know that I've assigned Kate to the Rastini case while we put our efforts into Millie Gwinn's claims. I've advised Kate to reach out to you should she need something, along with a priority rating of each request."

"Yeah, no problem. I'm a multitasking guru," Bit said distractedly. He was staring at the display of his phone. He finally handed it over as she tucked her own tablet and phone into the crook of her arm. "It's a coincidence, I'm sure."

Brook stared at the headline of the article, and her initial response was to head back to her office and place some phone calls. She forced herself to remain in place, just as she made sure not to show emotion. It was a force of habit that she was unlikely to change.

A renowned plastic surgeon located in the heart of Los Angeles had been killed during a carjacking. Brook skimmed the article, confident that Bit would have already added it to Jacob's files. The files would then be automatically updated to reflect on the murder board that was currently located in the smaller conference room.

"I'll look into it." Brook handed back Bit's phone. "I appreciate you keeping on top of this."

Bit merely nodded, though she could sense that he wanted to say something else. He must have thought better of it, because he turned around and headed for the kitchen.

"I'm grabbing an energy drink. Want anything?"

"I'm good, thank you."

Brook remained where she was to get her bearings.

CHAPTER SIX

The chances of the plastic surgeon being killed by Jacob were low. Her brother had always kept to his signature, and she highly doubted that he would vary from it. He preferred women who believed that their lives were without fault. While some serial killers would resort to desperation, Jacob wouldn't randomly begin to pick off potential surgeons out of some need to exact revenge on anyone attempting to aid Sarah Evanston.

"...and this one has a nutmeg flavor." Sylvie had come out of the kitchen with Bit, who wasn't carrying one of his usual energy drinks. Instead, he was holding a cup of hot tea. "You'll love it."

Sylvie smiled at Brook as she walked into the large conference room. Bit was pulling up the rear, staring at the hot beverage as if he wasn't quite sure how he'd ended up with it in his hand.

He hated tea.

Loathed it, really.

Only he refused to break that little piece of news to Sylvie for fear of hurting her feelings.

"You know, you could suddenly become allergic," Brook murmured as she passed him to enter the conference room. She didn't glance back over her shoulder to see if her advice was something that he was seriously contemplating, because she suspected that Bit wouldn't seriously take it under advisement. He liked that Sylvie believed they had something in common. "Alright, everyone. Let's get down to the business at hand."

Theo had his laptop open in front of him, and he'd been working in the conference room ever since he'd arrived at the office a couple of hours ago. He'd waited until Millie's lunch break to make the introductions to her protective detail.

"Sylvie, you spoke to Alex again?"

"Yes," Sylvie replied, setting her tea on a slate coaster that had the firm's logo lasered onto it. "Alex is providing Millie with a protective detail consisting of four former military personnel. Three men, and one woman. They will rotate twelve-hour shifts, working in twos.

Kate snuck in, even though she wouldn't be given too much responsibility on the case. She had her own workload with the Rastini investigation. Brook had been impressed with her abilities on a previous case that she'd been instructed to obtain background information on while the team had traveled out of state at the request of the Illinois governor. The intelligence had been well organized and thorough. Brook couldn't see any reason why the young woman couldn't do the same with this case, if not more so.

"I met Seth Sharman and Addy Boyce. They seem to be solid agents." Theo leaned back in his chair and looked up from his screen. "Also, Millie's front door was fixed by one of our contractors. The landlord didn't have a problem with outsourcing the task. Millie has a key, as well as her protective detail."

"Tyler Hendry and Giles Latty are the other two individuals who will be taking the second rotation." Sylvie motioned to the murder board behind Brook. "I've attached all four of their profiles to the case file labeled *Security Detail*."

Bit took his usual seat after setting his own cup of tea down on one of the slate coasters. The way he was staring at the four photographs on the monitor had Sylvie waiting for his question.

"How does that work? If Millie Gwinn lives in an apartment, will they stay inside with her or outside the door?"

"Both," Brook replied as she leaned back in her chair. She held the stylus to her tablet in her hand as she shared with them how the protective detail would work in a civilian setting. Theo and Sylvie were already aware of the routine protocols, but Bit and Kate had never been on a case that involved an outside firm. "They'll have one agent remain inside her apartment, keeping to the confines of the main living space facing the entrance. The outside agent will monitor the comings and goings of the building. Since it is a typical apartment building, that will consist of a walk around that particular floor, the lobby, and a brief check outside to monitor for any unusual vehicles that might be surveilling the exits. Everything is recorded. The agents are connected by encrypted frequency hopping radios. Transcripts will be reviewed daily by Alex or someone else in management. That documentation will then be forwarded on to us, with a list of license plates or descriptions of those of interest."

"I'm pulling surveillance from the building's security cameras surrounding the entrance of the building, but you should know that the back entrance has no working camera," Bit said with a disappointing shake of his head. "A tenant only needs a keycard to gain access to the back entrance, which means that there is a log kept somewhere. It's most likely a single layer of security provided by an unmonitored internal system."

"I'll reach out to the landlord to see if he'll grant us access." Sylvie jotted a note down on her electronic tablet with the stylus. The technological upgrade to their process was beyond efficient. "Don't go through any backdoors, and that pun was totally intended. See if they have another camera to swap out with the faulty one."

Brook didn't bother to turn around and look at the monitor. She hadn't contributed anything to the murder board quite yet, but she had her reasons for that. For now, she wanted to hear every single detail that the team had acquired in their research since last night, including anything that Bit's internal electronic surveillance had picked up.

"Let's start at the beginning," Brook suggested as she turned her attention toward Theo. "Millie Gwinn. What do we know about her background?"

"Mildred Anne Gwinn, single, thirty-nine years of age. Born and raised in Fairfax, Virginia," Theo responded, not needing to look at his laptop. He was a very eloquent speaker, and he always made direct eye contact with everyone present. "Parents still reside in the family home. Millie has one sister, who is married with two teenage children. Both girls."

Theo continued to divulge Millie's high school and nursing school credits, even going so far as to touch on the nurse's employment record. She was highly regarded by her peers, was bilingual, and maintained over a ninety-eight percent in patient satisfaction scores regarding compassionate care according to her hospital personnel file.

As for Millie's personal life, she was registered on two dating sites, had several social media accounts on numerous platforms, and a close-knit group of friends.

"Finances?" Brook inquired, still addressing Theo since he was the one who had completed an in-depth background check on Millie Gwinn. "Anything that should concern us?"

She didn't need to stress that the monetary status of their client was essential to their case. While Millie Gwinn was technically their client, it was best to ensure that she didn't have a hidden agenda. Dr. Kolsby was very prominent in the high society circles. At least, according to the newspaper articles regarding his car accident and the suicide incident that he had managed to prevent last year.

"Millie has a department store credit card to Macy's with a sixty-three-dollar balance on it, as well as a Capital One credit card that has a four hundred and sixty-five-dollar balance," Theo shared as he glanced at the screen of his laptop to confirm the figures. "She's current on all of her bills, doesn't overspend, and has a credit score that I'm jealous of if I'm being honest. Clean record, with the exception of two parking tickets over the last five years."

"That's good to know." Brook switched her focus over to Sylvie. Once she and Brook had driven back to the office, Sylvie had holed up with Bit to gather as much information on Dr. David Kolsby as she could in the few short hours they'd had today. "What were you two able to find out about the psychiatrist?"

CHAPTER SIX

Brook had taken a few minutes out of her morning to leave a voicemail for her own therapist. Dr. Neil Swift was a psychologist whose office was located right outside of D.C. While he was close to retirement and didn't work with the hospital in question, she'd hoped that he would have some scuttlebutt from other reputable colleagues regarding the man in question.

"Dr. David Oliver Kolsby is fifty-eight years old, divorced twice, and has three children. Two sons from his first marriage, and a daughter from his second." Sylvie paused to take a sip of her tea and to scroll down on the display of her tablet. She kept the cup in one hand, and Brook figured she liked the warmth from the ceramic. "His net-worth is listed at over six million dollars, and that is mostly due to speaking fees from around the country. We are looking to see if that figure was double before divorcing his first wife. He wisely had the second wife sign a prenup. Needless to say, he is very selective with his clientele. Politicians, government officials, and very high-net-worth individuals. Dr. Kolsby also has a very carefully managed social media presence, mainly restricted to friends and family. As you are all predicting, the man has a clean record. Not even a parking ticket."

Sylvie's tone indicated that the psychiatrist's connections played a part in that role, and she was probably right. Nothing in the man's past would suggest that he had serial killer tendencies.

"Kolsby didn't come from money, as one would suspect given his position." Sylvie took another sip of her tea before setting her cup back down on the slate coaster. A quick glance revealed that Bit hadn't touched his beverage. Brook lightly bit the inside of her lip so as not to show a reaction. "Kolsby was born outside of Philadelphia, raised by a single mother, and put himself through college mostly on scholarships, which allowed him to then use student loans for his doctorate. And yes, those student loans have all been paid off."

"If Kolsby didn't come from money, how did he make his connections?" Theo asked before reaching for his smoothie.

He usually made himself a protein shake or smoothie in the afternoon. He was a creature of habit. This particular drink happened to be bright green, and Brook didn't want to know the list of ingredients thrown in to make that peculiar hue. While she wasn't opposed to healthy eating, she also believed that everything should be consumed in moderation.

Well, except coffee.

Coffee was an essential food group all by itself.

"Kolsby met Senator Ponzio's son during grad school. The two became close, kept in touch, and remained that way after Dr. Kolsby moved to D.C." Sylvie held up a finger as if to say she had something else important to mention. Her black-rimmed glasses had slipped a little, but she didn't bother to adjust them as she continued to refer to her notes. "His main office where he sees his patients is actually separate from the hospital. He's on the board of directors at the hospital, which is why everyone on the staff seems to know him so well."

"Ponzio," Brook murmured, recalling that the senator had retired last year. "I believe that I met his wife once when I worked at the Bureau. Sylvie? Did you know her? I think she might have been an analyst."

"That was Stacey Ponzio, and she's the senator's sister." Sylvie scrolled to another screen, which was no doubt being displayed on the monitor behind Brook. "I'd like to stress that Bit did not obtain this information from the hospital."

Theo closed his good eye while he rubbed his temple and Kate discreetly coughed, while Bit crossed his arms and tilted his chin in pride.

"I didn't leave a digital fingerprint, no one will ever know, and we now have information on Dr. Kolsby that might come in handy. I get the whole HIPAA thing, but we're talking about a potential serial killer."

CHAPTER SIX

"Innocent until proven guilty," Brook stressed before nodding toward Sylvie. "What were you able to find without resorting to...setting the constitution on fire?"

"Dr. Kolsby had a ruptured spleen, some cracked ribs, and some facial lacerations from broken glass, but he suffered a brain bleed due to a severe concussion. Apparently, the doctors kept him sedated until the swelling in his brain receded," Sylvie explained, finally readjusting her glasses now that they were practically at the end of her nose. "These details were all procured from opensource social media and news sites."

The faint sound of the main line ringing could be heard through the door. Kate quickly vacated her seat, even though she could have answered the phone using the speaker unit in the middle of the conference room table.

"If Kolsby has ties to Senator Ponzio's family, there is bound to be pushback with our investigation," Theo surmised as he set his now empty glass on a folder that was next to his laptop. "We're going to have to be discreet in how we handle the questioning."

"While I agree that Kolsby might try to use his influence to get us to drop the investigation, I can also use that to our advantage," Brook reasoned as she mulled over the various ways that they could initiate contact. "If I word my request right, he'll want to quickly clear his name. Millie is scheduled to come into the office tomorrow. I want to know every word that was said in that hospital room."

"I have a list of family members and friends of Dr. Kolsby, along with the name of the woman who he is currently dating," Sylvie said as she glanced toward Theo. "Bit and I are going to divide the list in half. Theo, do you want the colleagues? I can easily take them if you want to switch."

"No, the colleagues are fine. I'll start with his assistant and work from there." Theo didn't miss a beat as he changed the course of the conversation. "Brook, do you mind if I'm the one who meets up with Officer Soerig tonight?"

Brook hadn't expected the request, though she didn't pause in giving her answer.

"That's fine," Brook responded, not unhappy with the change in schedule. She found it rather odd, though. "I'm going need the time to figure out what to do regarding a profile. It's rather hard to profile someone whose identity I am already familiar with, and one who could potentially be innocent."

"You told Millie that you believed her," Bit said with a frown. "Don't you?"

"I do believe that Millie overheard Dr. Kolsby's confession, but that doesn't mean it was real by any stretch of the imagination." Brook formulated her words carefully. "Kate mentioned last night that anesthesia isn't a truth serum. If it was, I'm sure that there would be a lot of people behind bars. What I do know for a fact was that someone did break into Millie Gwinn's apartment. Nothing was taken. I find it oddly coincidental that such a break-in comes so close on the heels of her accusation. It warrants a closer look. I'd rather err on the side of caution than to find Millie Gwinn missing or murdered in her sleep."

"Wait," Theo said as he held up a hand. "Does this case even need a profile if we already know the identity of the unsub?"

Brook finally turned around to face the large monitor that served as the team's murder board. Dr. David Kolsby's picture was front and center. His salt and pepper hair had been cut in a classic style, his eyes were brown, and he obviously preferred to spend time in the sun. Either that, or he was the type of man who used self-tanners. Either way, she got the sense that he cared about appearances.

Was she staring into the eyes of a serial killer?

She'd done so before and been none the wiser.

Well, technically that wasn't true. She *had* known that there had been something wrong with Jacob since childhood. Acknowledging just how much of a psychopath he was had been another matter altogether.

CHAPTER SIX

"I don't know, Theo," Brook answered truthfully. "I've never worked without a profile before. I'm not sure that I can start now."

Chapter Seven

Theo Neville
December 2022
Friday — 6:04pm

THE NOISE LEVEL OF the bar was somewhat louder than the establishment from last night. The weekend had arrived, and the patrons were unwinding from their stressful work week. The location where Officer Hadley Soerig had chosen to relax with friends was old-school, consisting of the bar and a few high-top tables near the far wall that allowed just enough room to reach the restrooms in the back.

People came here to drink, talk with friends, and then leave.

"...waiting for the defendant to arrive at the courthouse."

There was only one television in the corner due to the smaller square footage, and the channel had been turned to a local news station. A verdict was due in under an hour of a wife who had allegedly killed her husband and his mistress in a fit of rage. The trial had been all over the news for the past month, and the lawyers had given their closing arguments three days ago.

CHAPTER SEVEN

Theo thought he recognized a judge sitting at one of the high-top tables. This establishment serviced mainly law enforcement officials, and once that determination was made, it was a rare occasion that any other clientele would walk through the front door.

Theo hadn't even known this place existed, and he was well-acquainted with the downtown area. The bar had been discreetly tucked in between two takeout restaurants, and he was beginning to suspect the owner had chosen the locale for a reason.

The one thing he hadn't expected was to find Officer Soerig sitting by herself in a corner. She'd been observing him the entire time that he'd been standing near the front door and searching for her. She lifted her bottle of beer in salute, and he began to make his way through the narrow maze to her location.

While she was an attractive woman in uniform, she was even more beautiful in civilian clothing.

Her hair was longer than he'd originally thought, dropping a few inches below her shoulders. She currently had it secured with a hair tie on the left side of her neck so that the remaining strands rested against the fabric of her cream sweater. Since she was sitting at a high-top table, he could see her faded jeans and knee-high black boots. It didn't appear that she was carrying her firearm.

Theo was beginning to think that he shouldn't have requested this meeting. He'd done so under the pretense that his interest was solely due to the case, but that was far from the truth. Hadley didn't seem to be sending him the same signals, though. He'd keep things professional and then take his leave.

"Officer Soerig," Theo greeted before pulling out the chair opposite from her. She was still monitoring his movements, as if she was cataloguing every action he made. "It's good to see you again."

Theo hadn't bothered to take off his winter coat. He'd had to exchange his leather coat for a wool peacoat that was a bit longer at the waist. One, the lining was a hell of a lot warmer this time of year. Two, the length made it far easier to hide his firearm. Three, his mother had given it to him as a birthday present last year. No one could argue that she didn't have the best eye for design, which was where he'd gotten his penchant for style.

"Former Special Agent Theo Neville."

Theo tensed at the way Officer Soerig had used his previous title. He was used to long stares of curiosity due to his eyepatch, just as he was accustomed to people recognizing his surname. His father, who was on the cusp of taking over as the NYPD Commissioner, had been making headlines recently. He was more than deserving of such a title, and his dedication to the city had been his driving force.

"That's right," Theo stated cautiously as her tone solidified his plan to keep this meeting short. Still, he didn't want to come across as the rude one. He tried to lighten the mood. "I'm going to need a drink, aren't I?"

Officer Soerig finally broke their stare and caught the gaze of the bartender. She lifted her arm and signaled that she wanted two more drinks, presumably the same beverage that was in her hand. The gesture signified that she knew the bartender personally.

"Call me Hadley." She drained what was left of her beer and set the empty bottle near the napkin holder. "I'm curious. Why did you leave the Bureau?"

"Do you really have to ask that question?" Theo countered as he seriously debated calling Brook and letting her know that he'd made a mistake. He probably should have left well enough alone, but there had been something about Hadley that made him want to get to know her. To say that he was second-guessing himself now would be an understatement. "Look, I can have someone else take this meeting."

"I'm being serious." Hadley frowned, as if he was the one who had the problem. "I don't understand why you would leave the FBI. I get why they might not want you in the field, although I'm sure you can handle yourself just fine. Still, you can't tell me that they wouldn't have you working investigations from the inside."

"You mean a desk job?"

"Does it really matter if you're out questioning people or sitting at a desk? Either way, you get access to the files. Grunt work doesn't necessarily mean anything in the grand scheme of things."

Theo found that he might be having a change of heart.

He might actually enjoy the upcoming conversation.

He smiled as he stood from the chair. By the time that he'd removed his winter coat and placed it around the back of his chair, the bartender himself had delivered two bottles of beer.

"Hadley, don't forget that you're up in an hour. I owe you."

"No, Dad owes me a lot more than one. He needs to hire another bartender. I won't be available after this weekend." Hadley waited for the bartender to return to his post before she held up her beer. She waited for Theo to do the same. She then clinked the neck of her bottle to his before taking a healthy swig. "In all seriousness, I'd like to know why you gave up a career to go into the private sector."

Several things fell into place, and Theo was glad that he'd made the decision to meet with Hadley. He was attracted to her drive, her no-nonsense attitude, and her need to see that justice was delivered. He wouldn't deny that her beauty played a part in it, as well.

"Your parents own this establishment, the bartender is your brother, and you recently took the detective's exam. I'm guessing that you passed it with flying colors, and you're being transferred to homicide next week." Theo paused to take a drink of his beer. The cold, wheat beverage was most welcome after spending the majority of the day behind a computer screen. "As for your view of the FBI, I didn't take you for an idealist, Hadley."

Hadley returned his smile and sat back in her chair. She began to rotate the bottle in her hands as she replied to his conclusions.

"Two out of three," Hadley replied before giving him an in-depth analysis of his answers. "Yes, my parents own this bar. Yes, I took the detective's exam and passed with the highest score that they have seen in the past eight years. As for Hayden, he is my half-brother."

Hadley had waited until Theo had taken another swig of his beer, her words causing him to choke back his laugh as the liquid attempted to go down his throat. She handed him a napkin, her green eyes sparkling with mischief.

"You don't give an inch, do you?"

Whereas Hadley was biracial, Hayden was Caucasian. They shared the same distinct green eyes that resembled delicate jade crystals, which was how Theo had known that the two of them had been related by blood.

Theo came from a mixed family himself. While his father and mother were both African American, born and raised in Queens, his maternal grandmother was Asian. Both of Theo's parents loved New York City, but it had been his mother who had pushed him to pursue his dream of being a federal agent. His father would have preferred Theo join the NYPD.

"No, I don't give an inch. And I also don't consider myself an idealist, Mr. Neville."

Theo recognized her subtle hint that he hadn't invited her to use his first name. He rectified that as he made himself comfortable after adjusting his chair so that his back was to the wall. He had to turn his head to the right to address her, but he didn't like having his back exposed, even if they were in a bar full of law enforcement officers.

"What you consider yourself to be and how you actually view life are two completely different estimations," Theo pointed out before explaining his reasons behind such a drastic change in his life. "I'm not well-suited to be confined behind a desk. I'd go stir crazy. I prefer the field and interacting with people. To not do so would have me losing my ability to read any given situation. Facts on paper don't necessarily spell out the complete picture."

"Your father doesn't seem to mind a desk job," Hadley pointed out, revealing that she'd done her homework.

"My father is at a different stage in his life where it makes sense for him to take an alternative path." Theo was very proud of what his parents had accomplished, and he wouldn't begrudge them their personal choices. "My mother is a decorated officer, as well. She retires next month. It's my father who isn't ready to give up his career, and an opportunity opened up that he couldn't refuse. Much like the one that has been presented to you with your upcoming promotion."

Hadley picked at the label of the bottle as she studied him, not hiding her interest in his eyepatch. She was brazen, and that was one of the reasons that he was attracted to her.

Unfortunately, he had a job to do first.

"What was your impression of Dr. David Kolsby when you questioned him?" Theo asked, changing the subject so that he could report back to Brook. She would be in the office until late, and there was a chance that Hadley had information that could aid Brook in somehow creating a profile that could help determine the man's guilt. "You gave the impression that you believe Ms. Gwinn's claims."

"Kolsby is a borderline narcissist," Hadley declared with confidence as she leaned forward with interest. "I don't know how he could be one of the top psychiatrists in his field. He monopolized most of the interview, didn't come across as being very genuine, and became rather impatient when I pressed the issue."

"Could his reaction to you have been a result of the medication? I'm assuming he was still on some form of narcotic when you spoke with him," Theo surmised, knowing just how different one could be when in pain and on drugs. He hadn't been the most pleasant person to be around last year when he'd initially suffered his eye injury. "I take it you spoke to Kolsby when he was still in the hospital."

"Yes, but his reaction wasn't due to pain or any type of medication," Hadley refuted, scrunching her nose as she thought back to her interview. "Kolsby was a bit ruffled. I could see it in his eyes. His older son was in the hospital room at the time, too. Oddly enough, he didn't say a word. He just sat in the chair and looked down at his hands during the interview."

"The entire time?" Theo inquired, finding such behavior abnormal. "If my father was accused of murder, I'm not so sure I could maintain my cool."

"Agreed."

Hadley lifted the bottle of beer to her lips, giving Theo time to make another observation.

"You mentioned that he was impatient. How?"

"Kolsby didn't feel he needed to answer my questions. The formality of it seemed to be beneath him. He didn't want to be answering any questions, and he was definitely angry that a nurse whose job it had been to simply monitor his recovery would question his character. All normal reactions, but it seemed over-the-top." Hadley set her bottle back down on the table. "It wouldn't surprise me if he sues her for defamation. Trust me, if he can prove that Ms. Gwinn's words lost him a patient or tarnished his stellar reputation, he won't hesitate to go after her in court."

"Millie Gwinn seems genuine."

"She does," Hadley agreed. "It's the reason that I suggested to Ms. Sloane that we speak outside of work. I can give you my personal opinion, but it's basically her word against his, and I didn't find any reason to believe that he was involved with any criminal activity. There are no bodies, nothing to tie him to any open murder investigation, and no other potential leads to keep the complaint on the books. You have your job cut out for you if you're going to try and prove otherwise."

"I'll be honest with you," Theo said after he'd taken another swig of his beer. "I'm not so sure we would have taken the case if Ms. Gwinn hadn't called my cell phone this morning. She all but ambushed us at a pub near our offices. We were going to discuss her claims during our morning debriefing. Let's face it. You're right in that there are no bodies and nothing to point to any murder investigation."

"Do you believe her?"

"You mean about the break-in this morning?" Theo asked, waiting for Hadley's nod before continuing with his response. "I do. I also spoke with Ms. Gwinn's sister today. Millie spent the night with the family, and she didn't leave until an hour before she called me. The timing lines up. Someone definitely broke into her apartment, and I find it odd that nothing was taken."

"The neighbor to the right of Ms. Gwinn had already left for work, and the neighbor to the left didn't hear a thing over his music. As for the neighbor across the hall, the husband claimed to have heard something. Unfortunately, he got sidetracked by a phone call from his mother-in-law. He said that he forgot all about the noise by the end of the conversation." Hadley shook her head in amusement at recalling said interview. "I've decided that mothers-in-law can make or break a marriage. In all seriousness, you and I both know that the likelihood of us locating the perp is next to nil. Also, Dr. Kolsby is still recovering from surgery, broken ribs, and a head injury. Do you really think that someone in that state of health could go traipsing around the city and barging through doors?"

Hadley made a good point, but Kolsby could have easily paid someone to scare Millie Gwinn into recanting her claims.

They spent the next forty minutes talking about the case, Hadley's impressions of those who she'd interviewed, and her belief that there wasn't much that could be done with so little evidence.

Technically, there was no evidence that any crime had been committed by Dr. Kolsby, and it all came down to one person's word over another. Should S&E Investigations find that Dr. David Kolsby was nothing more than an upstanding citizen, they would have no choice but to close the case.

"Hadley?"

"I hear you," Hadley called out to her brother. She collected her two empty bottles, plus the one that Theo had drained before meeting his gaze. "I close the bar at two tonight."

Theo slowly smiled at her not-so-subtle hint.

Ever since his injury, he'd sworn off complicated relationships.

Maybe it was time to change his frame of mind.

"I could go for another round."

Chapter Eight

Brooklyn Sloane
December 2022
Saturday — 6:14am

The elevator doors slowly opened onto the first floor of Brook's building, giving her time to adjust her scarf. She was running later than usual this morning due to receiving a call from her father's nursing home in Morton, Illinois. He'd somehow fallen out of bed. The staff had immediately called 911, and he'd been transported to the hospital as a precautionary measure. X-rays and a CT scan had been ordered, and they should have the results relatively soon.

Brook had made sure the ringer on her phone wasn't set to silence before tucking it into the side of her purse. She didn't want to miss such an important call, and she once again debated with herself over whether or not she should continue to abide by her father's wishes.

He'd wanted to remain in Illinois.

He'd stressed his desire to do so numerous times during the earlier stages of his Alzheimer's Disease. She'd been assured many times over the last couple of years that he wouldn't know if he'd been moved to another facility in another state, but she wasn't so sure of that assumption. The bottom line was that she couldn't break the promise that she'd given her father after his doctor's initial findings.

Brook couldn't push back her concern that her father was nearing his eventual death. She'd wanted more than anything to one day be able to tell him that Jacob was no longer free to inflict pain on others. It didn't matter that he wouldn't understand in his physical and mental state. She'd just wanted to be able to say the words before he passed away.

Stepping out onto the marble floor, she pulled her leather gloves from the pocket of her winter dress coat. Since it was Saturday, she wasn't wearing her usual business attire. Instead, she'd opted for a pair of dark jeans, a brown turtleneck, and a tweed blazer. Professional, but casual since she planned on meeting with Millie later this morning.

Brook had just finished slipping her left hand into one of the leather gloves when she caught sight of Hadley Soerig. The officer wasn't in uniform, and she'd already opened the first door of the double entrance.

Officer Soerig hadn't noticed Brook at all.

It didn't take a genius to connect the dots.

Theo had moved into the building three weeks ago, wanting to be closer to work. A condo had become available on the tenth floor. They didn't even share an elevator bank, but such a sighting had Brook rethinking dinner with Graham on Wednesday night.

She wasn't the type of woman to second-guess herself, and what she did on her own personal time didn't concern anyone else. Still, it made her slightly uncomfortable to know something about Theo that he would no doubt like to keep private.

Brook paused as she stepped onto the industrial-sized grey mat that protected the marble tile throughout winter. She took

CHAPTER EIGHT

her time securing the second glove, not wanting Officer Soerig to still be outside waiting for a cab or an Uber.

"Good morning, Ms. Sloane."

Brook glanced over at the main counter where Charlie McPherson was standing with a smile on his face. He usually worked Monday through Friday, six o'clock in the morning until three o'clock in the afternoon.

Seeing him on a Saturday was unusual.

"Good morning, Charlie. Did Dennis call off sick?"

"Yes, ma'am," Charlie stated with a vigorous nod. "Lou will be working second shift, but we don't mind the overtime with the holidays so near."

"How are you doing in fantasy football this season?"

"Second place," Charlie boasted in pride. "Come tomorrow, I might be in first."

"Don't go rubbing it in Lou's face," Brook warned good-naturedly as she advanced toward the door. "Have a good day, Charlie."

The bitter cold wind stole Brook's breath, but she'd tucked her scarf into her dress coat as a barrier. She didn't waste time as she quickly walked to the corner before immediately crossing at the intersection. The pedestrian light had given her the right of way, and she wasn't going to spend one more second outside than was necessary. After a brief stop at her favorite café, she made it to the office building two blocks down in record time.

S&E Investigations was located on the fourteenth floor.

Since the first two floors contained a local bank, there was no real foot traffic this time of morning. While the bank had lobby hours from nine to noon today, the majority of their office space on the floors above would remain vacant until Monday morning.

The first thing she noticed upon entering the offices was the Christmas music drifting down the hallway. She presumed that Sylvie had discovered something, but Brook took her time to hang up her dress coat, change from her winter boots into her favorite pair of black ankle boots, and turn on the space heater to its highest setting.

Much to Brook's surprise, Sylvie's office was empty.

"What on earth are you doing here on a Saturday morning?" Brook asked Bit as she caught him playing an air guitar to "Santa Claus is Coming to Town" by Bruce Springsteen. He only ever played the air guitar when he was in a good mood. "You found something, didn't you?"

Brook had specifically told the team that they didn't need to come into the office this weekend. They weren't dealing with a typical case that had an invisible clock that was ticking away in the background. No one was in immediate danger, and they weren't even certain that there was a serial killer working in the D.C. area.

A lot of background investigations had to be completed before they came to any conclusions, and Brook's meeting with Millie today would give the investigation a bit more clarity.

"Morning, Boss!" Bit practically launched himself in his chair so that it rolled across the black antistatic mat. He always played music from the sound bar hooked up to the computer at the end of the long table. "I not only found something, but I might have a new theory."

"A new theory?" Brook inquired with interest.

She'd entered Bit's domain, noticing right offhand that he'd been busy with the decorations. While she'd known that he'd stapled garland to the ceiling, she hadn't realized that he'd acquired a Charlie Brown Christmas tree. It was on the back table surrounded by a mound of cotton balls that she assumed were supposed to mimic snow.

She grimaced when she counted four gifts tucked underneath the lower branches.

She hadn't had to buy anyone gifts for the holidays in too many years to count. Her father's annual gifts of socks, underwear, and t-shirts didn't really count in the grand scheme of things. There was a reminder in her calendar on the first of every December to place the same order.

Sylvie had been the one to mention that she'd found the perfect gift for Bit last month. Ever since, Brook had continually put off even contemplating any kind of holiday shopping. Such thoughts raised her stress level, and she was confident that she already had enough on her plate.

"Like I said yesterday, Millie Gwinn's apartment building only has a security camera in the front lobby." Bit pulled up a somewhat grainy photograph, and Brook realized it was a still from a video. "Well, I was able to pull several other camera angles from the time in question. See this sedan parked a block away? It's registered to Brett Kolsby. What if the good ol' doctor isn't a serial killer? What if Dr. Kolsby's son is the guilty party, and Dr. Kolsby was in the throes of some nightmare when he was mumbling those words to Millie Gwinn? I know, I know. It sounds like the plot of one of my sister's soap operas, but you've got to admit that it would make sense."

Brook stared at the license plate of the sedan in contemplation.

"Is there footage of Brett Kolsby actually entering Millie Gwinn's apartment building?"

"No." Bit motioned toward another monitor. He submitted a command on the keyboard, which in turn began to play a short clip from the security camera. "The oldest Kolsby son enters an apartment building across the street at one o'clock in the morning and exits a little before five. He supposedly spent four hours inside, but he could have easily walked out a side entrance, used a steam tunnel or something, and somehow made it around to the back entrance of Millie's apartment building."

Brook wasn't necessarily buying that theory.

"We could be looking at many possibilities here." Brook stared at the monitor as she gathered her thoughts. "One, Brett

Kolsby was simply in the wrong place at the wrong time. He could very well have a friend who lives in that particular building. Two, Brett believes that Millie could tarnish his father's reputation with false accusations. He went to her apartment, believed that she was home but purposefully not answering the door, and then took matters into his own hands. Three, there is something to Millie's claims regarding Dr. Kolsby, and Brett was purposefully seeking her out to either threaten or kill her to stop her from spreading the truth."

"All good theories," Bit said as he didn't bother to stifle his yawn. He even stretched in his chair with his arms high up in the air. "Do you know if Big T is coming into the office this morning? I was thinking of using his couch to catch some Zs."

Bit basically had nicknames for everyone, and the moniker Big T belonged to Theo for his muscular build. Sylvie's nickname was Little T due to her love for tea.

Somehow, Brook just got stuck with Boss.

"I doubt it. Then again, I didn't think you would still be here after pulling an all-nighter," Brook pointed out as she continued to stare at the monitor. "Before you do either hole up in Theo's office or go home for the weekend, would you please print that photo out for me, along with one of Brett Kolsby?"

"Sure thing, Boss."

"Go home, Bit," Brook recommended, giving him a pat of encouragement on his shoulder. "Great work, as usual."

Brook retreated and walked back to her office where her large caramel macchiato was still waiting for her on the desk. It was the first thing that she picked up before taking a seat. The rich, sweet flavor was most welcome. She sighed in appreciation before reaching for the remote control on her desk.

Before too long, she had settled into her regular routine.

Thankfully, a phone call thirty minutes later revealed that her father had been taken back to the nursing home with no broken bones.

CHAPTER EIGHT

A chime that she'd set on her tablet to alert her to any changes to the files of their investigations faintly rang out an hour later as she was in the middle of perusing Dr. Kolsby's background check. Nothing in it suggested the psyche of a serial killer.

Then again, working backward did have disadvantages.

Bit had brought her the printed photos that she'd requested before deciding that he was too tired to head home. He'd opted for Theo's couch. Brook wasn't sure how long he would be asleep, so she made sure to request that he close the door in case he was still sleeping when Millie came into the office for her ten o'clock meeting.

Brook relinquished her hold on the computer mouse and picked up her tablet. She couldn't stop the small smile at reading the name of the user who had finished inserting information into the Kolsby file.

Theo hadn't let his personal life interfere with the case.

He'd uploaded the notes from his conversation with Officer Soerig last night.

Brook quickly perused the notes, pausing when she landed on Brett Kolsby's name. He'd been in his father's room at the time Officer Soerig had questioned Dr. Kolsby. The officer had highlighted the son's unusual reaction by remaining completely silent during the interview. Accusations of murder had been discussed, and it was odd that the older son hadn't come to his father's defense nor basically made any comment at all.

Brett Kolsby could very well be the weak link that could either convict or exonerate his father.

Chapter Nine

Brooklyn Sloane
December 2022
Monday — 9:38am

A SMOOTH BLANKET OF snow covered the large front yard of Dr. David Kolsby's residence. The six thousand, four hundred, and eighty-three square foot house was grand in its stature. The beige and tan brick exterior had been professionally decorated for the holidays. Brook came to such a conclusion because no ladder that a regular homeowner owned could have hung the extravagant wreath from the high entryway. She could only imagine what it looked like at night with all its lights shining brightly.

She remained inside her Volvo S90 as she took in the sight before her.

She'd parked on the circular drive that had not one spot of ice or snow on its heated surface. There were no other vehicles nearby, but the driveway had forked a few yards back. If she'd veered left instead of right, she was almost certain the driveway would have taken her somewhere around the rear of

CHAPTER NINE 83

the property. She assumed that was where the large multi-bay garage was for the homeowner's fleet of vehicles.

Dr. Kolsby had most likely stayed in the residence after his second divorce due to the impression of owning such an estate conveyed to visitors.

After all, he had appearances to maintain.

The interview with Millie hadn't provided anything of relevance. While Brook had been hoping that Dr. Kolsby had provided more detail in his alleged confession, that hadn't been the case.

She'd also spoken to Millie's protective detail.

Nothing had seemed out of place since they'd started monitoring the woman's surroundings. It was all boiling down to Brook's opinion after she spoke with the good doctor himself.

Did S&E Investigations have any grounds to pursue the good doctor or not?

During Brook's interview with Millie, both scenarios had been laid out on the table. Millie was well aware that all the firm could do was look into her allegations. If it was determined that Dr. Kolsby was as upstanding as his reputation made him out to be, then it wasn't right to keep picking apart the man's life.

Brook didn't bother to put on her leather gloves before vacating her car. She didn't plan to be outside too long, and the walk to the front entrance was relatively close to the circular drive. Once she was standing in front of the oversized double doors, she didn't waste any time ringing the doorbell.

She didn't put too much stock in the fact that she was left outside longer than usual since someone was expecting her. From her understanding, Dr. Kolsby employed a housekeeper, as well as a professional cleaning service that came in weekly to clean the house from top to bottom. Sylvie's research had turned up a few more odds and ends of interest, but nothing that screamed the man's guilt.

"Hello," a beautiful woman greeted with a hesitant smile. "You must be Brooklyn Sloane. My father is expecting you."

"You must be Catherine."

Catherine Kolsby was the epitome of class. Money had nothing to do with how she carried herself, either. She was confident, and not only of her appearance. She was also a recent graduate from law school. She'd already passed the state bar, and she'd been hired as a first-year associate at a prestigious law firm in D.C.

She was definitely on the fast track.

"May I take your coat?" Catherine asked after she'd closed the door and taken a step back. "Peg, our housekeeper, is at a doctor's appointment. She made sure to set out refreshments for us before leaving. My father and brothers are waiting in the den."

Brook hadn't expected to speak with the entire Kolsby family. She found it interesting that Catherine lived elsewhere with her fiancé, yet she still referred to the housekeeper in a possessive manner.

Words were important in a case like this one, and Brook found herself wishing she'd brought Theo along for this interview. He and Sylvie had split up the list of hospital staff who had attended to Dr. Kolsby in the days after his surgery.

It was best that they were not questioned at the hospital.

Millie had already suffered a setback in her job, and it wouldn't be fair to have her completely ostracized by the hospital staff by announcing that she hadn't dropped her allegations like she'd been directed by her supervisors. It was best that the investigation be handled quietly and delicately for all parties involved in the case.

"Yes, please." Brook set her purse on the entryway table as she removed her dress coat and scarf. She'd worn a pinstriped pantsuit with high heels. She'd seen no reason to wear her winter boots when was simply driving from the parking garage of her building straight to a residence. That did not mean she hadn't brought along her tote bag in case of an emergency. "Your father has a lovely home."

Brook's adjective had been an understatement.

The foyer alone was as large as Brook's living room and dining room put together, causing an echo when someone spoke too loudly. Since Brook's condo was quite large and expensive in its own right, it had nothing on a house of this size. The décor was almost solely Victorian in nature, with a few deviances here and there for modern technology.

The ornate stairways on either side of the foyer led the way to the second story. The detailed trim of the banister and spindles was quite breathtaking. The splendor of the entrance was only enhanced by the lavish cut-crystal chandelier overhead. Brook guessed it was a 17th century French Empire Estate Style weighing in around four-hundred pounds.

A large Howard Miller grandfather clock was to the right, next to an irregular wall that was not uncommon with such décor. Inside the modest nook was a small oil painting no more than eighteen inches square that was highlighted by a hidden recess light. If Brook wasn't mistaken, it was either a Vermeer that was almost certainly part of the Frick Collection or a damned good replica. She would put her money on the former, which meant Kolsby's wealth had far more complexity than she'd previously understood.

"Dad couldn't part with the house after divorcing my mother," Catherine said as she took Brook's coat and walked over to an oversized closet. She took her time opening the door, choosing a wooden hanger, and carefully placing Brook's dress coat separate from the others. "Seeing as Mom wanted to move to South Carolina, it all worked out for the best. As I said, Peg set out some tea, coffee, and a pitcher of chilled water. Which would you prefer?"

"Coffee, please." Brook was a proponent for making others at ease, especially in a situation like this one. Giving a host something to do prevented them from overthinking their words or the uncomfortable situation before them. "It's quite cold out this morning."

"It seems like we might have a small break in the weather. I don't believe snow is in the forecast for the next week or so." Catherine made sure the closet door was completely closed before gesturing toward the left side of the home. She wore a pair of black slacks and a matching silk blouse, though the focal point was the unique width of the white belt around her waist. The contrast was only enhanced by the silver jewelry and rather large engagement ring on her left hand. "Please, follow me. Would you like cream and sugar?"

"Black is fine," Brook murmured as she fell behind Catherine.

They both rounded the corner on the left, and Brook didn't think she could be more impressed with the choice of décor. Catherine had led her to an exceptional library, which she'd referred to as a den. A blazing fire was flickering its flames in a hearth with a cherrywood mantel that had been decorated for the holidays. The green garland was nothing like what Kate had purchased for the offices of S&E Investigations.

This particular garland was thick, lush, and frosted with plump pinecones and sprigs of holly with red berries as decorative accents.

The Christmas tree was a Balsam Fir and stood at least twelve feet tall. It was difficult to ascertain if the tree was real or fake, but there was no doubt that the decorations were valuable. The gold and deep red bulbs weren't the kind of ornaments that children brought home from school. They appeared to be early 19th century handblown German glass ornaments.

The men must have previously been in deep conversation, although they'd all fallen silent the moment that Catherine and Brook had entered the room. The only sounds that she could

CHAPTER NINE 87

distinguish were the shifting logs, the rhythmic ticking of the mantel clock, and faint music drifting down from some hidden speakers in the ceiling. The holiday tunes weren't the standard songs on the radio, either. Instead, she was almost certain the music was the holiday collection of an orchestra.

"Ms. Sloane, thank you for driving all the way out here to speak with us," Dr. Kolsby said from a leather chair that was part of a seating arrangement in front of the magnificent fireplace. A cherrywood desk had been position near the far wall in front of a bookcase lined with what looked to be medical textbooks bound in leather, hardcover reference books of every sort, and cases of collective journals cataloged by publisher, author, and year. "I'm still recovering from—"

"Dad, you don't need to get up."

"I'm fine, son. I'm fine. Where are your manners?" Dr. David Kolsby stood, though it was clear such movement caused him considerable pain. Brook briefly shook his hand before stepping back. He still seemed weak from the accident. "It's a pleasure, Ms. Sloane."

"Dr. Kolsby, I appreciate you meeting me on such short notice. I was sorry to hear about your injuries."

"You've met Catherine, I presume." Dr. Kolsby nodded toward his daughter who had walked over to a credenza that held an ornate carafe and a tray of matching, porcelain mugs with a gold leaf family crest on them. "These fine young men are my sons, Brett and Nolan."

Brook remained silent as she shook their hands. The only animosity she could sense came from Nolan, who was the younger of the two. Both men resembled their father, without the greying hair and fake tan. They had his square facial features, large foreheads, and brown eyes. She studied each of them. While they had both met her gaze directly, Nolan was more direct of the two.

"Please, have a seat."

"I have to say that I'm surprised you were so willing to meet with me after hearing that Millie Gwinn sought out our services." Brook purposefully walked back to the second leather chair so that she wouldn't be caught sitting next to someone on the couch. It turned out that both Brett and Nolan remained standing near the fireplace. "As I mentioned on the phone, S&E Investigations is a private investigations firm. Ms. Gwinn came to us after the police determined that there was no validity to her claims."

"Ridiculous claims, you mean."

Dr. Kolsby raised his hand extending one finger when Nolan would have continued to respond in an impolite manner.

"I have nothing to hide, Ms. Sloane," Dr. Kolsby said confidently as Catherine brought over two cups of coffee. She handed one to Brook before relinquishing the second cup to her father. He was dressed in a pair of black pants with a burgundy cardigan sweater over a well-starched white dress shirt. Since a couple of weeks had already passed since his car accident, the lacerations on the left side of his face were almost completely healed. "The police have done their due diligence, and they have determined such accusations to be completely unfounded."

"I have spoken to Officer Soerig, and you are correct. She has concluded that Ms. Gwinn's accusations are baseless." Brook took a sip of her coffee and found that it was some of the best that she'd ever had the pleasure of drinking. The warmth from the porcelain cup was quite welcoming, but what she found she enjoyed most was the blazing fire. The heat permeated her clothes and swathed her skin. "Ms. Gwinn has simply hired my firm to fact check those findings. One of my colleagues has a family member in the medical field, and it is her firm belief that anesthesia doesn't act as a truth serum."

"Your colleague would be correct. You can imagine my surprise when the police were suddenly at the end of my bed, asking if I'd murdered someone. And not just one murder, but several supposed victims." Dr. Kolsby shook his head with just the right amount of disbelief. Brook had yet to notice any tell of his that indicated he was making false statements. "I've dedicated my life to helping others, Ms. Sloane. You may talk to my former wives. Unfortunately, they will confirm that I spent more time at the office than with them."

Catherine had taken a seat on the couch, and Brook had noticed the woman had chosen the cushion closest to her father. She'd even chuckled at his words, as if she could give his jest the weight of truth.

Maybe it was the truth.

"What I am telling you is that I could never harm another human being, physical or otherwise. The mental psyche is equally as fragile as the human body, Ms. Sloane. I believe in my oath, and I'm very good at what I do—helping others deal with their emotional and mental issues due to the harsh impact of the elements around them."

While Dr. Kolsby delved into numerous examples of how much he cared for his patients and how he had helped them overcome their tragic pasts, Brook monitored the reactions of the other three occupants.

Catherine clearly adored and admired her father without reservation. There was no underlying fear, no hesitancy, and no distrust in her gestures.

Brett held a coffee cup in his hand, but he hadn't once taken a sip of the beverage. He hadn't been focused on the conversation, either. From the time he'd greeted her, his attention had been on the orange flames flickering in the hearth as they searched for more oxygen.

Nolan, on the other hand, had his arms crossed and was standing with his feet shoulder length apart. Brook's presence had clearly irritated him beyond words, and he'd gone on the defensive. His dark eyes were practically drilling a hole into her head. He wouldn't remain silent for long.

"Is there a chance that you said something that Ms. Gwinn could have misinterpreted?"

"Certainly. It's possible that I had a nightmare," Dr. Kolsby replied smoothly before taking a sip of his coffee. He then shifted slightly to set his mug on the antique stand next to him with a noticeable wince. He rested his right hand on the left side of his ribs. "You must understand that I'm not calling Ms. Gwinn a liar. It's just her insistence that whatever was said reflects reality. From my understanding, she is a very responsible and experienced nurse. I could very well have muttered something I dreamt about while under the influence of something that she misconstrued in the moment."

"Dad, you've already spoken to the police. Ms. Sloane has absolutely no standing here. This interview is just a courtesy," Nolan exclaimed with impatience. He finally let his arms drop, though he slid his right hand into the pocket of his trousers. "You should be resting. Not answering pointless questions from someone who—"

"Enough."

Brook met Nolan's glare, and she wished that Dr. Kolsby had not interrupted his son. She was very interested in what he'd been about to call her, and she didn't need a doctorate in psychology to know that it had to do with her brother. Having been in many situations such as this one, she'd managed not to react too hastily. Instead, she took another sip of her coffee before meeting Nolan's scowl.

"I take you are acquainted with my personal history?" Brook asked directly, noticing how Nolan blinked his eyes several times before casting a glance toward his father. "You don't need to worry, Mr. Kolsby. I'm not on some quest to ruin the lives of innocent people due to some deep-seated fear that everyone I'm asked to investigate is some kind of psychopathic or sociopathic serial killer. I pride myself on my work ethic and my ability to see through the various obstacles and disinformation thrown my way regarding those involved in a case."

"My father has done nothing wrong, and I personally believe that woman should be fired for making false allegations and character assassination," Nolan stated as he straightened his shoulders. "If he did say anything resembling what this Gwinn woman was claiming, it could have been due to a drug-induced delusion, a conversation that he had with a patient concerning some messed up fantasy, or even a memory from some horror film he saw over the Halloween holiday. My sister has a fondness for them, although I don't see the attraction. She—"

"I beg your pardon?" Catherine snapped as the two of them then began to argue. "What is so wrong with…"

Brook settled back in the chair and enjoyed her coffee as she observed Brett's reaction to the squabble between his siblings. He'd given both his sister and brother a sideways look of frustration, but he intentionally didn't place himself in the middle of their verbal dispute. Officer Soerig had been accurate with her description of him. The oldest sibling was quiet, introspective, and preferred not to be caught in the middle of his family quarrels.

"There is no need for such formality," Dr. Kolsby said, causing his children to fall quiet. "First names, please. I take it your ability to see through the disarray of information comes from growing up with a troubled sibling?"

Dr. Kolsby's inquiry had promptly caused Nolan and Catherine to suddenly become quiet. Their father had clearly asked such a question to see if he could make a dent in Brook's composure. She'd been expecting such a query from him due to the way he'd been observing her in the same manner in which she'd been monitoring his children.

He'd obviously done so for one of two reasons.

Either he wanted to demonstrate his abilities as a psychiatrist, or he wanted to bait her into giving up information regarding Millie Gwinn. Giving it more thought, it could possibly be on the grounds of both.

"I would give credit to my childhood, yes," Brook answered truthfully as she crossed her legs, knowing full well that Dr. Kolsby would take notice of such body language. When an individual crossed one's legs, it displayed their relative ease with a situation. Basically, such a gesture meant a person was comfortable, and she wanted him to believe that the topic of Jacob didn't bother her. "I'm not naive enough to think that you didn't see my interview from earlier this year. Having a brother such as Jacob Walsh has given me specialized insight into the mind of a killer, but I credit my education and specific training inside the Bureau even more so. I've been able to sharpen my skills over the years, and my closure rate with the BAU speaks for itself."

Brook paused to take another sip of coffee, noticing that she'd garnered even Brett's attention. He was staring at her with sudden interest.

"I'll be frank with all of you," Brook said before waiting a heartbeat while she took her time debating which avenue to take this discussion.

She hadn't requested this interview with the family because she thought they would be forthcoming with the truth. She'd simply done so in order to get a sense of whether or not Millie's claims had any substance. With that in mind, Brook tilted her head slightly as she met Dr. Kolsby's curious stare.

"I don't believe that you should use your influence to fire anyone who was simply attempting to make sure no one had been hurt," Brook advised before turning the discussion up a notch. "Ms. Gwinn has also taken an oath, just as you have, Dr. Kolsby. The police have concluded that there is no basis to her claims. She most likely would have left things well enough alone, but she suddenly found herself being transferred out of the ICU to a different floor with less prestige. On top of that, she was given notice from upper management at the hospital to see a therapist to ensure that the stress of her job hasn't been taking its toll. You can imagine her reaction to such changes and stipulations."

"Now, wait a second," Catherine said as she reached over the arm of the couch in order to cover her father's hand with her own. "My father had nothing to do with—"

"It's alright, Catherine." Dr. Kolsby turned his hand over to squeeze his daughter's fingers in reassurance. "May I call you Brooklyn?"

Brook gave him a single nod, getting the sense that he'd expected her to argue at such informality. As long as she obtained the answers she sought, she couldn't care less what he called her.

"Brooklyn, I did not use my influence at the hospital to have Ms. Gwinn transferred from one floor to another, nor did I ask that she be forced to see a therapist once a week," Dr. Kolsby replied in a rather cavalier manner. She caught the slightest catch in his tone when she smiled at his rebuttal. "Any changes in Ms. Gwinn's employment was merely a coincidence."

"I didn't share the number of times that Ms. Gwinn was forced to see a therapist," Brook pointed out calmly, taking everyone by surprise. "See, Nolan? It's not always wise to use one's influence. Such a choice can cast a shadow on one's innocence."

Everyone broke out with their opinion at once, with the exception of Brook and Dr. Kolsby. He was too busy attempting to read her body language, which she'd made sure was the same as when she'd first settled into the chair.

"I said that's enough," Dr. Kolsby called out to his children when it was obvious they were just getting started with the defense of their father. "Cast a shadow on one's innocence? If you truly believe that I am not capable of murder, why have you agreed to continue an investigation that clearly has no merit?"

"First, everyone is capable of murder." Brook finished her coffee before setting her empty mug on the matching stand next to her chair. It was doubtful that she'd be offered another serving. "I see no reason not to be brutally honest with you, Dr. Kolsby. My second reason is that while you might be a narcissist, I doubt that you currently possess the physical strength to break into Ms. Gwinn's apartment."

Once again, Brook's statement was enough to cause a slight eruption from the others. They certainly were predicable.

"I meant no disrespect," Brook said loudly as she suspected that Dr. Kolsby had a difference of opinion from his sons and daughter. He preferred to deal with direct people. Brett was the one whose grunt of annoyance was last heard, but she ignored him to concentrate on the man in question. "Nolan's theory has piqued my curiosity, though. We all know that anesthesia isn't a truth serum, but Millie Gwinn didn't put words in your mouth, Doctor. I don't believe that she lied about what you said when you were coming out of your induced sleep, just as I don't believe she imagined a broken doorjamb. She came to my firm because she honestly fears for her life."

"What are you talking about?" Dr. Kolsby asked cautiously, letting go of his daughter's hand. He sat a little straighter in his chair while holding the left side of his ribs. "Has something happened to Ms. Gwinn?"

"As I just mentioned, someone broke into her apartment the night before last," Brook replied truthfully, seeing no reason to keep such knowledge under wraps. "Let's just say that Ms. Gwinn doesn't believe in coincidences."

"I can assure you that I had nothing to do with that, Ms. Sloane."

It was good to know that they were now back on formal ground. It made it easier for her to lay out the other details in order to solicit a reaction.

"I wish a simple denial took care of this situation, Dr. Kolsby. Unfortunately, a piece of information has been uncovered that puts your son at the scene of the crime."

Brook found it very interesting that everyone's gaze swung toward Nolan when she'd been referencing Brett. Even his attention was now on his younger brother, but it was the flash of fear in Dr. Kolsby's eyes that had her convinced this case wasn't going to be easy to solve.

Dr. Kolsby *had* uttered the words that had Millie Gwinn seeking out the police. From what Brook was witnessing in this intimate setting, there was some measure of truth to them, as well.

"My apologies." Brook waited for everyone's focus to be turned back toward her before she lit another match. "I wasn't referring to Nolan being seen near Millie Gwinn's apartment."

Catherine jumped to her feet in defense of her older brother, while Nolan was giving his brother advice on remaining silent until their lawyer could be contacted by one of them. Dr. Kolsby was urging Brett to deny such a charge. As for Brett, he wasn't inclined to remain so silent.

Brook had made her final determination.

There was no denying that Dr. Kolsby had information regarding a serial killer. Whether he was covering for a patient, a friend, or a family member was another matter altogether.

Chapter Ten

Sylvie Deering
December 2022
Monday — 10:02am

The quaint two-story residence had been decked out with holiday decorations. The front yard had inflatables that wouldn't be filled with air until sunset, a set of cute wire-framed lighted reindeer, and a string of colorful lights on the eaves that hadn't been set on a timer. It was the tilted snowman with a carrot for a nose that reminded Sylvie of her own childhood.

She tried her best to push away the memories, because every single one had been tainted by the image of her father behind bars. The decision on whether or not to visit him for the holidays loomed over her, and she was secretly wishing that this case bled over into the new year. It was a selfish bid, but she'd never claimed to be a saint. Technically, that was how her family and friends would have categorized her before her father's arrest for securities fraud, money laundering, false official statements. and a slew of other embarrassing charges that she'd rather forget.

"May I help you?"

CHAPTER TEN

Josh Perisot had been the ICU nurse working second shift when Dr. David Kolsby had been brought in after his accident. He most likely wouldn't have been admitted to that floor had he not had bleeding on the brain. Granted, a ruptured spleen could have serious complications even after surgery, but it wouldn't have warranted admission to the intensive care unit unless there had been complications.

"I hope so," Sylvie replied with a smile. "I'm Sylvie Deering, from S&E Investigations. I was hoping that you had a moment to speak with me regarding Millie Gwinn."

Upon hearing the name of his coworker, Josh had become instantly wary of Sylvie's visit. She happened to have lucked out and not have the door slammed into her face after the sweetest two-year-old boy attempted to make a dash for the snow. Josh had to relinquish his hold on the doorknob to capture the blond bundle of energy.

"I only have a few questions." Sylvie kept her smile in place, as well as her tone. "Ms. Gwinn's apartment was broken into the other night, and we're simply making sure that no one has noticed anything unusual of late."

"Someone broke into Millie's apartment?" Josh's concern was evident. He glanced over his shoulder when an odd noise filtered through the main level of the house. The little boy started to clap his hands as if encouraging further chaos. "Come on in."

Sylvie breathed a sigh of relief that she wouldn't need to push harder than necessary. She also hadn't been looking forward to staying outside another second longer. The cold gusts of wind were strong enough to pierce her scarf.

Josh Perisot didn't have to talk to her, but his view on what had transpired could put some context to the situation. Millie had provided Josh's name as one of the employees who she'd shared comments about what she'd overheard, and it would be to her benefit if he'd had a similar experience with Dr. Kolsby.

"Sorry for the mess," Josh muttered as he stepped over a plastic dump truck that had been filled with blocks in his bare feet. As far as Sylvie was concerned, he was tempting fate. "I worked the night shift. My mother-in-law was supposed to take Max for the day, but she claims that she has a mole on her forehead that is suddenly changing shape. We tried to tell her that it hasn't changed at all, but she wouldn't listen to anyone. She just had to make an appointment for the same day that my schedule overlapped with my wife's open house. She's a realtor in the area. My wife, not my mother-in-law."

Josh had been busy securing his son into a highchair that had been positioned next to the kitchen table. The open floor layout gave Sylvie the ability to observe both the kitchen and living room. Toys were scattered everywhere, the television had been set to the cartoon network, a basket of unfolded clothes was on top of the coffee table, and a bag of diapers with an open wipe's container was next to the couch.

Sylvie couldn't help but smile at the chaotic yet sweet existence the Perisots lived on a daily basis. Josh didn't seem to have a filter on the family drama, and she could only imagine how the mother-in-law fit into the scheme of things.

The woman sounded like quite the handful herself.

"You have a lovely home," Sylvie said, genuinely meaning the statement. Josh might not realize it through his haze of exhaustion, but he would look back on these days with fondness at some point. "I don't want to take up too much of your time. Millie mentioned that you were the one who took over Dr. Kolsby's care on the day in question."

"I was," Josh replied as he walked over to the kitchen counter. He took the two pieces of toast that had popped up out of the toaster and all but tossed them onto a plastic plate. He opened a drawer and pulled out a butterknife. "Millie was pretty upset. She said she waited for me to come on duty so that she could go and speak with the floor manager."

CHAPTER TEN 99

Max began cry at being trapped in the highchair. Sylvie instinctively leaned down and made a face. She was glad that Brook and Theo weren't here to witness her silliness. She'd never hear the end of it. While Max didn't laugh, he'd at least stopped crying as he studied her appearance.

"Did Millie tell you what she overhead Dr. Kolsby saying that day?"

"Just that she thought he was confessing to some murder. We all thought she was making too big a deal out of it, but she insisted that it was some type of confession." Josh began to put what appeared to be grape jelly on the toast. He was concentrating so hard that he'd tucked his tongue inside the corner of his lips. "Anyway, Millie wasn't in rotation on the ICU floor the next day that I went into work."

Sylvie hadn't realized that Millie's transfer had taken place at such a rapid speed. The timing of her removal from the ICU floor could be significant, and it warranted further investigation.

Sylvie had definitely captured Max's interest now. He was trying to reach for the hair sticks that she'd used in her bun this morning. They were the same exact gold color of her sweater, and she hadn't been able to resist buying them last week.

"Was Dr. Kolsby alert when you went in that night? Do you think that he may have requested that Millie be moved to another floor?" Sylvie asked as she pulled away from Max just in the nick of time. She'd thought that he'd wanted to grab the hair sticks, but what he'd really wanted was her black-rimmed glasses. "And did you hear him say anything similar?"

"Of course Millie's transfer out of ICU had everything to do with accusing Dr. Kolsby of being a killer." Josh had begun to cut the toast into miniature squares. "Beth is friends with the Kolsbys, so it makes sense. Millie didn't think things through when she escalated the situation."

"Beth?"

"Our floor supervisor."

Sylvie waited for Josh to answer her other question about also hearing Dr. Kolsby say something odd, but he was too busy washing his hands after setting the butterknife in the sink. Max's attention had been drawn to the sound, and it wasn't long afterward that his gaze landed on his breakfast.

He began to struggle once again, hoping to escape his confines.

"And was Dr. Kolsby alert when you began your shift?"

Josh waited to reply until he'd finished drying his hands on a dishtowel.

"I don't feel comfortable talking about one of my patients without their knowledge or consent." Josh picked up Max's plate and brought it over to the highchair. He set the jelly toast on the tray, not so distracted anymore. "Look, Millie made her bed, if you get my drift. Dr. Kolsby is on the board of our hospital. How did she think it was going to pan out?"

Sylvie stood slowly, her knees protesting a bit after how long she'd been kneeling on the floor.

Josh was no longer the distracted father.

"You still haven't answered my question," Sylvie countered, grateful that she hadn't taken off her dress coat or gloves. She had a feeling that she wasn't going to be welcome in the house for too much longer. "Did you overhear Dr. Kolsby say anything that could corroborate Millie's claims?"

"No." Josh had broken his stare before replying so that he could focus on his son. He was lying, but there wasn't a damn thing that she could do about it. "You mentioned that Millie's apartment was broken into. Is she alright?"

Sylvie mulled over her choices, but none of them resulted in Josh confessing that he'd heard Dr. Kolsby confess to murder. She could see why he would assume the break-in had something to do with Millie coming forward, and Sylvie regretted revealing such knowledge. Unfortunately, that lone fact was the reason that she'd garnered access to Josh in the first place.

CHAPTER TEN

Max hummed with each bite that he shoved into his mouth. Josh ran a hand over his son's brown curls. He had a son to protect, and it was evident that he wouldn't jeopardize his family's safety. She couldn't blame him, but such an assumption that someone would threaten another over what had transpired gave more credence to Millie's assertions.

"Millie is fine," Sylvie finally responded. "As a matter of fact, she went into work yesterday."

Sylvie gave Max one last smile as she turned away, fully aware that she wouldn't obtain any more answers from Josh. Unless she changed directions and didn't ask him anything. There was more than one way to build a fire.

"I appreciate you taking the time to speak with me." Sylvie made sure to step around the toy dump truck after searching her path through the array of blocks. "Millie spoke highly of you. She misses the ICU."

Sylvie waited until she was by the front door to turn around and face Josh. He was rubbing his forehead as he lagged behind, her words obviously having an impact.

"I'll be seeing her later today," Sylvie said, not quite sure there was any truth to her statement. There was always the possibility that she could see their client, though. Technically, it wasn't a lie. "I'll be sure to tell her that you said hello."

Sylvie gave a small wave to Max, who was too caught up in his food to even notice the gesture. To be so young and focused on what brought him joy was a sight to behold. Children understood the importance of living in the moment.

"Wait," Josh said right when Sylvie would have reached for the doorknob. He dropped his hand from his forehead in defeat. "Dr. Kolsby was completely aware of his surroundings by the time that I arrived at the hospital for my shift. Around seven o'clock that night and hours after Millie spoke with the floor nurse, Dr. Cranston came down to speak with Dr. Kolsby's older son. It wasn't long after their conversation that Millie was taken off the rotation for ICU."

"Dr. Cranston?" Sylvie repeated with curiosity. She'd seen the name somewhere in her list of hospital staff. "And who is Dr. Cranston?"

"Dr. Neil Cranston." Josh supplied the name with a grimace. It was evident that he had no respect for the doctor. "He's a cardiac surgeon, and a close friend of the Kolsbys."

Sylvie wasn't quite sure what she was missing. Josh seemed to be looking more pointedly at her, as if there was something more to the story than Dr. Cranston somehow having sway over Millie being transferred to another floor. When she continued to stare at him rather blankly, he finally caved and gave her something substantial.

"Dr. Cranston was a suspect in a missing person's case two years ago. He was involved with a lab technician, and one day she didn't show up for work. Her family reported her missing, and Dr. Cranston was questioned by the police. The hospital's PR team kicked into overdrive, and they did their best to minimize Cranston's involvement."

"What was the name of this technician?" Sylvie asked, wondering why Millie hadn't said anything to them about such an obvious link. "And what was the outcome of the investigation?"

"Natalie Thorne. And there was no outcome. She was never found."

Chapter Eleven

Brooklyn Sloane
December 2022
Monday — 1:57pm

"Brook, you have a call on line two."

"Thank you, Kate." Brook refocused her attention on Bit, who was busy writing down a list of internet searches that she would need results from by the end of the day. "Whatever you do, we cannot break any HIPAA laws nor violate the hospital's database firewall. I realize that will limit your search results, but we need to go about this the right way. Not working side by side with law enforcement inhibits our ability to gather certain information. If we do manage to be able to hand this case off to them, we want everything above board so that they can prosecute the guilty party in the court of law."

"You only need the patients' names," Bit said as his fingers skated across the keyboard. "You don't want access to their files. I have an idea that would give us the names of Dr. Kolsby's patients without violating their privacy."

Brook somehow managed to stifle a moan of future regret, but Bit had come a long way since the beginning of the year. While his methods to gathering intel were a bit unorthodox, he was finally understanding why it was so important to remain on the right side of the blurred line that was always presented to them in an investigation.

"I got it covered, Boss. Don't worry."

Brook *would* worry, but she had a call to take and a profile to draft.

She hesitated in her steps toward the door, but then thought better of turning around with another warning. She had to trust her team's decisions within the confines of a case.

As she made her way down the hallway past the various offices and conference rooms, she couldn't help but think back over the morning's events. Bit had already forwarded everything that he could find on Natalie Thorne to the shared documents. Sylvie had uncovered quite the motherload when it came to her meeting with Josh Perisot.

Natalie Thorne had been a twenty-nine-year-old lab technician who had gone missing after a shift at the hospital. Security footage showed her walking to her car and driving out of the hospital's parking lot. She never made it home, and her vehicle had never been recovered.

Was it a coincidence that Natalie Thorne had been a brunette?

A quick glance into Theo's office showed that he still hadn't returned from conducting interviews. The last she'd heard from Theo had been a couple of hours ago. He'd been having trouble locating Scott Crane, the thirty-six-year-old anesthesiologist who had been in surgery when Dr. Kolsby's spleen had been removed. Several of the hospital staff seemed to be difficult to locate today.

As Brook was about to enter her office, movement in her peripheral vision stopped her from crossing the threshold. Someone had walked off the elevator. Normally, anyone visiting the floor did so with the intent of visiting the hedge fund across the hall.

To Brook's surprise, Catherine Kolsby stepped off the elevator.

"Kate, would you please buzz Ms. Kolsby into the office? Oh, and please tell whoever is on line two that I will have to call them back."

Brook observed Catherine falter in her steps upon seeing the biometric scanner. She must have heard the lock disengage, though. The gentleman with her reached around and pulled on the handle, allowing Catherine to cross the threshold first. Her long brown hair swung lightly as she paused just inside the entrance so that her companion could join her.

"Miss Kolsby, what can I do for you?"

"I wanted to discuss something important with you in private. Something that I didn't want to bring up in front of my father." Catherine took the man's hand and squeezed his fingers. He whispered something to her, but since they were still near the entrance, Brook couldn't overhear him. "This is Stephen Averill, my fiancé."

"Mr. Averill," Brook said, not having to take a step forward to greet him. He was holding onto Catherine's fingers with his left hand, but he'd escorted her across the marble tile to shake Brook's hand. "Congratulations on your engagement."

"Thank you," Stephen murmured, releasing Catherine's hand so that she could walk in front of him. Brook led the way into her office, catching the sound of Kate giving an explanation to the caller on line two. "I had hoped to be at the house when you spoke with the family, but I had a meeting that I couldn't get out of. Catherine explained what took place this morning with Brett, and you should know that he had nothing to do with whatever break-in occurred at..."

"Millie Gwinn's residence," Brook filled in as she motioned for them to take a seat on the couch. She'd muted the television earlier, although the captions were on in case she wanted a summation of what was happening in the news. "And yes, I'm aware that Brett had picked up someone from the airport. Your sister, from my understanding. He stayed for a few hours, they talked, and then he made his way home."

Before Brook had left the Kolsby residence, she'd received a very detailed description from Brett on why he'd been parked in front of the building across from Millie's apartment complex. He'd claimed that he had no knowledge of Millie Gwinn residing across the street. Bit had confirmed that Celeste Averill was a resident of the building.

Considering that there was no evidence to the contrary, they would have to take Brett's explanation at face value. Unless, of course, evidence found at a later date proved otherwise.

The most frustrating issue for Brook stemmed from the fact that they still did not have a victim, let alone more than one. She'd driven back to the office to begin drafting a profile, but that proved too difficult to do without certain aspects of the case being run to ground.

"I take the reason that you are here has something to do with Brett and your sister?"

"No," Catherine responded as she set her purse on the glass coffee table. While Catherine and Stephen had claimed the couch, Brook had taken a seat in her favorite chair. It just so happened to face the foyer, allowing her to monitor the comings and goings from the elevator bank. "My father is dying."

Brook had let her gaze drift to Kate, who just so happened to still be on the phone. Whoever had called didn't seem pleased with an excuse as to why Brook couldn't take his or her call.

Needless to say, Catherine's statement had Brook's full attention.

"I'm sorry?"

CHAPTER ELEVEN

"My father was diagnosed with stage four pancreatic cancer," Catherine said after clearing her throat. Her affection and overly protective posture toward Dr. Kolsby this morning began to make more sense. She'd reached for his hand numerous times, as well as seen to his every need. Brook had merely assumed it was due to him recovering from surgery and his concussion. "He hasn't told my brothers yet, so I couldn't bring it up in front of them."

While Catherine came across as a very confident woman, she also naturally relied on her fiancé for support. She kept ahold of his hand on her knee while she evened her breathing before going into more depth on her reasoning for their visit.

"I want this case dropped," Catherine declared confidently, as if she had a say on whether or not Brook continued forward with the investigation. "Please ask Millie Gwinn how much it will take for her to drop this nonsense about my father subject to a nondisclosure agreement. I'll have my accountant wire the money over to her bank, and we can put this all behind us."

Brook remained silent while she mulled over Catherine's offer.

"Catherine," Stephen murmured as he tried to get her to see reason. "We need to bring the family lawyer into this so that he can draft a—"

"In case you have forgotten, Stephen, I *am* a lawyer," Catherine responded sharply, turning back into the woman who Brook had dealt with earlier. She refocused her attention back on Brook. It was almost as if the potential need for a negotiation put her emotions in check. "I'll draft up an NDA on my own. I'd rather no one else be involved with the contract. Basically, Ms. Gwinn agrees to stop slandering my father's name in exchange for a reasonable sum of money. Agreed?"

"I can't agree to that, Miss Kolsby. I run a private investigations firm. I'm not a lawyer, and I couldn't represent Ms. Gwinn in such a matter." Brook quickly ran through her options, because there was no telling what amount of money Catherine might offer Millie. Something told Brook that there was some validity to the case, but should Millie take the offer, there would be no grounds to continue investigating without their client. "If it eases your concern, I'll reiterate what I said earlier today. I do not believe that your father is a murderer."

Brook made sure that her words matched her opinion. While she didn't believe that Dr. Kolsby killed someone with his own hands, it was more than likely he knew of someone who had committed the brutal crime in question.

Was that someone a family member?

A friend?

A patient?

Brook had already come to the conclusion that she needed to speak with Dr. Kolsby again, but that would prove difficult if his daughter managed to keep him sheltered from calls or guests.

"I'm well aware of what you believe, Ms. Sloane." Catherine's tone was not just sharp, but her glare was meant to put the fear of God into Brook. Catherine would have to try a hell of a lot harder than that. "While I'm grateful that you believe in my father's innocence, that alone should tell you that we are striving for the same eventuality. It's time to end your involvement in this matter."

Brook maintained her focus on Catherine, never once breaking eye contact.

"My involvement comes to an end when my client decides to no longer pursue this investigation. Until such time, my firm and I will continue to follow whatever evidence we uncover to determine the truth."

Brook stood, signaling the end of their meeting.

Had Catherine and her fiancé chosen a different tactic to help close out the case, Brook might have been receptive to such a plea. Threats tended to do the exact opposite. It wasn't that she didn't feel for the Kolsbys having to deal with such a tragic diagnosis. Unfortunately, it didn't negate the possibility of them uncovering the remains of dead bodies buried somewhere, leaving the families of the victims without closure.

That was something that Brook couldn't...wouldn't...tolerate.

"I'm truly sorry to hear about your father's diagnosis, but you should know that any evidence this firm finds during the discovery process will be turned over to the police."

"Excuse me?"

Catherine quickly stood, her frustration evident.

As a matter of fact, Brook would say that the woman was close to expressing rage. Stephen slowly followed his fiancé's lead, attempting to calm the situation.

"Look, Ms. Sloane," Catherine declared as she angrily set the strap of her purse over her shoulder. "Whatever you have had to deal with in your past should have no bearing on my life or the lives of my family members. My father is dying. He only has a short time to live. Isn't that enough?"

"I have to believe that if you were one of the women who had been abducted and possibly murdered, leaving your father to languish away in his last days without seeking answers, that he would appreciate Ms. Gwinn's bravery in coming forward," Brook countered evenly as she walked to the door of her office. She opened it before delivering her final line. "I believe we're done here."

Chapter Twelve

Theo Neville
December 2022
Monday — 5:31pm

The monotonous click of the turn signal was slightly louder than the R&B music faintly drifting from the speakers of the radio. The warmth inside the Jeep Wrangler was a welcome respite from the bitter cold wind and falling temperatures.

Theo had been driving for a good twenty minutes since exiting the city. In that time, he'd come to the realization that their new case had finally grown some roots. All they needed to do now was follow those roots in hopes that they led to a full-grown tree.

In this case, the unsub.

As Theo continued to monitor the black BMW in front of him, he used his Bluetooth to call Brook's cell phone. The radio switched to the audio of a ringing sound that reverberated throughout the Jeep.

He'd basically spent the entire day interviewing hospital staff who had been present either during or after Dr. Kolsby's surgery.

CHAPTER TWELVE

That list had even included the paramedics who had been at the scene of the accident.

Theo and Sylvie had split up the names, each of them tackling the interviews that would bleed into tomorrow's schedule. First thing in the morning, Sylvie would be meeting with Dr. Kolsby's administrative assistant. Theo had already spoken to her, but she'd been tightlipped about her employer. Maybe Sylvie would have better luck, though it was doubtful that the woman would simply hand over the names of Dr. Kolsby's patients. Bit was currently working on an angle that would hopefully not end with any of them behind bars for violating telecommunications privacy laws.

"You could have given me a heads up about the background investigation," Brook said, forgoing the standard greeting. "Please relay my congratulations to your father."

Theo smiled as he glanced from the car in front of him to the red light above.

"Dad hasn't officially been appointed the NYPD Commissioner, but I will definitely let him know that we've started to receive calls." Theo had already been questioned, and it appeared as if the investigator was almost done wrapping up the vetting process. "Were you nice?"

"I'm offended that you would even ask me that," Brook replied wryly. "I'll be on my best behavior unless I find out that your father is still interested in having you move back to New York. In that case, all bets are off."

He didn't have to tell Brook that his father would never stop attempting to get Theo back to the city. It would never be in the capacity of an officer or a role that involved field work, which was why such a move had never been in consideration.

"Were you able to speak with Dr. Cranston?"

"Not exactly," Theo murmured as he was finally able to step on the gas. "Thanks to Bit's help, I was able to locate Dr. Cranston at a country club. Before I could park, he had already exited the building. I figured I'd follow him home, but he drove in the opposite direction. We're about to get onto the highway now."

"Not unusual," Brook surmised over what sounded like the office's coffee machine. She'd most likely be at work for another six to seven hours. On the bright side, at least she had started joining them for their Thursday night get-togethers. "I'm sure the man has a life. I was able to procure the missing person report on Natalie Thorne's disappearance. While Cranston was interviewed due to his relationship with her, he was ruled out as a suspect since he'd been the primary surgeon on a nine-hour emergency surgery the night that she supposedly went missing. His alibi was airtight."

"Something is off," Theo said with a bit of hesitancy, lifting his foot off the gas pedal to put some distance between his Jeep and Dr. Cranston's BMW. "Cranston looked around the parking lot for a good, solid minute before getting into his car. It was almost as if he thought that he was being watched. I just wanted you to know that I'm discreetly following him at a distance."

"Just be careful, Theo. We're already rocking the boat with the powers that be. I received a call from Senator Ponzio's younger sister. You know, the one who worked for the Bureau. She was putting out feelers as to the reason we would take Millie Gwinn's case when the police found nothing to substantiate a continued investigation."

"I bet that was a pleasant conversation." Theo frowned when Dr. Cranston passed an exit that could have potentially been a roundabout way to his home. "Your response?"

"Exactly what I told Catherine Kolsby today in my office. Millie Gwinn's apartment was broken into, she fears for her life, and she hired an outside firm to double check the findings of the investigation. And before you ask, the answer is no. I did not expand the conversation to include that we are providing our services pro bono." There was clanking of glass in the background, and Theo pictured Brook reaching into the cabinet for one of the white coffee mugs that had the firm's logo on the side. "I'm reading over Sylvie's notes from today's interviews. Keep me posted on your upcoming conversation with Cranston."

"Will do."

Theo disconnected the call, shifting in his seat. He might as well make himself a bit more comfortable. There was no telling how long the drive would be, especially given that Cranston had passed another exit. Theo glanced at the fuel gauge. He'd fueled up the Jeep earlier this afternoon, so he didn't need to worry about running out of gas anytime soon.

Theo found his thoughts drifting to Hadley, who had spent a couple of nights at his condo. They'd hit it off in more ways than one, but she always left before sunrise. He'd even offered to make her breakfast on Sunday morning, but she'd politely refused before walking out the door. She was also never the one to reach out first.

He got the sense that she wasn't looking for anything serious.

Theo was completely fine with that decision. Granted, he was finally in a good place with work and his health, and he'd finally found a nice place to live. He wouldn't mind finding something more than a one-night stand or a relationship purely based on sex. It would be interesting to see where Hadley wanted to take things over the course of the next few months.

Five minutes turned in twenty.

Eventually, Cranston flipped his turn signal on to exit the highway.

Theo gripped the steering wheel as he checked his rearview mirror. He'd hoped to find that someone else was taking the exit, but most of the vehicles were in the lefthand lane. He'd have a decision to make soon, because this exit seemed to be in the middle of nowhere. If he came to a stop behind Cranston, what were the chances that he would figure out that he was being followed?

Theo made the quick decision to pull up on the man's right side, purposefully turning right instead of passing underneath the bridge of the highway. He wasn't concerned that Cranston would see him due to the tinted windows on the Jeep. Considering it was quite dark outside with not a speck of moonlight, the only illumination came from the streetlamp on the opposite side of the road. There were no other vehicles around, so it wouldn't be that difficult to catch back up with Cranston.

Theo kept his gaze glued to the rearview mirror until he was able to execute a U-turn. If he'd continued straight, he would have hit a small town with what looked to be a lot of strip malls. As Theo passed the offramp from the highway, he noticed that there was still no additional traffic.

The BMW's taillights could be seen rounding a bend, so Theo sped up slightly to ensure that he didn't lose sight of the car. He was at least a good quarter of a mile behind. If Cranston was to turn off anytime soon, there was a chance that Theo could miss it.

After he'd disconnected the call with Brook, music had once again started to spill from the speakers. He used the button on the steering wheel to completely turn off the radio. His parents had used to do the same thing when looking for a destination, and he used to think they were foolish for doing so. One's hearing didn't mean one couldn't see what was right in front of them. He'd found himself doing the same thing recently, and he hadn't even turned thirty years old.

The quiet hum of the warm air coming through the vents eased the tension in his shoulders. It had also helped that he'd caught sight of Cranston up ahead. The problem was that they were the only two on the road, and it would have been all but impossible for the doctor not to have noticed the headlights in his rearview mirror.

Making a quick decision upon seeing a road to his left, Theo slowed down and turned on his signal. He veered left while

CHAPTER TWELVE   115

doing his best to keep an eye on the two red taillights. Theo managed to quickly execute another U-turn and douse his headlights. By the time that he was back on the road, he'd almost lost sight of Cranston's car.

Fortunately, the man was currently in the midst of making a righthand turn.

"You're going to get yourself killed with no headlights," Theo muttered to himself, hoping that there wouldn't be any oncoming traffic. They were far enough away from civilization that it had been at least two miles since they'd passed another vehicle. "Where are you going, Cranston?"

Theo witnessed the man's brake lights illuminate even more so than his taillights as he pulled off the road into what looked to be some type of clearing.

Theo slowed to a roll and let his engine idle.

The distance was vast enough that he wasn't worried about being seen or heard. It helped that he'd come to a stop underneath some low-hanging branches of a large tree. What turned out to be really beneficial was that Cranston hadn't bothered to get out of his car.

There had to be close to two inches of snow on the ground that hadn't been cleared away with a snowplow. Theo couldn't make out if there was a building of sorts off to the left. All he could do was wait for Cranston to make a move.

Was he meeting someone out here in the middle of nowhere?

Once again, time slowly passed by until the warm air from the vent started to somewhat cool down.

Five minutes turned into ten.

Ten minutes turned into twenty.

Eventually, Cranston remained in his car for over thirty minutes before driving off. Theo wasn't sure what had caused the change of heart, but he wasn't going to follow. As a matter of fact, he quickly turned his Jeep around and drove back toward the main road. Something told him that Cranston was going to backtrack, and Theo didn't want to be parked on the side of the road like a sitting lame duck.

Noting the time on the dashboard for his own notes, Theo eventually took the road that he'd veered off on originally. He made sure that he was close enough to monitor any passing vehicles, but far enough away to be discreet. It didn't take long for Cranston's BMW to pass by, heading back toward the highway.

He could have fallen right in behind without the doctor ever being aware that he was once again being followed, but something had Theo wanting to inspect the area where Cranston had been parked for over a half an hour.

Theo eventually made it back to the area, but he didn't notice anything out of place. There were no buildings, no houses, and no structures off to the side. There was an abundance of trees of various kinds, but mostly Red Maples that had long since lost their leaves due to the cold weather.

Theo remained parked in the darkness for some time, mulling over the possibilities of why Cranston had driven this far for basically no reason. He couldn't come up with a valid theory that didn't lead down a dark and twisted road...not that he'd been searching for puns.

As Brook had mentioned on the phone, she'd been going through Sylvie's notes from her interviews today. He'd had time to do so, as well, although not as in-depth as Brook was almost certainly doing at the moment. The only reason that Theo had Dr. Cranston on the list to speak to was due to what Sylvie had discovered today during her talk with Josh Perisot.

A young brunette had gone missing two years ago, and she'd never been found. Theo had read over the report, and the facts claimed that Cranston couldn't have abducted Natalie Thorne.

What if that alibi hadn't been double-checked by the officer in question? What was the likelihood of Cranston actually being

CHAPTER TWELVE

the one responsible for the woman's death? And what were the minuscule odds that he'd led Theo right to the burial site?

Theo placed another call to Brook.

It was his turn to not bother with a greeting.

"I'm not going to bother asking if someone owes you a favor at an independent forensics lab," Theo stated wryly, constantly amazed by how many favors that Brook had collected during her time with the Bureau. "What I'm wondering is if you're up for calling in a chip for a case unrelated to Jacob. There's a very slim chance that I know the location of where Natalie Thorne's body is buried."

Chapter Thirteen

Brooklyn Sloane
December 2022
Tuesday — 2:19pm

"WE CAN ALWAYS WAIT inside the Jeep," Theo suggested as his breath dissipated in the cold air. He moved his shoulders up and down, as if that would create a bit more body heat. "There's no telling how much longer they're going to be at this."

Brook was leaning up against the passenger side of Theo's Jeep. She'd ridden with him so that she could concentrate on making a few calls, lining up some additional help if Ezra Adler actually found the remains of Natalie Thorne.

By the time they'd driven to their destination, Brook was able to have Officer Soerig on standby. Granted, she'd just been promoted, but she wouldn't be the one covering a homicide. That responsibility would land with the homicide unit inside the sheriff's department that covered this jurisdiction.

"I thought I spotted movement through those trees. We should wait."

CHAPTER THIRTEEN

Brook and Theo had both dressed for the weather. She'd opted not to wear one of her usual pantsuits. Instead, she had put on a double layer of winter apparel underneath a pair of dark jeans and a black sweater. Her waist holster was secure on the thick belt that she'd thread through the loops of her pants. Instead of her dress coat, she'd opted for a winter jacket that could handle the cold temperature for an extended period of time. It also helped that she was wearing her winter boots with two layers of socks.

"You could have stayed behind, you know. This was merely a hunch, and it could turn out to be nothing but a waste of time," Theo theorized as he turned his focus toward her. Even though she was wearing earmuffs, she could hear him just fine. "We should have brought a thermos of hot coffee with us."

"Actually, I'm glad to be out of the office for a bit. There technically isn't a profile for me to draft, and it's driving me crazy. We have no victim, we're not sure that Dr. Kolsby is the responsible party, we might have a connected crime, or we might not. It's like we're chasing our tails looking for a ghost."

Although Brook had spent most of the drive making phone calls, they'd also had time to discuss the daily report sent over from DeSilva & Associates. Alex had been sending them over since his firm had taken over the protective detail. Nothing out of the ordinary had occurred that was cause for concern, although Millie had attended a therapy session as directed by the hospital.

Not surprisingly, Millie had met with Catherine Kolsby last night.

Fortunately, Brook had the foresight to share with Millie what had occurred during the encounter at the office, and she'd been adamant that no amount of money would get her to change her mind.

"This is basic investigative work." Theo shrugged off Brook's concern. "As long as we leave no stone unturned, we'll eventually figure out if this case has any legs to stand on."

"I'm sure if we decided to open a closet door of every individual residing in D.C. that we would find something that others would prefer we didn't," Brook countered, uneasy with how this case had evolved over the past few days. "Think about it. I could be in Dr. Kolsby's shoes right now. I could have had surgery, said something that stuck in my mind regarding my childhood with Jacob, and then woke up to find the police hovering over my bed slinging accusations concealing information dealing with a murder that he committed."

"Your point being?" Theo asked, playing devil's advocate. He shrugged again, this time using the movement to set himself into a rhythmic sway side to side in an effort to keep warm. "Jacob is a serial killer, and he's on the FBI's radar. We're looking for him. You're hunting him. It's not like you are colluding with him. If Kolsby has information of previous murders, he has a duty to come forward and report what he knows."

Brook didn't often talk about her childhood with others.

Unless, of course, it benefited the search for Jacob.

"Dr. Kolsby wouldn't need to come forward if what he said was in relation to a patient."

"While there is such a thing as doctor and patient confidentiality, that is waived if said doctor believes that his patient is a danger to others and likely to reoffend," Theo pointed out.

He shifted to the side when a gust of wind came from the West, ending up side by side with Brook. They were now both staring into the desolate woods. Brook once again caught sight of Ezra's bright red jacket. He must have left his technician and the large machine they had brought with them back aways.

"What if that's what we're dealing with in this situation?" Brook asked as she took a step forward. Theo fell into step beside her as it went unspoken that they would meet Ezra near the tree line. "What if Dr. Kolsby brought up something from a past patient, but who would—"

"Rehabilitated?" Theo asked wryly with a shake of his head. "Serial killers are a special breed of monsters, Brook. You know that more than anyone. They don't stop until they are made to stop. There's something wrong inside their minds. A disconnect, of sorts. It is Kolsby's responsibility to come forward if he's aware that a patient went on some killing spree, especially if Catherine Kolsby is being truthful about her father's prognosis. Time is of the essence. He owed it to humanity to be honest about what he knows."

Brook agreed with Theo's opinion, but it still didn't negate the doctor and patient bond if Dr. Kolsby didn't feel there was an immediate threat to others. It was a fine line, much like the one Bit was walking when it came to gathering pertinent information during an investigation.

"Brook, you're going to want to call in the police," Ezra stated in his usual nasally tone.

Ezra Adler was approximately forty-five years of age, and no more than five feet and five inches. There was a bald patch on top of his head, he constantly had a red nose that leaked, and the lenses of his glasses were constantly smudged with skin oil. He might have a unique way of doing things, but he was the best in his field.

After parking behind Theo's Jeep in the clearing behind them, Ezra and his colleague had unloaded a ground penetrating radar set. It worked basically on the density of the ground and the ability of the radar to penetrate the soil. Disturbed ground allowed the radar waves to reach deeper into the ground quicker. Thus, the correlated data created a picture of the surrounding underground, possibly down to bedrock if the earth was shallow enough. Fresh bodies absorbed radar waves and returned as a void or darker images. Bones buried in shallow graves came back as very distinct reflections.

"You found a body?" Theo inquired before Brook could ask the question. "Seriously?"

"Most likely skeletal remains, to be more exact," Ezra corrected as he motioned behind him. "Four, at last count."

A burial site.

Dr. Cranston had led them straight to a burial site.

Brook should have experienced some type of elation in regard to the shocking discovery, but she'd learned the hard way that nothing was ever what it seemed when first presented on a silver platter.

"Did you…" Theo met Brook's stare. "Four?"

"Maybe more." Ezra sniffed before pulling his hands out of his pockets. He must have taken his gloves off while working with the machine and his laptop. He took a few moments to blow into the tissue and then wipe his nose. "I'd place that call now if I were you."

Chapter Fourteen

Brooklyn Sloane
December 2022
Tuesday — 8:17pm

THE HEAT RADIATING FROM Brook's space heater was the only reason that her teeth weren't still chattering after being outside most of the afternoon. She and Theo had spent an hour waiting for the police and the lead homicide detective to arrive, another hour giving a detailed account of what had led Theo to the location, and then another two hours standing around for the state forensics team to make an appearance.

Brook had already warned Theo that their services wouldn't be required nor desired, and she'd been right. It wasn't that Detective Mike Raines hadn't been professional. He'd handled everything by the book. The problem was that there was a good chance he would be turning the case over to the FBI.

She would have been perfectly fine with such a decision, but Supervisory Special Agent Matthew Harden was currently on sick leave. Brook would have easily been able to surpass the state level altogether if he'd been back at work.

Unfortunately, her former supervisor was still at home recovering from a heart attack that required bypass surgery. She'd spoken to him just last week, and he wasn't slated back into the office until the first of the year.

Since there had been many changes at the Bureau recently, Brook had no connection to the agent who had stepped into the interim supervisory position. Not wanting to upset the status quo, she'd gone through the proper channels.

"I just received confirmation that there are only four skeletal remains," Theo said as he walked into her office. He paused midway between the door and the couch. "Brook, it's got to be a hundred degrees in here."

Brook didn't bother to reply, because she had no intention of turning down her space heater. He would just have to suck up the heat.

"It looks as if Raines is going to take lead instead of handing it off," Theo divulged as he laid down on the couch and stretched out his legs.

She almost made a quip about how he might not be so tired if he didn't have guests spending the night and leaving before sunrise, but she thought better of it.

Graham was due into town tomorrow.

Should she still go ahead with their dinner plans, there was a chance that Graham would be seen by Theo in the lobby of their building. She wouldn't want him to bring up the topic in the office.

"That's probably for the best," Brook said as she saved her profile draft. Once she was confident that her outline had been stored to the file, she focused on Theo. He had made himself very comfortable on her couch. "If Detective Raines had turned the scene over to the feds, we would have lost complete access. Harden isn't in the office, and the upper brass brought someone in from Quantico due to the length of his absence."

"Do you think this Raines will work with us?"

CHAPTER FOURTEEN

"Yes," Sylvie responded before Brook could answer Theo's question. Brook would have said the exact opposite, which meant that Sylvie had an update on the case. "Apparently, Officer Soerig knows Detective Raines from another investigation that crossed through both of their jurisdictions. Everyone has agreed to loop the other in, and the same goes for us. Believe it or not, that last benefit is due to Officer Soerig going to bat for us. She's officially reopened the case now that she has been made detective."

Brook wasn't surprised when Theo's legs swung back around to land on the floor. Sylvie had been too busy entering something in on her tablet to notice his reaction. She ended up taking a seat in one of the leather chairs. Kate had left the office for the evening an hour ago, and Bit had followed in her footsteps moments later citing dinner plans with his sister.

"Raines brought Dr. Cranston into the station for questioning, but the surgeon lawyered up immediately without saying a word." Sylvie finally looked up from the tablet before resting it against her stomach. "There's not enough evidence to arrest him, so Raines is hoping that the forensics team turns up something from the scene. Unfortunately, it could take days to excavate the burial site. The ground is frozen solid. They've tented the entire area and have forced heated air running twenty-four-seven."

Theo and Sylvie continued to talk over the latest turn of events. Brook picked up her coffee mug that was mostly empty and stood from her chair. She stretched a bit before walking around her desk.

"We need a new strategy," Brook advised them as she came to a stop near the coffee table. She didn't bother joining them, though. She wanted another cup of coffee and to also grab the take-out menu for a new Chinese restaurant that had opened a few blocks from the building. "Detective Raines is going to focus on Cranston, Officer Soerig will want to reinterview Dr. Kolsby, and Millie's break-in seems all but forgotten. We're footing the bill for her protective detail. The faster we can put all the pieces together, the sooner we can close this case."

"Do you have a strategy in mind?" Theo asked, linking his hands behind his head. His dark eyes narrowed in her direction. "You do, don't you?"

"Yes, but I need the rest of the evening to hammer out a solid game plan. You two call it a night, and we'll regroup in the morning." Brook's phone rang, prompting her to turn back to her desk. "I'm serious. We had a long day, and the rest of the week promises to be much of the same."

"Tell me about it," Sylvie muttered as she rubbed her neck. Brook's cell phone continued to ring, and Sylvie took the opportunity to head for the door. "I think I need to invest in one of those massage chairs. Did you know that they have heated ones now that…"

By the time that Brook made it around her desk, Theo and Sylvie's conversation had all but faded away as they exited her office.

"Sloane," Brook greeted once she'd set her mug down before reclaiming her chair.

The warmth from her space heater elicited a chill through her body. It also could have been due to the number that she'd recognized on the display of her cell phone.

"Ms. Sloane, do you have a moment?"

"For you, Agent Houser…yes." Brook leaned back in her chair, deciding to preface something first. "If I recall, we did agree that I had a week to think over your proposal."

"That's why I'm reaching out to you, Ms. Sloane. The U.S. Marshals refuse to take part in such a sting under any circumstances." Agent Houser's sigh of disapproval came across the line loud and clear. "I couldn't get them to agree, so I'll have to go back to the drawing board."

Brook might have been focused on their current case, but that didn't mean she hadn't been mulling over Jacob's recent actions. She'd jumped to the conclusion that her brother would want to locate Sarah Evanston through her surgeons, but no marshal in North Dakota would have had access to such information. Not unless someone from that specific office had been assigned to Ms. Evanston, which was doubtful.

"The answer to what Jacob was looking for resides in the location. North Dakota isn't one of the major cities, nor is it a secure data depot, yet it was close enough to the state where Evanston's half-brother lives." Brook sat forward and leaned her forearms on her desk. "He was killing two birds with one stone."

"It doesn't matter," Agent Houser stated in defeat. "Ms. Evanston will remain in witness protection, she'll get the surgeries that she needs, and we'll be left to figure out another way to apprehend Jacob Walsh."

Brook didn't have the energy to think back over their past conversations. He had a tendency to rub it in her face that she was the sister of a serial killer. If she wasn't mistaken, Agent Houser might be warming up to her. She couldn't say the same, because she still believed that he was fully in over his head.

Jacob was running circles around him, but it wasn't like she had much room to talk.

Brook had attempted for decades to locate her brother to no avail. He'd stood in the middle of her condo, and she still hadn't been able to bring him to justice.

"He's patient."

"Excuse me?"

"Jacob is patient in ways that you could never understand," Brook said as she picked up her coffee cup. Theo had already grabbed his coat and left the office. She hadn't seen Sylvie leave just yet. "While I do believe Jacob will try to figure out which surgeon has been assigned to Sarah Evanston's procedures, he wouldn't be able to surveil each of them. He'd want more information to whittle down his percentages."

"Like?" Agent Houser prompted, his interest unmistakably piqued. "We've already agreed that Jacob would be well aware of the procedures regarding the U.S. Marshals Service. The moment we realized that he'd accessed their computer systems, Evanston was given a new handler."

"Exactly." Brook walked past Sylvie's office, noticing that she'd taken a phone call. "Jacob could very well be gathering every single piece of information in order to connect the dots. Think about it. If I was able to narrow down the surgeons to three in the entire country, Jacob would be able to do the same. If he had a comprehensive list of handlers, he could start weeding through them one by one."

"Do you know how many handlers there are in the U.S. Marshals Service, Ms. Sloane?"

"What I know is that Jacob would focus on those three plastic surgeons, research exactly what hospitals they worked out of, and then compare that to the handlers' current locations. And before you give me all the reasons why that would be improbable, you should know that Jacob possesses one thing that you don't have—patience. My brother has all the time in the world, and he isn't even giving you one moment of his time. He's not worried about you finding him or ruining his plans, because by the time you figure out what he is up to...he'll have already completed his mission and faded back into the darkness. His plans are highly detailed, multifaceted, and in place far ahead of your reaction time."

"Even if I were to entertain the idea that Jacob Walsh was able to download a list of names from the system, you expect me to believe that he can locate their whereabouts?"

"I suspect most senior handlers have families, don't they?" Brook countered, reaching for the glass carafe that was on the burner. She'd made a fresh pot of coffee upon returning to the office. There was basically enough for one more cup. Seeing as she planned to be working until well after midnight, she might as well brew up another pot. "Jacob will monitor every single family member of those men and women until he figures out where Sarah Evanston is located. Trust me, Agent Houser. Jacob is always two steps ahead of us."

Agent Houser fell silent as he took her words under advisement.

"You might as well start calling me Russell." Another resigned sigh came through Brook's cell phone. "Goodnight, Ms. Sloane."

Agent Houser disconnected the call before Brook could respond in kind. She'd do so in their next phone call. Unfortunately, there was no doubt that there would be more on the horizon. That was a given, not that she'd been prepared to be on a first name basis of the federal agent in charge of her brother's case. She and Agent Houser couldn't be more different in their approaches to investigations if they tried, but she found herself getting used to the oddity of late.

As a matter of fact, her entire life had done a one-eighty recently.

She somehow had to find time to either stop by a grocery store or have groceries delivered to her condo. She didn't consider herself much of a cook, but she had memorized her mother's lasagna recipe back in her teens.

"Heading out," Sylvie exclaimed from the hallway. "See you in the morning."

"Goodnight," Brook called out, finally pressing brew now that she'd prepared the coffee machine for another carafe. "Drive safe."

She wasn't sure that Sylvie had heard her parting words.

Brook picked up her topped-off coffee mug before making her way back to her office. She paused just outside the conference room. Having a change of heart, she crossed the threshold and didn't stop until she was standing in front of the large monitor. She turned it on and stepped back, waiting for the touchscreen to display the latest case files. Once they had the appropriate time to load, she then opened the four files that she had created less than thirty minutes ago.

Four victims.

Brook now had something to work with in order to build a profile.

She was finally back in her element...her true element.

Although there were other details floating around in the background, she purposefully pushed aside thoughts of Dr. Kolsby and Dr. Cranston. For all intents and purposes, all Kolsby had done was bring a killer to the attention of the police. All Cranston had done was pull off on the side of a desolate road. It didn't matter that he'd been seeing one of the alleged victims two years before she'd gone missing. Even if Natalie Thorne's remains were included in the ones that had just been located, there just wasn't enough evidence to make an arrest.

It was best to start at the very beginning.

Chapter Fifteen

Bit Nowacki
December 2022
Wednesday — 10:47am

"What are you doing?" The abrupt question startled Bit to the point where he almost dropped the aluminum can he had in his hand. He'd just popped open an energy drink. He hadn't even taken a seat in his chair before Sylvie had snuck into his office behind him.

"I'm young, Little T," Bit exclaimed as he hastily pressed the escape key on his keyboard so that she wouldn't get a better look at the video that he'd had on the screen. From her knowing expression, he hadn't been quick enough. "I'm not supposed to die from a heart attack at age twenty-four."

"You're rewatching the security footage from the house in Illinois, aren't you?"

Bit could have attempted to deny such an allegation, but Sylvie was already pushing him aside with her hip so that she could reach for the computer mouse. She navigated directly to the video that had shrunk to the lower righthand corner of the screen.

"Did you find anything?"

Bit had to lean forward so that he could catch a glimpse of her blue eyes.

Sure enough, she wasn't expressing one sliver of fear at the reminder of what had to be the worst moment in her life. She'd been abducted by a lunatic who had believed her soul had been possessed by another woman. There were still red marks from the abrasions on her wrists from when she had tried to escape the confines of zip tie cuffs. The scars would probably always be there as a reminder, but her inner strength wouldn't allow her to be seen as a victim.

The only time that he'd ever experienced such fear was the day that his sister had called him over to her apartment to tell him that she had cancer. Primary Mediastinal B-Cell Lymphoma. A mouthful that he'd never said aloud. It wasn't until her oncologist had determined that only an expensive, experimental rituximab enhanced anthracycline chemotherapy treatment could potentially save her life. He'd wasn't proud of the way he'd gone about getting the money, but he didn't regret a thing. Besides, it had led him here...to the team.

To Sylvie.

"Not yet," Bit replied in resignation as he shooed her away from the keyboard. She immediately grabbed one of the other chairs that he'd made sure was available to the other team members. It wasn't long until they were side by side. "I've been dissecting the footage. Basically, I've been pulling it apart frame by frame. Nothing shows up in the seconds leading up to the static, which is when I'm positive that the porcelain doll was moved from the closet back to the curio cabinet."

The state police of Illinois had requested help on an investigation a couple of months prior, and the team had rented out a house in the heart of a small roadside town. Unfortunately, the renter had passed away in the months preceding their arrival.

Bit had always been the type to err on the side of caution, so he'd purposefully set up a camera inside the living room where he'd opted to sleep on the couch. While he'd been ninety-nine-point-nine percent certain that the team had played a prank on him by putting an antique doll back inside the curio cabinet after he'd stuffed her in a closet, there had been a margin of error.

For once, technology had failed him.

The camera had seemingly been working fine the entire time, with the exception of those few moments where odd things had happened during their time in the house. Bit was beginning to resign himself to the fact that he might never know what had truly transpired in Illinois.

Unless, of course, one of the team members fessed up to a prank.

"Were you the one who took the porcelain doll from the closet and put it back inside the curio cabinet?" Bit asked before holding his breath in anticipation.

"Bit, I did not touch that doll," Sylvie said as she raised her right hand in oath.

He believed her, which left Theo or Fritz.

Detective Roger Fritz came across as a stuffed potato, but sometimes those were the very people who had a sick sense of humor. Bit narrowed his eyes as he thought through the various types of revenge he could enact.

"Great job in getting the list of patients, Bit," Brook said as she strolled through the doorway. She hadn't been in the best of moods lately, but she seemed to have gotten her spunk back. He wouldn't go so far as to say she was jovial or completely vested in the holiday spirit, but at least the perpetual frown lines on her forehead had vanished. "We can't interview them, but it still gives us something to work on. Theo has decided to question

Dr. Kolsby's assistant again since Sylvie wasn't able to fit her in yesterday, so he'll be out of the office most of the day."

Sylvie and Bit both turned their chairs around to face Brook.

When it came right down to it, he hadn't broken any laws in obtaining the patients' names. He'd gone about doing so in a roundabout way by contacting the software company that Dr. Kolsby's private practice hired to store their patients' information. Bit had been truthful in that he worked in IT. He wasn't to blame for their misunderstanding that his position wasn't technically with the psychiatry practice.

While he was going over the phone conversation in his head once more to confirm that the firm couldn't get in trouble should it ever get out that he'd acquired the names of Dr. Kolsby's patients, he caught Brook staring at him as she stood behind Sylvie's chair. It was almost as if she'd asked him a question and was waiting for his reply. It wasn't until her focus drifted toward the monitor over his shoulder that he sprang into action.

"Is that security footage of—"

"Nope."

Bit breathed a sigh of relief when Sylvie came to his rescue. He'd witnessed the crease in Brook's forehead, and he didn't want to be the reason that her bad mood the last few days returned with a vengeance. He'd didn't need that kind of negativity during the holidays.

"Does anyone want a cup of tea? Coffee? Brook, can I bring you back a cup?"

"No, thank you." Brook shook her head as if to say the previous subject wasn't worth bringing back up. "Bit, *you* texted *me*. Remember?"

"Yes!" Bit exclaimed, snapping his fingers when it hit him why she'd been staring at him so intently. "Kolsby and Cranston have been friends for years. They were actually hired the same year by the hospital back in the day. It wasn't until seven years afterward that Kolsby started his own practice, although he still consults for the hospital. Get this. Brett Kolsby and Cranston's only son—Devin Cranston—were best friends in high school. They still run in the same circles."

By the time that Bit was able to catch Brook up on what he'd discovered through various search engines, Sylvie had exited his office. He hoped that she wasn't making him a cup of tea. His stomach couldn't handle any right now, especially when he'd just placed an order for chicken tacos. It was a little early for lunch, but he was starving after skipping breakfast. A chime rang out from one of the sound bars, and he rotated the chair around with a single push off the floor.

"Uh, Boss? You're going to want to see this." Bit scooted to the side so that Brook could step closer to the monitor. "I created a program to match other missing women with Natalie Thorne's physical description. Needless to say, a lot of people go missing in any given year. But, I narrowed the field by age, distance, and any connection to the hospital or Dr. Kolsby's private practice."

"And?"

"A twenty-two-year-old woman by the name of Laura Keery went missing nine months ago." Bit stared at the one detail that separated the woman from the other missing persons that the search program was sorting through. "Boss, get this...she was a nursing student who interned for the same hospital."

Chapter Sixteen

Brooklyn Sloane
December 2022
Wednesday — 7:52pm

Light jazz music drifted throughout the condo, its soothing sounds falling somewhat short of its desired effect. After giving the upcoming dinner arrangements more thought, Brook had found herself picking up the phone on several occasions to cancel on Graham. It would be a pointless meal when neither one of them could plan more than a week at a time. He'd lost his wife and daughter in the span of a very short time. Back-to-back funerals had been held, and the emotional trauma that he'd been handed would have crushed the soul of a weaker man.

The last thing that Graham should be doing was getting involved with a woman whose only commitment in life was to her brother's capture and subsequent punishment. It didn't matter that her intention was to bring Jacob to justice. Whether that would be behind bars or six feet under was still up for negotiation, but it didn't negate the fact that he was her sole focus.

CHAPTER SIXTEEN

She spent almost every waking moment thinking about Jacob.

Obsessing over him.

Even she could recognize that her fixation wasn't healthy, but she wasn't going to alter her objective.

Brook took a hefty sip of her cheap Moscato wine that she'd purchased earlier today. She hadn't bothered to give a reason as to why she'd been leaving the office earlier than usual. Considering she was usually still at her desk well after midnight, she could see the team's cause for concern. Still, it was no one's business but her own who she had dinner with and what she did on her personal time.

"Who are you kidding?" Brook murmured to herself as she pulled on the oven door to get a better look at the top layer of cheese that had melted over the meat sauce and lasagna noodles. "They probably think that you're having a mental breakdown."

Brook closed the oven door.

Needing something to do besides question her own decisions, she walked out of the kitchen toward the dining room table. She'd removed her laptop, all the files that she'd had in numerous stacks, and the various spools of color-coded strings that she used when pinning something to the murder board.

Technically, the dining room wall *was* the murder board.

The wall that she and Graham would be staring at during their dinner.

"This was a terrible idea," Brook whispered as she took another sip of her wine. "This is what happens when you veer off course, Brook. You crash and burn."

She didn't even want to imagine what her therapist would think about her having a conversation with herself. It was probably best if she didn't even bring up this dinner. Dr. Swift would only try to put an odd DMS-inspired label on it.

Brook glanced at the table setting one more time to make sure that she'd set out everything needed during their meal. As she leaned forward to straighten one of the butter knives, she thought she'd caught the sound of Graham's voice.

She tilted her head at an angle, but all she could hear was the music that she'd chosen from her playlist. The walls in this building were not only thick, but also well insulated. Crossing the hardwood floor while being mindful not to spill any of her wine, she opened the front door to her condo.

Sure enough, Graham was pacing in the hallway while holding a bottle of wine in one hand and his cell phone in the other.

"...any movement on the western border?"

Graham must have heard the door open. He swung around to meet her gaze, lifting the corner of his mouth in regret. She nodded her understanding before gesturing that he should step inside. There was no reason why he should be carrying on an important conversation where her neighbor might hear him.

"Did you confirm this intel through NRO?"

Brook stepped back while keeping her right hand on the doorknob. Graham crossed the threshold, his gaze focused on the table settings. He continued discussing the latest emergency with one of his government contractors as he handed her a bottle of her favorite sparkling wine. She held back a grin knowing full well that he'd had to grit his teeth upon paying for the bottle at the checkout counter. It wasn't like him to spend so little on a California vintage, especially when his preferences were so refined.

Thank you.

She'd mouthed the words, which caused his dark gaze to linger on her lips.

"How long do you think we have?"

Brook motioned that she would take his dress coat as she set the bottle of wine down on the entryway table, along with her wineglass. She wasn't going to look a gift horse in the mouth.

This muddled greeting had some of the tension easing from her shoulders.

She hadn't been looking forward to answering the door.

Brook technically didn't date, and she'd never made dinner for a man before. She had sex with men who had the same expectations as her—no strings, no regret, and certainly no thought of breakfast the morning after. Somehow, Graham managed to remove his black dress coat without moving the phone from his ear.

"Have you touched base with Lucas? He should still be at the airport." Graham loosened his tie as Brook kept herself busy sliding his coat onto a hanger. She then hung it in the small closet next to the front door. "No, don't do that. His wife is eight months pregnant. I'll catch a flight back. Advise JSOC to spin up a team ASAP. I want a fresh intel from Creech before I arrive."

When Brook would have turned around to retrieve his dress coat, Graham reached out and wrapped his warm hand around her wrist. She had on a pair of brown jeans and a cream-colored sweater. She'd pushed the sleeves up onto her forearms when she'd been cooking, so the contact of his touch was startling.

"I'll let you know when I'm back in the air," Graham advised whoever it was on the other end of the line. She stepped back, letting his arm fall. "I'm going to enjoy a delicious dinner before going home to change out my suitcase. If anything else happens, let me know."

Brook cleared her throat before stepping around him and picked up her wineglass. She made sure to also collect the bottle of wine, not that she would pour him any of the contents. He preferred whiskey, and she'd made sure to buy a bottle of his favorite brand. He'd mentioned that he was staying for dinner, but she doubted that he would have a drink if he needed to head home afterward in order to pack for an emergency trip.

"I take it that you need to go save the world once again?" Brook asked with a touch of humor as she crossed through the dining room and into the kitchen. The open layout of her condo worked for her current lifestyle. She was able to see her dining room wall from practically every vantage point, with the exception of the bedroom and main bathroom. "The lasagna only needs a few more minutes."

"It smells delicious in here," Graham said as he removed his suit jacket. He hung it on the back of a dining room chair before following her into the kitchen. "And I don't know about the saving the world, but I am contracted to make sure a small piece of it doesn't get reduced to nothing but a wasteland."

Brook set her wineglass on the counter. Having something to do with her hands was most welcome, so she concentrated on brewing up a carafe of coffee. He'd need some fuel to keep him going if he was going to turn right around and hop another flight. She understood that his line of work required a top secret sensitive compartmented information (TS/SCI) clearance, and she'd never ask him to betray his security agreement.

"How did the meeting go with Alex DeSilva?" Graham asked as he leaned back against the island. "The firm's lawyers sent me a copy of the contract that you signed. I'm surprised that he was willing to compromise on such short notice."

"I think that Alex is hoping to get into *your* good graces," Brook replied wryly as she cast a glance over her shoulder. This type of casual conversation was something that she could handle. She closed the lid on the filter before taking the glass carafe by the handle. "His colleagues' reports are quite extensive. They are well-trained, and such a partnership could benefit us in the long run."

"Agreed. Alex has a good reputation, and he does his damnedest to employ the best of the best."

CHAPTER SIXTEEN 141

Brook filled the carafe up with water before pouring the contents into the reservoir. He liked his coffee strong, which was something they had in common.

"How is the case going?"

"Let's just say that it took a curve at a rather high speed," Brook said as she slid the carafe onto the burner. She then pressed the brew button. "We went from allegations to actual evidence of several murders."

"Are you talking about the four bodies that were found about twenty miles outside of the city?" Graham asked as he pushed off from the counter and began to take the saran wrap off the small salad that she'd made while boiling the noodles. "Is that related to your case?"

"Yes, although I'm not sure if the psychiatrist was responsible for the murders. I'll be honest," Brook said as she reached for the oven mitt that she'd placed on the counter next to the stove. "I've been struggling with this investigation. I'm used to profiling the crime scene and the victims. Starting with no scene, no burial site, and no victims...well, let's just say that I've been out of my element. Locating the burial site should help, though."

Graham took the small salad bowl and placed it on the dining room table while Brook removed the glass baking dish from the oven. She ignored how natural it seemed to discuss her day while doing something so mundane as serving a home-cooked meal. She'd never been traditional in that sense, but she found such an extreme rather soothing. No longer was she pent up with the previous tension that had plagued her all day long.

"I take it that you can start drafting a profile?" Graham asked as he returned to the kitchen to grab the tongs that she'd set on the island countertop.

"I already started, but I'm waiting to gather more information from forensics." Brook used a second oven mitt and was able to carry the glass dish of lasagna into the dining room. She carefully placed it on the large potholder that she'd placed on the table when she'd arranged their place settings. "I don't even know their cause of death yet, and that makes all the difference dictating which direction I take the profile."

Brook had already made the garlic bread and made sure to cover the basket with a small cloth napkin. With everything in place, she gestured that he should take his seat. He didn't immediately sit down, but instead pulled her chair out so that she could be the first to sit at the table.

And there went her relaxed stance.

Talking business had allowed her to treat this as an ordinary meal that she might have had with one of her team members. Graham pulling out her chair took this evening into intimate territory.

She pushed aside her unease as she murmured her appreciation.

"I apologize for the scenery," Brook muttered as she gestured toward the dining room wall. She removed the silverware from the cloth napkin before unfolding the soft material and spreading it across her lap. "It's not exactly a relaxing sight."

"You could always put a Christmas tree in front of it," Graham suggested with a bit of humor. She appreciated that he didn't make the situation uncomfortable. Not a lot of people would understand her need for such a display. He was the first to grab the spatula and use the end to cut the lasagna into pieces. He then served one to her before filling his own plate. "Not big on decorations?"

"I'm just not here long enough to enjoy them. I take you aren't decorating, either?" Brook passed him the garlic bread. "You haven't been home for a week, and you were traveling quite extensively before that."

"I managed to put up both Christmas trees right after Thanksgiving." Graham must have caught her surprised expression, because he laughed. She was usually better at hiding her reactions. "You heard that right. I have one in the formal living and a smaller one in my office. Christmas was Kelsey's favorite holiday."

Kelsey had been the name of his daughter. He spoke about her differently now that her killer was rotting in the lowest pit of hell. Graham's words, of course. Brook had been meaning to ask about Austin Ridley, the man who had been wrongfully convicting of Kelsey Elliott's murder.

"How is Austin doing? Last I heard, you mentioned that he was working with his father. Are they still running a construction company?"

"Austin has decided to go to law school," Graham replied as he poured them both a glass of ice water from the pitcher that she'd filled earlier. "He received a settlement from his wrongful conviction, and he's using that money to pay his way through college. I have no doubt that he'll be successful."

Brook was grateful that Graham hadn't pushed on the holiday decorations topic. It was hard for her to celebrate any holiday knowing that Jacob was out there hunting innocent victims.

Right now, he had his sights set on Sarah Evanston.

Brook pushed her brother to the back of her mind in order to stay in the present. She and Graham discussed many topics over dinner, although the one that had fascinated her the most was Graham's view on fruitcake.

"You don't actually eat it, do you?" Brook asked with incredulity as she sat down on the couch with a cup of coffee in hand. She and Graham had cleared the table, but she hadn't allowed him to do anything more. She was well aware that he would have to leave soon, and he was going to need some caffeine for the long night ahead. "I had one bite when I was seven years old and can still remember how awful it tasted. Fruitcakes are terrible."

"It depends on how you make it," Graham said with a laugh as he settled onto the couch. They had each taken an end cushion, which enabled Brook to pull her legs up underneath her while facing him. He had also shifted slightly so that his right arm rested on the back of the couch. "If I have time, I'll make you one."

"Oh, you don't need to go out of your way," Brook assured him as she took a sip of her coffee. She could have stuck with wine, but she also had a long night ahead of her. She'd looked at her phone after dinner, and Bit had uploaded the first autopsy report. "I'll just eat up the cookies that Bit keeps bringing into the office. His sister has been on a baking spree."

"Speaking of siblings, has Agent Houser reached out to you lately?"

Brook explained her most recent phone conversation with Russell. It was still hard for her to call the man by his first name, but he'd had a point about dropping their formalities.

"Two siblings," Graham read from the dining room wall. Brook had tacked up a piece of paper and written a slew of words in capital letters. "Same parents. Same household. Same town."

"It's something that I don't think I'll ever understand," Brook said quietly yet comfortably. He'd allowed her to be back in her element. Whether that was by design or not didn't matter. In her mind, the dinner had been a success. She'd allowed a small part of herself to have a semblance of a normal life, and that was something that she'd never thought possible. "It's not like Jacob suffered some tragedy that changed his personality. Trust me, I've combed through every event in his childhood. There is nothing there that would explain why and how we turned out so differently."

"Do you recall when he began to change?" Graham didn't seem to be in any hurry to drive home, pack, and then head back to the airport. Brook found that she was fine with him delaying his departure, though she wouldn't put too much thought into the reason why. "I know that your father can't answer any of your questions, but what about another family member? Maybe they can recall an event or some type of accident that could explain his personality change. You mentioned to me before that he used to join in on family movie nights or watch Sunday morning cartoons with you."

"I've already asked questions from every family member possible," Brook replied with a small shrug. "At least, the ones who would sit down and talk to me. Let's just say that I'm not invited to the family reunions that are held every five years or so."

"And Jacob's friends?" Graham prodded as he continued to stare at the large murder board. "I take it you've spoken with them?"

Brook narrowed her gaze at Graham's sudden interest in the scenery that she'd already apologized for before dinner. It dawned on her that he had an ulterior motive for wanting her brother apprehended, but she couldn't really hold it against him.

Her obsession kept her from moving forward in her life.

Without it, she might be more willing to venture forth and try a piece of that horrendous fruitcake. While anyone else listening in on the conversation wouldn't have thought anything of her dismissal of such a gesture, Graham had seen the underlying truth.

Her cooking for him was one thing, but the other way around contained more intimacy than she was comfortable with right now. In her head, she understood such a distinction made little sense. She'd already warned him that she carried ugly scars underneath the surface.

"Right after I finished college, I called up Scotty and Daryl," Brook informed him. "Neither one of them were very forthcoming, not that they were rude to me. They answered my questions as best they could, but let's just say they didn't volunteer anything substantive."

"When did they stop coming around the house?" Graham asked after he savored some of his coffee. "I see some newspaper articles on the wall dating back to 1997."

"Some are from 1995 and 1996," Brook admitted, having combed through every criminal report that she could get her hands on from those prior years. "It wasn't a sudden thing. It's hard to explain, but I guess the two of them gradually stopped coming around about a year or two before 1997."

"And you don't recall anything unusual that might have caused their disassociation?"

"No," Brook replied, frowning when she tried to bring back memories from so many years ago. "We used to go to summer camp in the mid-nineties. I interviewed every camp counselor from those years a long time ago, but no one could remember a situation or event that involved Jacob."

"Was there an event that occurred *without* Jacob?"

Brook slowly shook her head, but the truth of the matter was that she wouldn't have been privy to such a thing. While she'd attended the same summer camp throughout their childhood, she'd been with a different age group.

"Not that I'm aware of," Brook replied cautiously, her mind working overtime now that Graham had planted a few more seeds. She'd overturned every part of their lives, including that specific camp. Had she missed something? It was a question that she often asked herself. "Did you ever go to summer camp?"

Graham flashed her a wicked smile before sharing stories from his own childhood. He full admitted to being a handful, but that didn't surprise her.

A half an hour turned into an hour and then some.

He had the ability to make her want to forget her obligations and the promises that she'd made to herself so long ago. It was as if time had suspended, and while she wasn't one to get into the spirit of the holiday, she found that she wanted to give herself a small present...a short break from her life.

CHAPTER SIXTEEN

"And your mother?" Brook asked. "You mentioned that your father has passed on, but what about your other family members?"

"No one can keep up with my mother," Graham said with a laugh. He rubbed his eyes with exasperation. "She's on a European cruise, but she's scheduled to be home in time for Christmas."

"Does she live in D.C.?"

"My mother lives on my estate," Graham divulged with a grin. Brook had a background check conducted on him last year, and she didn't recall that piece of intel being included in the reports. "I have a few aunts, uncles, and cousins in the area, as well. Mom travels so much that it seemed pointless for her to have a house of her own sitting empty all the time. The estate has two smaller homes on the back of the property with their own entrances. It seemed simpler to have her close by, too."

Brook tried to picture Graham's mother to no avail.

"You haven't been out to the estate." Graham finished off his second cup of coffee without taking his gaze off her. "We'll have to remedy that soon."

And just like that and with those few choice words, the bubble around Brook's small break from reality burst.

There was no need to meet Graham's mother.

None.

Besides, Brook was confident that Graham and his mother would want to share the holidays without interference from their business.

Brook was his business partner.

"I should be back early next week." Graham leaned forward and set his empty mug on the coffee table. "Christmas is in a week and a half. You haven't mentioned a holiday party for the firm."

"A holiday..." Brook let her voice trail off as she struggled with a reply. She cleared her throat as she attempted to put herself back into her normal routine. Graham had obligations to fulfill when it came to his contract with the government, and she had a profile to draft. "We technically only have four employees, Graham. Six if you include both of us."

"I know for a fact that the Bureau hosts holiday parties, but I'm going to go out on a limb and say that you never attended one." Graham rested his left forearm on his knee as he quietly regarded her before continuing. "We also have a law firm representing us, an accounting firm that handles our business, and now a private security firm that we have contracted out for the next three years. Social events like a holiday party display how we value those relationships. On a side note, there is also nothing wrong with having a small celebratory drink with the team right before the three-day weekend, as well."

Brook tucked a strand of her hair behind her ear, struggling against the urge to get up off the couch and find a hair clip. While there were some workdays that she could leave her long black hair free from containment, there was something said for composing oneself into a professional package.

Business suits were her armor.

They gave her a sense of control, which she had sorely lost throughout the evening somewhere between fruitcake and parties. Maybe between fruitcake and his mother. She wasn't sure which, and it didn't matter. Right now, she had the urge to defend her choices when she'd worked for the Bureau.

"A lot of those holidays were spent working long hours," Brook amended, recalling one Christmas how she'd spent days locked up in her tiny office that should have remained a storage space. "Cases like the one we're working now don't take days off, if you know what I mean."

"I'm heading back into what could potentially be a war zone. Trust me, I know exactly what you mean. Still, give it some consideration."

CHAPTER SIXTEEN 149

"It's a little late in the month," Brook pointed out as she stood from the couch. She'd only been following his lead, but she didn't want his departure to be uncomfortable. She leaned down and picked up his cup, along with hers. "Don't you think?"

"What about a New Year's gathering at the offices?" Graham suggested as he followed her across the hardwood floor. "Would Kate be willing to put together something small? An open house, maybe?"

Graham was giving her an out, and she would happily take it. She didn't mind doing what was necessary for the firm, but she'd rather it be on her terms. An open house for the outside firms was something that she could manage. She also didn't mind a small gathering with the team before the three-day weekend.

"I can arrange that," Brook said as she carefully set both of their mugs in the sink. She left her wineglass on the counter, though. She'd enjoy one while getting back to the profile. Of course, that would be after she cleaned off the kitchen table so that she could have her workspace back. "How does your schedule look in January?"

Because Brook had been a consultant for the FBI, she understood how contracts were negotiated with government contractors. Graham had mentioned previously that his contract was set to expire at the end of the year, and another one had already been presented to him for review.

He hadn't replied to her question, so she turned around only to find him studying her closely. Too closely.

"You simply tell me the date of the open house, and I'll make myself available." Graham was close enough that he could have reached out to her, but he seemed to sense that she'd already closed herself off. "Thank you for dinner, Brooklyn."

The way he'd said her full name had her almost changing her mind in regard to him leaving. Something told her that if she asked him to stay, he wouldn't have hesitated to push off whatever emergency was taking place halfway across the world.

That knowledge was dangerous, and it was something that she would rather not be privy to after such a nice evening.

"You're welcome."

Graham slowly nodded before turning and walking back toward the dining room table. He collected his suit jacket before slipping his arms into the sleeves. He adjusted the collar and lapel before then following her to the front closet. She opened the door and took his dress coat off the hanger.

Though the two of them had lunch together twice over the last two months in between his business trips, they had always been conducted in public settings. It had kept their dealings on a platonic level, which was where she'd been most comfortable with him.

"If you need anything while I'm gone, you know how to reach me."

Graham hadn't made a move to take his dress coat from her. As a matter of fact, he closed the distance between them, but not enough to back her against the doors of the closet. She stilled her movements when he slowly lifted a hand before gently running a finger down the side of her jawline. He then leaned forward until his lips were brushing against her ear.

"Breathe. It's only me."

Graham waited patiently to hear her soft exhalation.

He then pressed a soft kiss to her cheek.

"Goodnight, Brooklyn."

Without another word, he took his dress coat from her hands.

In seconds, he was gone, and the door had quietly closed behind him. Only then did she draw oxygen into her lungs. She stood there for some time, the evening replaying over and over in her mind.

It had been a simple dinner.

Nothing else.

CHAPTER SIXTEEN

Brook had a feeling that she would be telling herself that lie multiple times until their next dinner...one that did not include fruitcake.

Chapter Seventeen

Brooklyn Sloane
December 2022
Thursday — 7:59am

"No cause of death?"

"Not yet," Theo stated as he took a seat at the conference room table. Everyone on the team was in attendance with the exception of Kate. She'd already been on the phone for a good half an hour in regard to the Rastini case. "It took them two days, but they were able to excavate three of the four remains. They've been examined, and we have preliminary results. It could be days before we receive the toxicology reports."

"Have identifications been made?"

Brook continued to read over the notes that Theo had inserted into their files. She slowly scrolled up on the display of her tablet so that she could read over the findings.

"Again, three out of the four," Sylvie replied as she wrapped the string of her teabag around her index finger. Bit also happened to have a cup of tea in front of him. "Natalie Thorne, Lau-

CHAPTER SEVENTEEN 153

ra Keery, and Andrea Firth. Detective Raines is in the process of notifying the families."

Brook sipped her coffee as she skimmed the photographs that Bit had managed to produce from an online search.

All the victims had been brunettes.

Considering Millie had made mention that Dr. Kolsby had said she reminded him of someone who he'd allegedly killed, the fact that the three victims had been brunette didn't come as a shock. Brook had spent last night drafting her profile, but she'd run into a few bumps along the way. Unfortunately, those hesitations were due to Dr. Kolsby's so-called confession in the hospital and Dr. Cranston posing as some sort of tour guide.

"Give us the run down, Sylvie," Brook instructed as she turned her chair so that she could see the large 4k monitor. "Theo, jump in when necessary."

"Andrea Firth went missing two and a half years ago." Sylvie paused long enough to take a sip of her tea before diving into the heart of the data. "She was twenty-three years old, and she worked as a phlebotomist at the hospital. Single, brunette, and lived with a roommate."

"I already have a meeting scheduled with the roommate for later this morning," Theo interjected.

"Natalie Thorne went missing two years ago," Sylvie continued, keeping the same format to make things easier. "She was a twenty-nine-year-old lab technician. Brunette, and she lived alone."

"The only thing we know so far is that she was involved with Dr. Cranston at the time that she went missing," Theo tacked on. "He was technically cleared of any wrongdoing due to his alibi. I'll start diving into the lives of the other victims today."

"Laura Keery went missing nine months ago. Twenty-two years old." Sylvie paused as they all studied the young woman's photograph. "Laura was a nursing student who was interning at the hospital. Single, brunette, and still lived at home with her mother. Father wasn't in the picture."

"When you say that Miss Keery was interning at the hospital, was her internship in the cardiac unit?"

"No," Sylvie replied as she reached for her tea. Brook spun her chair around so that she was once again facing the others. "Pediatric floor."

Brook reached for her coffee mug. She'd already finished her caramel macchiato over an hour ago while sitting at her desk and watching the local news. Footage from the crime scenes had been the focal point as a local reporter covered the story, highlighting Millie Gwinn and Dr. David Kolsby.

Someone had let it leak that Millie Gwinn had gone to the police with suspicions of Dr. Kolsby having killed someone. Whoever had leaked the information had also known that Millie had been assigned a protective detail. It wasn't long after that statement that the reporter had included S&E Investigations role in the investigation.

Brook had muted the television after that small detail had been broadcasted, because it inevitably led to Jacob. The media coverage would only intensify from there, and it wouldn't surprise Brook if Graham started to receive a bit of pushback from Senator Ponzio. Then there was the fact that the Kolsby children would want to sue Millie for defamation. In Brook's opinion, it was only a matter of time before they filed suit.

"No cause of death? That doesn't make sense," Brook stated as she glanced up from her tablet. "Millie's statement regarding the day that Dr. Kolsby was brought out of his induced coma specifically described the blood of his victims. Even if their throats had been slashed, there would have been forensic evidence left behind on the skeletal remains."

"Is it possible that we're dealing with two different killers?" Bit asked without looking up from his phone. "Dr. Cranston obviously killed the four women. I mean, he drove Theo straight

CHAPTER SEVENTEEN

to their location. That's some crazy ass shit...pardon my French. Maybe Dr. Kolsby has his own personal burial site."

Bit lowered his phone, but Theo was too late to stop one of Bit's conspiracy theories from being floated around. Brook had seen some astonishing things when she'd profiled for the Bureau. She wasn't willing to stifle anyone's theories.

"Here me out. Maybe the killers are in some sort of competition with one another," Bit said eagerly, sitting forward and leaning his forearms on the table. "You know, to see who can rack up the most kills. I'm pretty sure that I saw a movie that had two killers trying to one up the other. Boss, have you ever dealt with something like that at the FBI? A set of killers linked by their passion for murder?"

Brook parted her lips to respond, but then thought better of it. It was one thing to stifle someone's idea, but she also didn't want to encourage the team to veer from the profile...not that she had a complete one to hand out.

"Brook, you realize how ridicu—"

"Everyone is free to share their opinions," Brook advised as she held up a hand in acceptance. Theo rubbed his temple, leaving Sylvie to smile behind her teacup. "We can't sweep any possibility under the rug. Millie specifically said that she heard Dr. Kolsby talking about blood, Dr. Cranston shows up to speak with Brett Kolsby, and then Dr. Cranston drives directly to the location where four remains have been buried. Bit's scenario might seem farfetched, but we're clearly missing something."

"Well, we can't ignore the background of these victims," Theo pointed out before gesturing toward the murder board. His gaze shifted to focus on the screen over Brook's shoulder. "They all had ties to the hospital. I can reach out to Had—Detective Soerig. She'll most likely be the one who starts to interview the victims' colleagues, friends, and family members since Detective Raines has agreed to work this case interagency."

Brook kept her attention on the display of her tablet. She wasn't one to talk about bringing personal business into office matters, so she wisely remained silent on the subject. Sticking to their formula worked best, and that was what she fully intended to do during this investigation.

"So, the fourth body has remained unidentified," Brook stated with curiosity. "Has the medical examiner been able to determine the *time* of death?"

"Roughly three years ago," Sylvie chimed in, glancing over at Bit. He'd gone back to looking at his phone. "Bit? Anything on Jane Doe?"

Had they found their first victim?

Brook put heavy stock into the initial victim, because that was where all the answers were usually found. Until forensics came up with something solid, patience was going to play a big role in this investigation.

"I'm running multiple searches on missing persons from three years ago and cross-referencing them with the hospital, Kolsby, and Cranston." Bit hadn't missed a beat. "Oh, and I threw in the other Kolsbys, as well."

"And Stephen Averill, Catherine's fiancé?" Brook asked since they were expanding the scope of their investigation. "He doesn't work at the hospital, but I'd like to make sure we cover our bases. Averill works for an insurance company, so there is bound to be connections to the hospital."

The team spent another half an hour going over specifics of the case, what directions each of them should take, and what leads would be more beneficial in the hands of Detective Raines and Officer Soerig.

For all intents and purposes, Hadley Soerig was now a homicide detective.

Seeing as the majority of the answers could be found with the first victim, it would be beneficial to have a name and cause of death for Jane Doe. Was she the first victim? Or had she only been the first one buried in that particular spot?

The longer this case went on, the more questions that seemed to arise.

"Bit, what is so interesting on your phone?" Brook asked with no judgement in her tone, only exasperation. She wasn't faulting him at all due to his ability to multi-task. The question was more to soothe her curiosity. "You have barely looked away from your phone all morning."

"What are you getting the General for his Christmas present?"

"I'm sorry?" Brook asked in disbelief. She immediately sought out Theo's gaze, but he was too caught up in gathering his things from the conference room table. "What?"

It was best to keep her questions short.

"Well, I have presents for you, Bit T, Little T, and Kate," Bit explained as he stood from the table, pushing his chair away with the back of his knees. "The General is another matter altogether. He's a tough one."

Brook resisted the urge to place her hand over her stomach. It had taken her a long time to accept that she needed to buy presents for the team this year, but she hadn't given a thought to buying Graham a gift. Her life had certainly been simpler when her only focus had been on Jacob and the cases given to her by the Bureau.

"I'm sure you'll come up with something," Brook murmured, collecting her own items to take back to her office. "I need coffee."

Sylvie had already vacated the conference room, Theo was one step ahead of Brook, and Bit slowly brought up the rear. Kate was still on the phone, but it dawned on Brook that there was a reason that the firm had hired an assistant. Would it really be so bad to delegate a bit more, especially since they were involved in a case? Kate had proven on multiple occasions that she was smart and creative, so chances were that she would excel at picking out gifts.

As Brook entered her office, her cell phone rang. She answered it as she rounded her desk.

"Sloane."

"You'll be getting a call shortly from Millie Gwinn," Alex DeSilva stated without offering the standard greeting. "The hospital has cancelled her mandatory therapy sessions and moved her back to the ICU that will commence upon her next shift."

"Seriously?" Brook carefully set her tablet, stylus, and mug down on her desk. A brief glance at the television showed a commercial airing during a break in the national news. "Kolsby apparently doesn't view her as a threat anymore now that all eyes are on Cranston."

"Do you still want two teams in rotation?"

"Yes," Brook replied after she'd thought over the possible scenarios. "I appreciate you wanting confirmation, though."

"Firms such as ours can easily go into the red unnecessarily. I know this is a pro-bono case for you. With that said, I'd like to make sure we both benefit from our contract."

"I knew I liked you for a reason, Alex," Brook said with a touch of humor. "Thanks for the call."

Brook spent the rest of the morning trying to piece together a profile, but doing so still proved difficult with Millie's claims of blood. By the time lunch rolled around, Brook had decided to ignore Dr. Kolsby's so-called confession and concentrate on the hard evidence being presented to them by the medical examiner's office.

Was it possible that a surgeon could slice someone's throat without leaving a mark on the skeletal remains? Brook would reach out to the forensics anthropologist for possible scenarios.

"Boss?" Bit had entered Brook's office after opening her door. "Cause of death just came in for the fourth victim. Unofficially, she was stabbed in the abdomen. The blade nicked one of her ribs. There was also mention of the clothes that the bones were found in as having a great deal of blood on them."

"That would explain the blood that Dr. Kolsby was rambling about, though not how the other victims were killed. The medical examiner will no doubt go back over the other remains to see if he missed anything," Brook replied as she leaned back against her chair. She also held up a hand to stop Bit from diving deeper into his conspiracy theory. "The likelihood of Kolsby and Cranston working together are low, Bit. But..."

"But?"

Brook lowered her gaze from Bit to her computer. She had multiple files open as she'd attempted to piece together the profile.

"I don't know," Brook murmured, still not getting a sense of the bigger picture. "Something doesn't add up. Please keep me posted on when the other remains are reexamined. It would help to be certain that they were all stabbed to death, because that would present a signature of the unsub. You should—"

At first, Brook thought that lunch was in the process of being delivered to the office. Kate had come around earlier with a menu from a local sandwich shop. Surprisingly enough, the individuals getting off the elevator weren't delivery people.

"Do you want me to get Sylvie, Boss?"

Catherine and Brett Kolsby stood in the main foyer outside of the elevator bank waiting for Kate to buzz them inside. Catherine seemed agitated, while Brett seemed more resigned about whatever reason it was that caused them to once again pay Brook a visit.

"No, Bit," Brook replied as she remained seated. The Kolsbys weren't their clients, and Brook saw no need to bend to their wills. "I can handle this. You can leave my door open."

Brook began to shut down the files that she had opened on her computer as Kate went ahead and buzzed the siblings in through the glass entrance. The upcoming conversation should be very interesting, especially since Millie Gwinn had turned down their offer of money in exchange of leaving well enough alone.

Brook could hear Kate ask Catherine and Brett to remain in the waiting room, but neither one of them seemed inclined to respect the professional setting. Catherine led the charge and walked through the open doorway with her head held high. There was a small hitch in her step after she'd already advanced into the office. Brook figured it had to do with the noticeable change in temperature, but Brook wouldn't apologize for how she liked to keep her office during working hours.

"Is there something that I can help you with?" Brook inquired as she stood from her chair. She made her way around her desk, not wanting to give them the sense that they were driving the conversation. Brook had no use for others who preferred to use intimidation as a tactic. "May I offer you coffee? Water?"

Brook's offer of a beverage had Catherine hesitating prior to her possible tirade.

"No, thank you," Brett responded for both of them before glancing at his sister. "Catherine?"

"We heard about Dr. Cranston. We find it hard to believe, of course. So does our father, and he's decided that he would like to see you," Catherine stated before taking a seat in one of the two guest chairs. Brett followed suit, but Brook wouldn't be forced back behind her desk. She chose to remain standing. "Considering his recent diagnosis, we have some stipulations before such a visit can take place."

"I'm listening."

Chapter Eighteen

Brooklyn Sloane
December 2022
Thursday — 5:42pm

THE FIRST AROMA TO hit Brook when she stepped through the front doors of the Kolsby residence was a complex mixture of various herbs and spices. She'd yet to have dinner, and the delicious fragrance was downright mouthwatering.

"You must be Ms. Sloane. Please, let me take your coat."

Brook almost turned down the request, but then thought better of it. It occurred to her that it would be beneficial to get someone else's insights into the Kolsbys, especially from an individual who was basically inserted into the family's daily lives.

The meeting with Catherine and Brett hadn't gone as well as they had hoped, but at least they now understood where Brook stood in regard to the situation. While it was their right to try and shield their father from as much stress as possible, Brook's independent investigation and the two police agencies had a job to do.

Unfortunately, their father's health didn't enter into the equation. Brook wasn't running for office nor looking to win a popularity contest. She didn't need to bend over backward to placate anyone's sensibilities.

One good thing had come from the discussion, and that was the knowledge that Dr. Kolsby had shared his diagnosis with his entire family, his friends, and his colleagues. There wouldn't be a need to tiptoe around such a sensitive topic when questioning anyone connected to him.

"Thank you so much," Brook murmured as she took her time removing her leather gloves. She made it seem as if she wasn't aware of the woman's identity. "You have me at a disadvantage, though. Are you Dr. Kolsby's—"

"No," the woman replied with a stiff smile before allowing Brook to ask her full question. The woman clearly wasn't one to make small talk. "I'm Dr. Kolsby's housekeeper. You're thinking of Cecilia, the woman who was briefly involved with Dr. Kolsby."

According to Sylvie's research, Peg Stockerman was in her late fifties. She'd been with the Kolsby family for the past twenty-four years, which meant that she'd been under the employment of Dr. Kolsby through at least one of his marriages and had been a part of his children's lives since they were very young.

As for Cecilia, Peg had been speaking about Cecilia Hemsworth. She had been linked to Dr. Kolsby romantically, although that relationship was apparently extinguished in light of the most recent circumstances. The woman had left the city and had been in Aspen, Colorado for the past month in order to spend time with her family for the holidays. She'd yet to return Sylvie's call.

"It's very nice to meet you." Brook shoved her leather gloves into one of the pockets on her dress coat. Wanting additional time with the woman, Brook then removed her scarf before slowly folding it into a square. "I must have missed you on my last visit. Do you reside in the residence, as well?"

"No, Ms. Sloane."

Brook tucked her scarf into the other pocket of her dress coat. Peg had been around long enough to know when she was being played, so it wasn't likely that Brook would be getting complete answers to any questions any time soon.

She tried a different approach.

"I was very sorry to hear about Dr. Kolsby's diagnosis," Brook said softly, completely abandoning the sets of questions that she'd thought of on the drive over. "I can only imagine how hard it was for you to hear the news."

Peg looked down at her hands as she fought for composure.

"Dr. Kolsby is a good man," Peg replied after clearing her throat. "He's also a fighter. I have faith that he will face this diagnosis head on and come out the other side of this."

"I've only had the privilege of speaking with him once. I would agree with your assessment. He comes across as someone who is not willing to give up quite yet."

Brook could sense that she'd taken Peg by surprise. Not wanting to push too hard, Brook concentrated on unfastening the button on her dress coat.

"I was under the impression you had a different opinion of Dav—I mean, Dr. Kolsby."

"While my firm was hired by the nurse who took care of Dr. Kolsby after the car accident, we only seek the facts concerning the matter at hand," Brook stated truthfully. She'd chosen her words carefully. "My colleague was the one who located the four women's remains, and that part of the investigation points into another direction."

By this point, Peg had taken Brook's dress coat and was gripping the fabric in relief. This woman might have been employed by the Kolsbys for many years, but she didn't see herself as part of the staff. It was also evident that she viewed Dr. Kolsby through rose-colored glasses.

"I heard on the news that Dr. Cranston was being questioned." Peg seemed to be willing to talk more now that she didn't view Brook as the enemy. "I can't say that such a turn of events is surprising. I never cared for that man."

Peg opened the large front closet and proceeded to store Brook's dress coat inside on a wooden hanger. She then closed the door and turned back around as she gestured toward the den.

"Did Dr. Cranston stop by the house often?" Brook inquired, keeping her tone light. She fell into step with Peg as they advanced across the marble tile of the grand foyer. "It's my understanding that he is close friends with Dr. Kolsby."

"You must be referring to Devin Cranston. He and Brett are close friends, although I'm not fond of that young man, either." Peg came to a stop outside of the door to the den to face Brook. "What is it that you would like to know, Ms. Sloane?"

Peg was very astute, and Brook respected the woman for calling out such an obvious attempt at gathering facts.

"You've made your opinion of Dr. Kolsby known, but what about the rest of his family and friends? Stephen Averill? What about the Cranstons?" Brook asked bluntly, getting right to the heart of the matter. "I believe the ICU nurse is telling the truth about what she heard while taking care of Dr. Kolsby. I also believe that his confession can be explained away, because being privy to such horrific details can weigh on one's conscious. Is there a chance that Dr. Kolsby could be protecting a patient or a close personal acquaintance?"

"Dr. Kolsby would never do such a thing," Peg disclosed with a bit of hesitation. She wasn't confident in her answer, but she clearly wanted to be. She laced her fingers in front of herself as she provided Brook with much-needed information. "Brett is our peacemaker. He has good intentions, although he doesn't always make the wisest of decisions due to his reliance on his emotions. Nolan, on the hand, could care less about anyone but himself. He's selfish and somewhat entitled. Catherine was our wild child until she met Stephen during her first year of college. It was then that she began to take her life seriously and not view her father as an endless pot of gold. She's come a long way, and we are proud of the life that she's built for herself."

"And the Cranstons?"

"Dr. Cranston has an inflated ego that has nothing to do with money. The root of which comes solely from his skill as a surgeon and his belief that he is a beautiful man."

"I'm sorry?" Brook hadn't expected Peg to go in that direction. "His appearance?"

"He loves women, and the women adore him," Peg explained with a ting of disgust. "Every time that Dr. Kolsby would host a dinner event or a party, he would inevitably get into an argument later that night with one of his wives regarding their blatant, flirtatious behavior with Dr. Cranston."

"And Dr. Kolsby didn't take issue with his colleague?"

"No." Peg coughed discreetly before continuing. "I'm aware that I shouldn't air the dirty laundry of the Kolsbys, but if it means that Dav—the good doctor can conserve his energy for his upcoming chemotherapy treatments, then so be it. Someone has to watch out for his best interests."

The dig that Peg had just given was toward Dr. Kolsby's' children.

While Brook would have loved to hear more, the door to the den flung open.

"...believe what you want," Nolan exclaimed in anger. He'd been looking over his shoulder, so he hadn't realized that Peg and Brook were standing right in front of him. He came to an abrupt halt. His facial features were twisted in anger, and it was clear that he didn't care who heard his parting line. "If you believe that, Dad, go ahead and have them arrest me."

It wasn't long before the front door of the house slammed shut.

Peg cleared her throat once more before calling out to Dr. Kolsby.

"Ms. Sloane is here to see you."

"Send her in, Peg," Dr. Kolsby called out from his chair near the elegant fireplace. "Would you please be a dear and bring us some fresh coffee?"

"Of course, sir."

Brook stepped into the den. The warmth from the fire was a nice touch, but she instantly chilled when she caught the hardened stare of Dr. Kolsby.

"I apologize for my son's behavior. These past few weeks have been hard for the family."

"No apologies necessary."

Brook had expected Brett, Catherine, and Stephen to be in attendance. They'd been adamant about how Brook should conduct this meeting, and they had even expressed their need to limit what could be asked during this interview.

Of course, Brook had made no such promises.

The lack of attendance by his children gave more credence to the fact that they no longer believed the police were interested in their father. Brook believed that their absence had more to do with their father's directions than beliefs.

"I appreciate you meeting with me again."

Brook set her purse down next to the leg of the chair that she'd sat in previously. Instead of claiming the same seat, she walked over to a small table that housed several framed photographs.

"We have things to discuss."

"Yes, we certainly do." Brook decided to clear the air before getting down to business. "Brett and Catherine came to see me in my office earlier today. They had stipulations for this meeting, such as I shouldn't bring up Nolan and his past troubles with the law. I reassured them that I wasn't looking for a scapegoat."

CHAPTER EIGHTEEN

Brook leaned down for a closer look at the family pictures. There were various shots taken throughout the children's lives. Some had been taken with their mothers and some without, but an outsider looking in would have said that they were a happy family based solely on appearances.

"Let me guess," Dr. Kolsby said as he seemed to relax a bit now that Nolan had left the house. "They're concerned for my health, and they didn't want you to stress me needlessly."

"That about covers it." Brook had appeased her curiosity about the photographs, so she turned and made her way back to the chair. "How *are* you feeling?"

"Better with each passing day, although I'm not looking forward to my cancer treatment, whatever that might be. I have a meeting with the head of oncology next week to lay out a plan." Dr. Kolsby did seem to be in better health, all things considered. "Getting back to Nolan, his behavior has improved considerably since he cut ties with Devin Cranston. Brett was the one close with the Cranston boy, but my oldest has a good head on his shoulders. He knew when to cut bait. Nolan can be...well, Nolan can be impressionable. Eager to please. I believe you'll find that out yourself with a bit of digging."

"Which is why you had Catherine and Brett come to my office in the first place. You wanted me to find the link between Devin Cranston and Andrea Firth, but you didn't want anything found to tarnish Nolan."

Dr. Kolsby remained silent, though he refocused his attention from Brook to the flickering flames. Embers floated into the air occasionally, giving the doctor something to focus on. It was obvious that he didn't expect Brook to call him out on such a glaring misrepresentation of the facts.

Brook had Bit look into Catherine and Brett's claims that their brother had once been in trouble with the law. No charges had ever been filed against Nolan, which was why the cursory background didn't reveal the numerous times that Dr. Kolsby had used his connections in the city to protect his son from the consequences.

Devin Cranston, on the other hand, had been publicly arrested for being drunk and disorderly while at a hospital event with his father. Devin and Nolan had gotten into a physical altercation over Andrea Firth, who just so happened to be one of the four victims discovered at the burial site.

"If you'd like to recant your earlier denial over what you said in front of Millie Gwinn, I won't judge your motives." Brook sweetened the deal. "My investigation is technically independent from that of the two police agencies that are currently investigating the four remains that we discovered."

"Two?"

"Officer Soerig recently made detective, and she has reopened her investigation into Millie Gwinn's claims. I'm sure that Detective Soerig will be in touch with you, if she hasn't already attempted to do so." Brook paused for effect. "Detective Raines is overseeing the four homicides discovered in his jurisdiction. They decided to work jointly together instead of independently. After all, there is cause to link the two cases."

"Me," Dr. Kolsby theorized before compressing his lips in frustration. "To answer your question, no—I don't want to change my statement. I do not recall saying anything of the sort, I have not harmed anyone in such a manner, and I will continue to defend my reputation against any slanderous statements."

"Good to know," Brook replied, crossing her legs while she studied him. "I also won't compromise my beliefs, Dr. Kolsby. I don't like being used as a pawn, and I'm giving you fair notice that such a stunt won't end well for you or yours."

Dr. Kolsby seemed to mull over her words, and he continued to do so even after Peg had brought in a serving tray filled with coffee cups, a carafe, sugar, and cream. She set it down on the beverage cart before pouring the hot beverage.

CHAPTER EIGHTEEN

"Thank you," Brook murmured as she carefully took a cup from Peg.

"I'll hold dinner for you, Dr. Kolsby," Peg said as she set his cup down on the table next to him. "Can I get you anything else?"

"No," Dr. Kolsby replied softly, still staring at the blazing fire. "Thank you, Peg."

Brook took a few tentative sips of her coffee as she waited for Dr. Kolsby to do the same. It became clear that he'd thought she would take the information about Devin and run with it. Dr. Kolsby hadn't expected her to continue down the path that led to his own door. It wasn't her intention to come across as rude or unsympathetic, but she also wouldn't disrespect him by handling the situation with kid gloves.

"If you're aware of something about Dr. Cranston or his son, it would be best for everyone involved if you come forward," Brook advised, thinking over Nolan's recent exit. He must have discovered that Catherine and Brett had all but thrown him under the bus, and he'd put two and two together. Nolan was being used as a pawn to steer the investigation, and he clearly wasn't happy about it. Who could blame him, really? "No one has to know that the information came from you."

"Neil has been a friend of mine for many, many years." Dr. Kolsby frowned as he met her gaze, not even bothering to drink the coffee that he'd been given by Peg. "I've had a couple of weeks to digest the news regarding my cancer, Ms. Sloane. I've had many revelations since then, and I've come to the conclusion that nothing is more important to me than my family and friends. Of which, I realize that I have short supply. My three children, Neil Cranston, and two old med school friends who moved away many years ago. We still keep in touch, but it's not the same as having them here in my home. I worked long hours, wasn't the best father, neglected my ex-wives, and spent more time on superficial relationships than fostering the ones that meant the most. I'm not sure how much time that I have left on this earth, but I refuse to be remembered in the hideous light that Millie Gwinn would like to paint me in."

"You had no trouble throwing Devin Cranston under the bus, Dr. Kolsby." Brook didn't bother to sugarcoat her opinion. Now that her coffee had cooled somewhat, she took a healthy drink of it before setting the mug to the side. "I find it difficult to believe you are sincere when you went to such extremes to divert my attention."

Brook uncrossed her legs and stood from the chair.

"My mother passed away from cancer some time ago, Dr. Kolsby." Brook made sure her suit jacket was fastened before she continued. "I can recall her last days as if they had happened yesterday. While she held onto her illogical belief that the evidence against my brother was somehow staged or misunderstood, she had never once played word games. She had also become brutally honest toward the end. I don't believe that she wanted any more regrets than she'd already racked up in her life. I'm merely offering you that same opportunity to clear the air."

Brook nodded her goodbye before she began to walk toward the door. The moment her high heels hit the dark hardwood floor, Dr. Kolsby's next words lent themselves to explain why he'd wanted to separate himself from any type of insinuation.

"Devin Cranston isn't Neil's biological son, Ms. Sloane. Do with that information what you will."

Chapter Nineteen

Sylvie Deering
December 2022
Friday — 9:29am

THE LOW MURMURS OF conversation being carried out by the crowded café practically drowned out the holiday music spilling from the hidden speakers. Red garland was strung somewhat haphazardly from the ceiling with tiny, silver jingle bells dangling every two feet or so. Most of the baristas had on Santa Claus hats, while two others had opted for red noses and reindeer headbands.

"Susan!"

Sylvie stepped to the side so that an older woman could collect two hot beverages after the barista had called out her name. She must have been out Christmas shopping, because she had two department bags slung over one forearm and a plastic bag with some type of toy inside on the other.

"Joey!"

Sylvie stayed where she was now that Susan had headed for the exit. Joey, on the hand, was grabbing two hot chocolates to bring to the table that his wife had snagged at the front of the café.

Sylvie's focus was on the small table tucked into the back corner where two men were having a deep discussion. She'd expected to find Devin Cranston here, but she hadn't counted on Nolan Kolsby. It shouldn't have come as a shock, though.

Brook had texted everyone last night after her meeting with Dr. Kolsby. First thing this morning, Bit had delved into the background of Devin Cranston. If he was the biological son of another man, there was no hard evidence to back it up other than obtaining the permission of a DNA test through the courts. That wasn't even in the realm of possibility, but that didn't mean that the question couldn't be asked outright.

As for friendships, Brett had distanced himself from Devin. While the same had been assumed of Nolan, those supplying such information either had the wrong assumption or they'd purposefully mislead the investigation to protect the middle son.

"Sylvie!"

She stepped forward and grabbed her Chai tea. She'd been monitoring the couple at the table closest to Devin and Nolan. According to their body language, they were about to throw away their cups and leave. Sylvie slowly began to make her way over so that no one could cut in front of her and lay claim to the table.

Her cell phone vibrated, but she didn't reach into her purse.

Sylvie gave the man at the table a small smile so that he would realize someone was waiting for the table. He motioned to his wife to grab the sugar packets that she'd used, as well as the wooden stir stick. Before too long, Sylvie was a mere five feet from Devin and Nolan.

"...questioned your dad yet?"

"Dad was brought into the station yesterday, but he made sure that his lawyer was there to fend off any questions," Devin said,

CHAPTER NINETEEN 173

keeping his voice low. Sylvie could sense the weight of his stare, but she paid him no mind as she pulled out her phone. She'd already taken off her gloves and shoved them inside her purse. "They didn't have enough to arrest him. He didn't do this, Nolan. Is that why you called me? To see if I'd rat out my own father so that you could take the heat off your family?"

"No." It was Nolan's turn to see if Sylvie was paying them any attention, so she purposefully dug her earbuds out of her purse. He seemed to wait to continue until she appeared to be listening to music on her phone. She even tapped her foot in rhythm as she stared at the door, making it seem as if she was expecting someone to join her. "Look, you and I haven't seen eye to eye on a lot of things, but don't you find it odd that your father gets a call to meet someone right where there are four bodies found the next day?"

Sylvie almost dropped her phone, because she hadn't expected to gather much information from today's run-in let alone something so substantial. Detective Raines had been able to get a warrant for Devin's phone logs, which meant that Bit had been able to track Devin's phone itself. It had been her intention to question him, but this was extremely more beneficial. As far as Sylvie was aware, Dr. Cranston hadn't said a word about receiving a phone call the evening that he'd driven from the country club to the burial site. She'd have to double check the report that they had received from Detective Raines.

"I don't think we should be talking about this in public," Devin replied as he glanced over the numerous tables in the café. Sylvie could once again sense the weight of his stare, but the two men seemed satisfied that she wasn't listening in on their private conversation. Their voices were rather low, and Sylvie had to strain to hear each and every word. "I'm telling you that my dad was set up. Maybe the same thing is happening with your dad. You said that his nurse was the one to report those things to the police. Have you checked into her?"

"Dad was the one who suggested my brother and sister throw me to the wolves, not that nurse." Nolan pushed back his chair. "I'm sure it's only a matter of time before the police reach out to me, and I have no reason not to tell them about you and Andrea."

"We didn't—" Devin had raised his voice, but he quickly stopped talking. "I never saw Andrea after that night, and I had no idea that she was missing, let alone dead. I just assumed she'd quit after we got caught that night. Wait a second. Nolan, are you telling me that you think I'm respons—"

"I don't know what to think, but I know one thing," Nolan stated as he stood and tapped the table with his knuckle. "I'm getting my own lawyer, and it certainly won't be my sister or my dad's team of shysters."

Sylvie looked down at the display of her phone to give herself something to do while Nolan grabbed his jacket from the back of his chair. He didn't wait to hear what Devin had to say as he pushed aside anyone who got in his way as he headed for the exit. She would need to explain the situation to the team before suggesting that Theo be the one to speak with Devin. It wouldn't be wise for him to discover that she was employed by S&E Investigations.

There was no need to add fuel to the fire.

Devin remained at the table, his decision to do so essentially keeping her seated as well. His cell phone had been on the table, but he didn't pick it up until Nolan had left the café. He quickly called someone before impatiently waiting for the other person to pick up the line.

Sylvie reached for her Chai tea now that the beverage had cooled off a bit. She savored a long sip while feigning interest in one of the apps on her phone. In her old life, she never would have considered eavesdropping the way she'd just done in order to obtain information. She had mostly been assigned to a desk, given the appropriate spreadsheets and documents to peruse then correlate the data into a cohesive report, ultimately ex-

CHAPTER NINETEEN   175

pected to provide her opinion on an investigation. It had usually been either for the Bureau's white collar or counterintelligence units.

"Dad?" Devin stood and grabbed his jacket before following in Nolan's footsteps. "I'm going to need my own lawyer. I just spoke with Nolan, and..."

Devin's voice trailed away, but Sylvie didn't follow him. She had inadvertently obtained information in a public setting, and she didn't see the need to push a conversation into a direction that would likely only cause more friction in their case. She was finally able to text the team the details on what she'd overheard between the two men.

She eventually removed the earbuds and stuffed them back inside her purse before planning out the rest of her day. Clearly, something had transpired between Devin, Andrea, and Nolan on the night in question. The two men had gotten into a physical altercation, but had there been something more to it? The fact that Devin had reached out to his father regarding a lawyer told her that the two were close, unlike the impression that Dr. Kolsby had given Brook last night. Sylvie had also had the ability to peruse the facts behind Andrea Firth's disappearance.

Would they match that of Natalie Thorne's case?

Why would Devin not have been privy to the facts? Why hadn't he been questioned regarding Andrea's disappearance? While Sylvie could have made some calls, she was close to the police station. It would be easier to stop in and speak with the officer who'd handled the missing person's case.

With the right questions, maybe there was another way to solve their investigation.

Chapter Twenty

Brooklyn Sloane
December 2022
Friday — 1:26pm

"Brook, we need to—"

She held up a hand as she turned toward the entrance of the conference room. Theo returned the gesture to say that he apologized for the interruption. She was on the phone with her father's nursing home. Lilith, one of her father's nurses, was in the middle of explaining how he'd taken a turn for the worse in recent days following his fall.

Lilith was in the middle of suggesting hospice care as a possible avenue in the near future.

Brook had already anticipated that this decision would inevitably come, especially after her last visit. Her father had lost so much weight that he didn't even resemble the man he'd once been. He could no longer bath himself or feed himself. She'd already been explained in detail how the last stage of Alzheimer's Disease affected the body. Soon, her father would forget how to swallow...and then eventually forget how to breathe.

CHAPTER TWENTY

"I trust the doctor's opinion, Lilith." Brook noticed that Theo was no longer standing in the doorway. She reached for another yellow string to attach Dr. Cranston's photograph to Natalie Thorne's picture. "Please do what is necessary to make sure that he's comfortable."

Brook spent the next ten minutes listening to Lilith explain what to expect over the coming weeks. By the time that she'd disconnected the call, there were voices from somewhere inside the main offices that were vaguely familiar. She quickly set her phone down on the conference room table as she made her way out into the hallway. Because she'd unconsciously wrapped the yellow string around her finger while digesting the change in her father's care, she hadn't bothered to take the time to unwind the thread.

"...last week. I was wondering why you would need a firm like this, but it makes sense now," Kyle said as he stood facing Millie. Two men stood off to the side. "The media is saying that you were the one who came forward about the bodies that were found in a remote area outside the city. Is it true that one of the surgeons you worked with is a serial killer? I can't imagine what—"

"Millie, is everything alright?" Brook asked as she came to a stop in front of the firm's client. She looked good considering the changes to her daily life, and she nodded her reply leaving Brook to be able to address Kyle. "You mentioned last week that you recognized Millie at the pub. I didn't realize that the two of you were so well-acquainted."

"We have some friends in common." Millie shot Kyle a warm smile. "We haven't seen each other in years, though."

"How about grabbing a coffee after you're through here?" Kyle asked as his gaze darted to the two men who served as Millie's security detail. "Unless now isn't a good time?"

Brook caught Kate's expression of disbelief, but she wisely concentrated on the computer screen in front of her.

"Maybe in a couple of days?"

"Of course. And if you ever need anything, don't hesitate…"

Brook turned to leave Kyle and Millie to finish their conversation, almost running into Bit as he emerged from the hallway.

"Boss?" Bit glanced over Brook's shoulder to make sure that he wasn't overheard. "The fourth set of remains had some pins and a plate attached to the radius. They were able to get the serial number and link it to an orthopedic patient at the hospital. She also happened to be an employee."

"Name?"

"Margo Urie, twenty-five years old, and she worked in admissions."

"Thanks, Bit."

Brook didn't have to ask if he'd already informed the others. As he walked back down the hallway, she retreated to her office. Millie wasn't far behind, and she ended up taking a seat in one of the guest chairs in front of the desk instead of the seating area. Her protective detail remained in the foyer to allow for privacy while being able to keep an eye on their subject.

"I'm glad that you stopped by the office, Millie," Brook said as she took a seat at her desk. She'd unwrapped the yellow string from her finger before setting it aside so that she could pick up her tablet. "I have a few questions that I'm hoping you can answer."

Millie had already touched base with regards to her reinstatement on the ICU floor. Everything had gone back to normal, although Brook had convinced her to keep the protective detail for the time being.

"Did you happen to know Natalie Thorne, Laura Keery, Andrea Firth, or Margo Urie?" Brook was able to access the most current information that Bit had already uploaded to everyone's tablets. It didn't take her long to access Margo Urie's picture. "They all had connections to the hospital."

CHAPTER TWENTY

"Laura Keery rings a bell," Millie said as she furrowed her brows in concentration. "I believe that she was a nursing student. Why?"

"Those four women have been identified from the remains found at the crime scene." Brook kept Margo's picture on the display as she set it down in front of Millie. "This is Margo Urie."

It didn't come as a surprise that Millie bore a striking resemblance to what was now the first victim. Her physical appearance must have been a trigger of some sort for Kolsby.

"Ms. Urie worked in admissions, and she's been missing for three years," Brook explained before leaning back in her chair.

"We look so much alike," Millie whispered in what could only be taken as fear.

"I can only guess why you're here, and I'd like to go on record that I think it's a bad idea." Brook glanced out in the foyer to see Kate speaking to the two men. No doubt that she was offering them coffee or water. "I understand that it's an inconvenience to have them around all the time, but we're talking about your life. Four murders in the span of three years, and you are the sole reason that those victims' families can now have some peace."

"Does that mean you know for sure that Dr. Kolsby is the one responsible?" Millie asked, a tinge of hope in her voice that the situation would soon be over. "I saw on the news that Dr. Cranston was brought in for questioning. I heard that the hospital assigned another surgeon to his scheduled operations. You have no idea the amount of guilt I had over the last few days believing that I accused the wrong man."

"We aren't sure who killed any of those young women. The point that I'm trying to make is that you could still be in serious danger." Brook stood from her chair before walking around her desk. "Millie, regardless if Dr. Kolsby is involved with these murders, the bottom line was that he knew about them. Your physical appearance is very close to that of Ms. Urie, and I'm assuming that is what prompted Dr. Kolsby to say the things that he said to you last month as he was coming out from under sedation. The hospital's board must agree with my assessment. Otherwise, they wouldn't have fully reinstated you without any restrictions."

"They don't want me to sue now that the spotlight is on them and their actions," Millie replied wryly as she sat back in her chair. She still had her dress coat on, sans any gloves. "Why would I still be in danger, though? Everything is already out in the open."

"I agree, but I say we err on the side of caution. The unsub may try to eliminate anyone who could testify against him in court. Then there is a very real possibility that he needs to feed his addiction."

"Because I look like them?" Millie asked, referring to the victims.

"In part." Brook hadn't been able to finish the profile due to several things, but now that the identity of Margo Urie had been established, there was a starting point. "Serial killers have a signature. In this particular case, the victims are all brunette, and they all worked at the hospital. You fit that signature."

It was evident that Millie had come to the office with expectations that her life would finally return to normal. That could be a dangerous assumption, and Brook needed her to see reason.

Witnessing Jacob go to the extreme to finish what he'd started with Sarah Evanston, Brook couldn't allow the same thing to happen with Millie. Until an arrest took place, it was best to keep things status quo.

Brook spent the next five minutes making her case.

"Okay," Millie said almost in a whisper. "Let's keep the protective detail in place for now."

"Good." Brook had been leaning against her desk, so her tablet was in easy reach. She tapped on the display until Margo Urie's picture reappeared on the screen. "You said that you were

CHAPTER TWENTY 181

familiar with Laura Keery. What can you tell me about her and possibly the other victims?"

"Our hospital employs over a thousand employees," Millie said reluctantly. "Laura Keery had an internship, but I had no idea that she'd gone missing or was presumed dead. You mentioned that Margo Urie worked in admissions, but I only know a handful of admissions personnel. Darla and Francis, mostly."

"Did Laura work with you at any point?"

"No. She followed Josh around for a few shifts, though."

"Josh Perisot?"

"Yes."

"What about Natalie Thorne or Andrea Firth?" Brook asked as she picked up her tablet. She typed in a note regarding Laura Keery and Josh Perisot so that Sylvie could follow up on the connection. "Did you ever meet them?"

"No." Millie gave a rather hopeless shrug. "I'm sorry. I wish I could be more help."

"Millie, what you've done for the families of these four victims can never be put into words," Brook praised as she placed the tablet back on the desk. "If you hear anything around the hospital regarding this case or any other woman who might have left without notice, please give me a call. I'll keep you posted on the progress of the investigation, as well."

Brook walked Millie out of the office to where her protective detail waited, noticing that Kate was near the Christmas tree. She was putting a few gifts on top of the red tree skirt. Not needing the pressure of the holidays, Brook started to walk back to her office to grab the yellow string that she needed to finish the impromptu murder board.

While the 4k monitor had everything that she'd ever need in that regard, creating a murder board from scratch helped her see details that she would otherwise might have overlooked…such as the fact that two of the victims had gone missing right after a social event at the hospital.

Chapter Twenty-One

Brooklyn Sloane
December 2022
Friday — 11:02pm

"How did I know that you would be here?" Theo asked as he took a seat at the conference room table.

He'd changed clothes since leaving the office around five hours ago. He sported a mustard yellow sweater that had a thick collar with two wooden buttons near the neck. Not a lot of men could pull off such a color, but Theo managed to do so in spades.

"Your amazing skills as an investigator, I'm sure," Brook quipped as she reached for her coffee mug. She'd brewed a fresh pot about twenty minutes ago. "Why aren't you out painting the town?"

Brook kept to herself that she knew he was seeing Detective Hadley Soerig.

"My parents are driving in tomorrow morning from New York. We're going to do a bit of Christmas shopping together. I forgot to grab my laptop before I left the office earlier, so I figured I'd

CHAPTER TWENTY-ONE

stop by now instead of having to make a separate trip in the morning." Theo studied the massive murder board that she'd put together. He didn't say a word about how redundant it was when the same information resided on the monitor, which she had turned on so that she could look through her notes. "Getting anywhere?"

"Not really." Brook had kicked off her high heels hours ago. She crossed her ankles as she rested her feet in the chair next to her. "I'm going over the missing person reports. I think we can safely determine that the women went missing after hospital charity events. Bit was able to gather information regarding the fundraisers, but Detective Soerig promised to send over a list of attendees by Monday."

"Dr. Cranston had an alibi for the night that Natalie Thorne went missing, and it doesn't appear that he was at the charity event, either."

Theo had followed the light blue strings that led to Dr. Cranston's photograph that Brook had pinned to the wall. Several blue threads also led to Dr. Kolsby, but he'd been out of town when Laura Keery had gone missing.

"Dr. Kolsby garnered our attention due to his so-called confession to Millie Gwinn," Brook pointed out after taking a sip of coffee. "Dr. Cranston led you directly to the burial site, but he received a call from someone, asking him to meet in private. Blackmail? We won't know until Detective Raines calls Cranston back in for questioning."

"I spoke to Raines earlier today." Theo must have taken off his winter coat before walking into the conference room. She'd heard someone activate the biometric scanner, so she hadn't been startled by his presence. He didn't seem to be in any hurry to leave, though. "Raines was hoping to wait for potential DNA evidence from either the skeletal remains or what remained of their clothing."

"That could take weeks," Brook said with a grimace. She rested the back of her head against the chair. "Given what Sylvie overheard at the café earlier today, Raines certainly has enough to bring Cranston back in for questioning. Sylvie was finally able to upload everything about Andrea Firth's disappearance."

"I saw that Sylvie stopped into the police station to speak directly to the officer in charge of Firth's case. Apparently, Andrea Firth was caught stealing drugs from the hospital's pharmacy. She showed up at the event to talk to her supervisor, hoping to salvage her job, I guess. The officer had no idea that Andrea had any kind of friendship with Devin or Nolan."

"I'm sure their fathers did what they could to avoid that from happening, but it still doesn't explain why these missing person cases weren't connected by law enforcement. They all worked for the hospital."

Brook was well aware that a lot of crimes slipped through the cracks, but the hospital should have been able to connect the dots. It shouldn't have mattered that each of the women had worked in different departments. Millie made mention that over a thousand employees worked at the hospital, but someone still should have found it odd that four staff members had gone missing in the span of three years without giving notice or providing a forwarding address. Do they really believe employees with professional degrees just leave and never use the hospital as a reference?

"Let's start at the top," Theo said as if it wasn't closing in on midnight on a Friday night. He even reached for the carafe that she'd set down in front of her. Kate always made sure that there were a few clean mugs positioned on a small tray in the middle of the table. "Our first victim, based purely on time of death, was Margo Urie. What do we know about her?"

"Brunette, twenty-five years old, and she worked in admissions." Brook didn't bother to lift her head. She just tilted her face toward the murder board that she'd worked on all day while

CHAPTER TWENTY-ONE

keeping her coffee cup steady. "We know from the examination of her skeletal remains that she was stabbed on her right side. From the missing person report, she went to a fundraiser for the new pediatric ward a couple of days before she disappeared."

"From the hospital?"

"According to the report, she left her shift at the hospital and didn't make it home."

"Car?"

"Never found."

Theo frowned as he reached across the table for the remote. Brook was well-acquainted with that knowing expression, so she lowered her feet to the ground and slowly rotated her chair so that she was facing the 4k monitor.

"Brook, all four vehicles of the victims were never discovered." Theo's attention averted from the screen to her. "What are the chances of that? Hiding a car has got to be even more difficult than hiding a body. VINs are hard to erase."

Brook continued to sip her coffee as they let the details of such an anomaly settle over them. Different scenarios played through her mind, and she kept coming back to the one that made the most sense.

"The unsub could be setting up meetings with the victims."

"What does he do with the vehicles afterward, though?" Theo asked as he set down the remote. He'd accessed each and every missing person report that Sylvie had uploaded into the file. He left all four tabs open as they stared at the lines that he'd highlighted. "Lake?"

"Some of these women were abducted and killed in the dead of winter," Brook countered, though she wasn't ruling out Theo's theory. "First thing Monday, start looking for large bodies of water. It can't hurt to check them out while we're waiting for the police to figure out which gear this investigation should be in."

"Do you think they're getting pushback from the brass?"

"I think they want to make sure that they have all their ducks in a row before they get their hands dirty," Brook clarified as she pulled her tablet closer. She was mindful of spilling her coffee as she quickly typed in some instructions for Bit. "I'll have Bit comb through the victims' cell phone locations, DMs, and emails for any sign that they were meeting someone. Each of them disappeared either on their way home from work or vice versa."

"Are you suggesting that the fundraising events don't come into play?"

"Quite the opposite, Theo," Brook said as she finished typing her note. She shifted her focus back onto the screen where the important sections remained highlighted in the reports. "It's all connected. We just need to figure out how and why."

Chapter Twenty-Two

Brooklyn Sloane
December 2022
Monday — 7:11am

"Your ex-wife had an affair with Dr. Trenton Yackley, she became pregnant with his child, and she never blinked an eye when she lied to your face about you being the father." Brook kept her voice low, but she made sure to maintain direct eye contact with Dr. Neil Cranston. "To this day, she doesn't know that you are sterile."

"I'll call security," Dr. Cranston warned quietly as he finally glanced away to see if anyone had overheard her. "You can't talk to me without my lawyer pre—"

"I'm not with the police, Dr. Cranston. I don't have to follow their rules."

Brook had taken a guess that a man like Dr. Cranston would have a hard time forgoing his daily routine just because he wasn't performing surgeries at the hospital. Every Monday, Wednesday, and Friday, he arrived at his exclusive country club to meet with his personal trainer. His dedication to his health routine was admirable.

She could sense that he was aware of her identity, which meant that he'd spoken to Dr. Kolsby at some point regarding her involvement. Odds were that was before Dr. Kolsby decided to throw Devin Cranston under the bus.

"I can see from your expression that you've connected the dots. You would be correct, by the way." Brook had taken off her leather gloves upon arrival, so she was able to slip her hands inside her pockets without any restriction. She'd been early to make sure she could catch the surgeon before he walked into the men's locker room of the country club. "I imagine that Dr. Kolsby was hoping such a diversion would take the limelight off of Nolan."

"What the hell are you talking about?"

Brook lifted the corner of her mouth at how astute Dr. Cranston was even while being taken by surprise. Now that she had his attention, she turned and walked over to a private area where they could continue their conversation without being overheard.

She had no doubt that he would follow.

"Tell me about the call you received last week requesting a clandestine meeting out in the woods," Brook instructed as she took a seat in one of the two chairs in front of a coffee table. They were close enough to guarantee that their voices wouldn't drift across the large foyer. "I take it that you didn't recognize the number, but did you recognize the voice?"

Dr. Cranston sat in the other chair, though he took his time doing so. She figured that he was trying to process her words, but she'd thrown a lot at him in a short amount of time. Brook set her purse next to the chair. Her phone was tucked into the side pocket and set on vibrate.

"Talk to my lawyer."

CHAPTER TWENTY-TWO

"Dr. Cranston, I might be the only person involved in this case that doesn't believe you killed those women," Brook said honestly as she casually reached for one of the fastened buttons on her dress coat. Once she was more comfortable and her words had a chance to penetrate the man's frustration, she continued. "I believe it's in your best interest to answer my questions."

"Or what? You'll tell the world that Devin isn't my biological son?"

Brook had been monitoring the man's body language, and he wasn't just frustrated over the situation. He was terrified, but not for himself.

"Devin has no idea that you're not his biological father, does he?" Brook asked cautiously, wanting to ensure that she'd read the signs right. She was coming to the realization that Dr. Kolsby had taken his life-altering diagnosis and chose to protect his family above all else. Instead of Nolan being the center of attention, the spotlight was now on Devin. "Dr. Cranston, I'll say it again. I'm not here to trick you into confessing to a crime that I highly doubt you committed. While it is true that killers return to the scene of the crime—in this case, the burial site—I don't believe that you would be foolish enough to do so after you were identified as a suspect in Natalie Thorne's disappearance."

"I had nothing to do with Natalie's disappearance," Dr. Cranston said with a touch of desperation. He ran a hand down his face as if he couldn't believe that his life was disintegrating right before his eyes. "I was fond of Natalie. We weren't serious, but it could have turned out that way. As for Devin, no…he doesn't know that he's not my biological son, and I don't want him to find out. He's my son in every way that counts. He doesn't need the trauma of finding out about his mother's infidelities under these circumstances."

"Did you kill those women?" Brook asked directly.

"No. God, no. I'm a surgeon," Dr. Cranston exclaimed as if that made all the difference in the world. He spread his fingers wide and held up his hands. "I swore an oath, Ms. Sloane. And I know my son. I'm not saying that he's an angel, by any measure. He has a wild streak a mile long, but he could never do what you're suggesting."

"What happened with Andrea Firth?"

"Andrea was stealing drugs from the hospital and selling them to whoever had the money and desire to distribute them." Dr. Cranston finally lowered his hands, but he didn't take his gaze off them. "Devin was one of her customers. I put him into rehab shortly after that night."

"Was she fired?"

"Yes, from my understanding." Dr. Cranston shrugged, as if anything was possible. "I'm sure you'd be able to get more information from one of the board members or the HR department."

"Andrea was fired the day before a fundraising event, yet she still made an appearance. Why? And what happened that night that would prompt Devin to get into an altercation with Nolan?"

"How the hell would you know that?" Dr. Cranston asked with disbelief. "Are our phones tapped?"

Brook weighed her options, but it wouldn't do to have Dr. Cranston paranoid. She decided to tell him the truth.

"One of my investigators overheard a conversation that Devin had with Nolan last week at a café. Dr. Kolsby was the one who informed me about Devin not being your biological son, but you already knew that, didn't you?"

"I still don't know why David would..." Dr. Cranston let his voice fade as realization set in. "Son of a bitch. He's setting me up. Or my son."

"We don't know that, but I do believe that Dr. Kolsby doesn't want Nolan to be the focus of the investigation." Brook tried not to inhale too deeply. Fresh coffee was being made across the foyer, and this place clearly didn't skimp on their food or

CHAPTER TWENTY-TWO

beverages. The display being set up was quite grand. "Devin also spoke to Nolan about something taking place the night of the charity event. Can you enlighten me? Help me look beyond what's being served up to the authorities as the facts?"

"I didn't know about Andrea until last week when Devin called me," Dr. Cranston revealed as he finally leaned back in the chair. He still wasn't completely comfortable in her presence, but at least she had been able to get him talking instead of trying to communicate through his lawyer. "Apparently, Devin and Nolan attended this charity event that you're referring to in order to buy some pills from Andrea. She showed up, demanding that one of them help get her job back. She knew who their fathers were, and she thought that she'd use that knowledge to blackmail them. They got into a fight—mostly verbal, I might add, but it got out of hand enough that the police were called. She left the event prior to the police arriving, and they never saw her again."

Brook mulled over Dr. Cranston's words, attempting to find holes in his story. There could technically be many, but she didn't get the sense that he was pushing the issue. If anything, he still seemed concerned with Devin potentially discovering that he had a different biological father.

Devin and Nolan didn't have day-to-day contact with the hospital. During the investigation into Andrea's disappearance, she'd already been fired from the hospital. The detective in charge of her case had spoken to her previous employers, but he also hadn't spent a lot of time on them once he'd learned the reason for her termination. Her friends and family had insisted that she wouldn't just up and leave, but seeing as no vehicle had ever been located, the detective had been leaning toward Andrea pulling up stakes and leaving town after losing her job.

"You said that you're not working with the police," Dr. Cranston said as he misconstrued her words. She didn't correct him. She didn't see a need to at the moment. "Do they know about Devin not being my biological son?"

"Yes," Brook replied truthfully. "I can speak with them, though. I'll ask that they use discretion when the time comes, although I'm sure you saw to it that Devon has legal representation. Tell me about this call that you received that had you driving miles out of your way outside of the city."

Dr. Cranston hesitated, which told her that there was more to the story.

Brook could feel the vibrations of her phone through the leather of her purse. She made no move to answer the call. She was afraid that if she interrupted Dr. Cranston, he wouldn't divulge the much-needed information to move forward on this part of the investigation.

"My lawyers have advised me—"

"I'm sure they have given you sound advice, but I'm not a lawyer. I'm an investigator, and there are four skeletal remains of young women whose families only want answers. If you didn't kill them, then it was the person who called you and asked you to meet them in that location. The unsub set you up, hoping that the police would look no farther than what was served up to them on a silver platter with you visiting the grave site right in front of them. Again, I'm not the police. I want to look beyond how you were obviously being manipulated, Dr. Cranston. Help me do that. Help me clear you and your son."

Dr. Cranston became slightly agitated at the situation that he'd found himself in, and he started to jostle his right knee. He was wearing a pair of jogging pants, and she assumed that he had on the matching sweatshirt. She couldn't tell, because he was still wearing his winter jacket. It bunched up in the middle as he leaned forward to rest his elbows on his knees.

"I didn't receive a call. It was a text message, and from a number that I didn't recognize. It stated that they had information regarding a past incident with...a young woman. Should those allegations become public, it would ruin my career. They wanted a hundred thousand dollars, and then they gave me the name of a road. Said that I should drive a quarter of mile and park in the small pull-off on the righthand side of the road. I did that and then waited for at least a half hour. No one came, so I left. I still have the money in cash, but I haven't received another text."

"I take it this so-called incident actually took place?"

"It was an allegation, not an incident. And I decline to answer that question." Dr. Cranston seemed to think better of such an evasive response. "Wait. You should know that this allegation has nothing to do with those murders. Again, I took an oath. I would never harm another human being."

"Do you still have the text message?"

"I deleted it once the meeting fell through."

Brook made a mental note to have Bit locate the number from the service provider. They would have a list of numbers listed for incoming messages. She had to assume that the text had been sent via a burner phone.

"Who knew of this allegation from your past?"

"No one."

Brook arched an eyebrow. While most everyone had skeletons in their closet, very few had all the bones in one place.

"My first wife and D—"

Dr. Cranston had been going to name David as the other individual.

"I need to call my lawyer." Dr. Cranston's voice left no room for argument. "I'm sure you'll receive a call from him at some point today. He won't be happy that I spoke with you, but our conversation has been very enlightening."

"I appreciate your time, Dr. Cranston." Brook reached for her purse. She stood before securing the strap over the shoulder of her dress coat. "I do have one more question, if you don't mind."

"Look, I—"

"Why did you stop by the ICU and speak with Brett Kolsby the day that his father was brought out of the induced coma?"

"Because that is what concerned friends do, Ms. Sloane."

The anguish and remorse that laced his words was palpable.

"May I give you a piece of advice?" Brook could see that any suggestion wasn't really welcome, but she found herself parting with some wisdom that he really should take to heart. "It's actually an old adage. Keep your friends close, but your enemies closer."

Brook wasn't sure the lengths that Dr. Kolsby would go to if he thought that Dr. Cranston would push back against the clear onslaught being waged against him. She now had no doubt that Kolsby was involved with the four skeletal remains found at the burial site, but there were still so many unanswered questions. She'd been able to work up half a profile based on Millie's recount of what she'd overheard and the death of Margo Urie. So far, she was the only victim whose cause of death had been given. The other remains were currently being looked over by a forensics anthropologist.

There were a few more stops that Brook had to make before heading back into the office, but it was clear to her that she needed to start from the beginning. She needed to ignore everything and everyone involved in the case with the exception of Margo Urie. Brook needed to start from the very beginning, because the profile that she'd drafted wasn't showing Dr. Kolsby as the unsub, even when all the leads they had gathered indicated his involvement. In turn, Dr. Kolsby was willingly and eagerly pointing a finger at Dr. Cranston.

A vicious circle had formed around every suspect, and it was time for Brook to shatter it.

Chapter Twenty-Three

Brooklyn Sloane
December 2022
Monday — 12:27pm

"I FOUND TWO POSSIBLE lakes near the burial site that could potentially be where the unsub dumped the vehicles," Theo said as he walked into the conference room. "I've already put a call into Detective Raines. Both bodies of water are in his jurisdiction. Detective Soerig is meeting us there in about a half hour."

Brook had everything up on the monitor that had to do with Margo Urie's disappearance. If she were to include the other three victims, then it was possible to throw out the previous profile and start anew.

The woman's facial features were very close to those of Millie Gwinn, so it could be understandable how Dr. Kolsby managed to get the two of them mixed up when he was coming out from under the effects of anesthesia. The question remained whether he was commenting from being up close and personal, or if he had simply connected the two women based on hearsay from a patient, a family member, or a friend.

The pool of suspects was vast.

"Can they send a diver down in this weather?" Brook asked as she reached for a slice of the medium pepperoni and mushroom pizza that she'd had delivered to the office. The others had chosen subs from a local sandwich shop, but she worked better with a pizza box nearby. "I heard that we're supposed to get some snow later today."

"Only an inch or two." Theo crossed his arms as he stared at the far wall. Brook had finished tacking the appropriate strings to the associated pictures, facts, and locations. "The major part of the stormfront is moving slowly in from the West. Should be here before Thursday, but we should have answers by then. First, Detective Raines will have a technical team use sonar equipment before sending a diver down. Who knows how long it will take to extricate the vehicles if we actually find them? They have the specialty dive equipment that can work in freezing water, but their time under will be limited. Has Bit forgiven you for the manual murder board?"

"He will by this afternoon," Brook quipped after she'd swallowed a bite of her pizza. She wiped her fingers with a napkin before turning back to the 4K touch screen monitor. She pulled up a schedule that she'd had Bit upload into the files. She then pointed toward the last date on the document. "The hospital has a fundraiser tonight. If the unsub is still active, we might be able to apprehend him in the act."

"On a Monday?" Theo asked before recognition dawned regarding the direction that she was taking this conversation. "You're going to have Bit use the tech van, aren't you? What are you looking for? Those events draw hundreds of people, mostly high-net-worth individuals."

Brook addressed his first question.

CHAPTER TWENTY-THREE

"Fundraisers are mostly scheduled around either grand openings or specific times of years...like the holiday season in December."

Theo snapped his fingers.

"Tax write-offs."

"Exactly." Brook turned once again, pulling up a guest list. She zeroed in on specific names. "The Kolsby family has been invited, and I confirmed that Dr. Kolsby will be in attendance. He's scheduled to give a speech, although I'm not certain about the topic. It would be rather difficult for him not to mention Millie Gwinn, especially since it leaked to the press that she had gone to the police with accusations of murder."

"Kolsby has been doing his best to steer the unwanted attention toward Cranston. Do you think he'll try to put the final nail in the coffin?"

"Funny that you brought up the subject," Brook said as she finally took a seat at the table. She pulled her plate closer as Theo remained near the door. He'd need to leave soon if he was going to meet up with Detective Raines. "Dr. Cranston's lawyer called a few minutes ago. It appears that a board member called and advised him that it wouldn't in the hospital's best interest for Dr. Cranston to make an appearance tonight."

"They think that one of their top cardiac surgeons is under suspicion of being a serial killer. They are minimizing the damage to the hospital's reputation."

"I don't blame them, but since I don't believe that Dr. Cranston has anything to do with this case, the fundraising event gives us an opportunity." Brook focused her attention on Margo Urie's photograph. "Each of these victims went missing days after a hospital event such as the one this evening. Eliminating everything else and focusing on Margot, we're left with a very cunning unsub who has a way of manipulating any given situation to their advantage. The unsub has managed to pit two powerful families against each other who had once been very close. That means the unsub is intimately close with both families. Since I would categorize both doctors as narcissists, I believe that the unsub is using that specific characteristic against each of them. Margo Urie was stabbed, which means the unsub obtains a personal gratification from a victim's death. Take in the other victims, the unsub's preferences are an open book."

"But not the unsub's signature?"

"Not until we have confirmation that the other three victims were stabbed to death. I'm holding off on a specific signature." Brook glanced at the clock on the wall. "You should get going. Let me know what you and Raines find, because some of these murders took place in the winter. If the vehicles are at the bottom of those lakes, then that means there's a place where the ice is either thin or a portion of the water doesn't freeze over for whatever reason."

"I'll keep in touch, but you're robbing me of witnessing Bit's reaction to the news," Theo said before stopping short of the doorway. "By the way, what exactly will he be monitoring? You already have a guest list."

"I want him to monitor the Kolsbys' comings and goings, as well as their communications during the event. And yes is the answer to the question that is floating around in that head of yours," Brook said wryly as she lifted what was left of her slice of pizza. "Detective Soerig was able to obtain warrants to tap every single phone that is involved in the case, including the burner number that the text was sent from to lure Dr. Cranston into the woods."

"Tap whose phones?" Sylvie asked as she came to stand beside Theo. She grimaced at the pizza, indicating her displeasure at the mushrooms. "I might have a name to add to that warrant."

"Dr. Kolsby and his children," Theo answered before gesturing toward the kitchen. "Kate put your sub on the counter in the breakroom."

CHAPTER TWENTY-THREE

"Thanks." Sylvie was still wearing her cream-colored dress coat, matching scarf, and earmuffs, minus the gloves. Her hands were tucked into the pockets. "My lunch might have to wait."

"What name?" Brook asked, wanting to get back to Sylvie's previous desire to tack on a name to the warrant that Detective Soerig had already put in front of a judge. "And will this individual be at the fundraiser tonight?"

"Fundraiser?" Sylvie pulled her right hand out of the pocket to hold it up in warning. "Stop. I'm confused. What's going on?"

Brook quickly filled Sylvie in on the plans for the evening while Theo vacated the conference room to gather his belongings. There was a good chance that he wouldn't be returning to the office today.

"Now it's your turn," Brook said as she tossed her napkin onto the plate. She leaned back in her chair, sensing that Sylvie had come across something in her interviews today. "Who did you want to try and add to the warrant?"

"A man by the name of Gary Heinsel. He is one of Dr. Kolsby's patients, and he is the man who tried to jump off the roof of the hospital." Sylvie removed her earmuffs. "Care to guess why he was going to jump?"

"No idea whatsoever," Brook said, knowing that the reasons for such a decision were too many to count. "Let's have it."

"Gary Heinsel was due to go to trial for murder the day after he tried to commit suicide. Get this," Sylvie said as she tucked a loose strand of her blonde hair behind her ear. "Gary stood accused of murdering a twenty-six-year-old woman who just so happened to be a brunette with the same basic description as our victims."

Chapter Twenty-Four

Brooklyn Sloane
December 2022
Monday — 3:46pm

B<small>ROOK OPENED HER OFFICE</small> door to the sound of holiday music. If she heard Jingle Bells one more time today, she wasn't going to be responsible for her actions. The cheerful tunes had been the reason that she'd closed her door in the first place. It wasn't that she begrudged anyone their sense of Christmas spirit, but it was rather difficult when her father had been assigned a hospice nurse, her psychotic brother was still in the wind, and there were two cases that were looking more and more likely that they wouldn't be solved before the new year.

"Brook, the accountant had this envelope couriered over about an hour ago," Kate said as she pushed a yellow envelope toward the edge of her desk. "Your door was closed, and I didn't want to disturb you."

"Thanks, Kate." Brook was glad that she'd chosen to hole herself up in her office instead of snapping at Kate over the music coming from the overhead speakers. Granted, it wasn't

CHAPTER TWENTY-FOUR   201

like they had guests in the lobby throughout the day, but the tunes made the rest of the team happy. She wouldn't dampen their holiday spirits. "How are you doing on the Rastini case?"

"Good," Kate responded as she flashed Brook a smile. "Great, in fact. I think I might have narrowed down the list of people who could be responsible for Kyle's death. I still have to put together some timelines, but your profile has been amazing when weeding through the vast array of people in his life."

Brook paused as she picked up the envelope. While Kate's words should have been a compliment, all Brook could focus on was the way that Kate had personalized the victim. She'd done that over the past week, which indicated that she was getting too close to the case. Brook had learned long ago to contain her emotions. Otherwise, she would have burnt out a long time ago.

It wasn't that Brook didn't immerse herself in each of her cases. Far from it, because she'd come to find that she was very possessive when it came to the victims and the unsub. Still, she was able to put up a professional barrier that kept her from being swallowed whole.

"Kyle's timeline doesn't necessarily match up with what his parents gave us originally. I caught the mistake when I was speaking with a friend of his, who mentioned that Kyle actually left town three hours later than what we were initially told. It's hard to confirm, but I think those missing few hours could be key."

Brook decided to postpone discussing the boundaries needed in their profession. It would do nothing right now except impede the investigation. Kate had the ability to use the intel that the team had gathered, the interviews that they had conducted, and the profile that had been crafted on the unsub to see the case through to the final stages.

"I'll be in the conference room if you need me."

Brook retreated to her office briefly so that she could lock the envelope in her desk. The accountant had sent an email stating that the year-end bonuses would be couriered over this afternoon. Graham's suggestion of a New Year gathering for the team and the firm's partners was a wise one. At least, she had convinced herself that it would benefit the firm from a business standpoint.

Brook had also recognized that the team deserved something a little more personal, so she was having lunch brought in next Friday before the three-day weekend. She would hand out the bonuses that afternoon, as well as have the gift exchange that they were all excited to conduct. The stress of having to figure out what to get everyone was heavy, which was why she was going to add it to her official procrastination list.

By the time that she'd joined Sylvie in the conference room, the electronic murder board had the most recent and pertinent information displayed for all to see. Bit had joined them, though she still hadn't informed him that he would get to use the van in real time.

"What have you found?" Brook asked as she picked up a bottle of water off the entry table before pulling out her usual chair. She turned it sideways so that she could get a better look at the screen. "Gary Heinsel, forty-six years of age, and..."

Brook let her voice trail off as she digested the bullet points underneath the man's picture. The sentiment went against what Sylvie had insinuated earlier this morning.

"Heinsel isn't currently serving time in prison for murder?"

"No," Sylvie responded as she picked up the remote. She scrolled down to a newspaper article. "This is why Dr. Kolsby's actions turned out to be quite heroic the day that he talked Heinsel out of jumping off the hospital roof. While the man was admitted for a psych evaluation right after his attempt to commit suicide, his lawyer was somehow able to get the case tossed out on a technicality. The media took that as a sign of the

CHAPTER TWENTY-FOUR

man's innocence, which was why the following articles hailed Dr. Kolsby as a hero."

"What did you find out about the victim?"

"Donna Laurel was twenty-six years of age, an x-ray technician at an urgent care facility, and the girlfriend of Dr. Lance Heinsel." Sylvie paused as she set the remote down on the table. "You heard right. Dr. Lance Heinsel. He's a doctor in the emergency room, and he's the one who paid for Gary's defense lawyer."

"Cause of death?" Brook asked as she unscrewed the cap of the water bottle.

"Ms. Laurel was stabbed to death," Sylvie revealed as she sat back in her seat, though Brook got the sense that something wasn't quite right about the murder. "Her body was discovered in her apartment by her mother."

"That isn't the unsub's M.O." Bit switched his focus between Sylvie and Brook. He hadn't been on his phone, which meant that he almost certainly had figured out what to buy Graham. If only she could do the same, then she might not be so stressed out over the holiday music. "Right? I mean, are you thinking that this Heinsel guy killed four other women and took the time to bury their bodies and dump their cars?"

"It's unlikely." Brook made herself comfortable as she turned on her tablet and unhooked the stylus. Ever since she'd lost her favorite pen, she'd gotten more accustomed to fidgeting with the stylus when she was thinking over scenarios. "Had Heinsel murdered Donna Laurel five or six years ago versus twelve months ago, I might have a different opinion. If that had been the timeline that we were dealing with, it would be a logical assumption that Heinsel discovered he needed to hide his crimes. He doesn't present as a serial killer, especially the suicide attempt right before a court proceeding."

"Could he have been the patient that caused Dr. Kolsby to react in such a way upon being brought out from under sedation?"

Sylvie asked as she reached over and grabbed one of the M&Ms from the small yellow bag that Bit had brought into the room. "I mean, that part of the case would make more sense."

"Cranston was led to the location of the burial site," Brook pointed out as she twirled the stylus in between the fingers of her right hand. "Whoever was able to blackmail him was close to him, which I believe brings us back to Kolsby."

"I thought you weren't convinced that Kolsby was the unsub," Bit pointed out skeptically as he ever so slowly separated the yellow M&Ms from the other colors. He had the oddest quirks. "I'm getting whiplash."

"That's too bad," Brook said as she observed him pass the yellow M&Ms over to Sylvie. She took them as if this was a normal routine between the two of them. "I was hoping that you were in good enough health to work the tech van this evening."

Brook's words had registered immediately, causing Bit's hand to retract at lightning quick speed. The other M&Ms went flying off the table, but he made no move to pick them up off the floor. From his expression, he reminded her of a kid in a candy store.

"Wait. Little T, did you hear that or am I experiencing a sugar rush?"

"You heard right," Sylvie said with a laugh as she pushed back her chair from the table so that she could come around and help pick up the chocolate candies. "I want in on this surveillance gig. This is going to be fun."

"Boss, I need specifics." Bit hadn't wasted any time getting down to business, completely ignoring the fact that Sylvie was picking up the M&Ms. His entire attention was focused on Brook. "Who, what, and where? I've got the how covered."

"There is a fundraising event tonight being hosted by the hospital for their new pediatric neuro center," Brook explained as she reached for the second remote on the table. Bit had thought of everything when he'd installed the 4k LED monitor. She quickly pulled up the list of attendees. "The Kolsby family has been invited, and the doctor himself is also set to give a speech. Dr. Cranston has since been disinvited as of this morning, but you'll notice that Dr. Lance Heinsel will be attending, along with a date and the same brother who Dr. Kolsby saved from taking his own life. I think this event is also being used in an attempt to repair some of the damage that has been done by the negative press generated by our investigation. It would certainly explain why Gary Heinsel was issued an invitation."

"Which of these individuals will we be monitoring?" Bit asked as he stood from his chair. Brook figured that he'd be busy for the next few hours, double and triple-checking every technical component in the van. "If you're asking me to do this, I take it we have warrants that cover the scope of this type of surveillance?"

"We will be monitoring the comings and goings on all of them, and the warrants are vague enough to include individual electronic surveillance, as well as telephonic intercepts," Brook replied truthfully as she set down the remote. She kept the stylus in her right hand as she reached for her tablet. "That works to our advantage. I'll send you the address of the venue, and you'll await any instructions from me as to who you might be surveilling should someone decide to leave the event earlier than expected."

"You're going?" Sylvie asked as she threw away the M&Ms that had been on the floor. "As in, dressing up and mingling with the hospital staff and donors?"

"I managed to finagle an invitation or two from—"

"Someone who owed you a favor," Sylvie and Bit said in unison.

"It's called networking, and it wasn't a favor," Brook pointed out wryly as she entered the address and other pertinent information into the tablet. Each of the team members would receive an alert. "I hadn't planned on attending, but Millie Gwinn called me about an hour ago. She received an invitation, and she's currently planning on attending the fundraiser."

Brook nodded toward Bit, who could barely contain his excitement regarding the tech van. He didn't waste a minute longer before exiting the conference room, mumbling something about getting to the nearest cell tower next to the event to install a monitor to intercept cell phone traffic for their list of numbers.

"Is that wise? For Millie to attend, I mean," Sylvie clarified with concern as she returned to her place at the table. She didn't take a seat, but instead began to collect her items. "Also, I thought only the executive staff members and doctors attended such events."

"That's why it is such an unusual invitation. It's also the reason that I told her to accept it. Someone wanted her there," Brook explained, comfortable with such a decision due to their client's protective detail. "I'll also keep a close eye on her, but I'd like to see the reaction of those involved when they see me there. Bit will need to loop in the protective detail's communications into the van. They will most likely be encrypted using burst transmission."

"What about your profile? I saw you added some specifics, but you also left a few details out that are pretty crucial to all investigations."

"Until I have the full reports on the three other skeletal remains from the forensics anthropologist, I'll hold off filling out the profile so that we aren't chasing our tails looking for false indicators." Brook recalled something that Theo had said last week. "Until then, we work this case a bit different than the others."

Brook's phone rang, and it wasn't a surprise to find that Theo's name was on the display. When she finally answered, she made sure to put the call on speakerphone to include Sylvie.

"Were you able to locate the victims' vehicles?"

"No," Theo said a little breathlessly. The cold temperatures most likely hadn't made the day any easier. "Both lakes have clear, sandy bottoms with no large hits that would indicate vehicles. Locals implied the public access ramps were dredged only last year on both lakes as part of a state fisheries initiative."

Brook met Sylvie's disbelieving gaze.

"Four vehicles up and vanish into thin air," Sylvie said with a shake of her head. "How is that even possible?"

"We're widening the search of the landscape by another ten-mile radius," Theo divulged over the sound of his Jeep's door slamming closed. "The unsub had to have dumped the cars somewhere or buried them with heavy equipment you might find on a farm. Come sunrise, I'll be joining Detective Raines at another possible site."

"Does that mean you're done for the day?" Brook asked as she powered down her tablet and hooked her stylus to the side.

"It does," Theo responded as the engine of his Jeep roared to life. "Do you need me to pick up something on the way back?"

"That depends," Brook said lightly as she stood from the chair. "Do you own a tux?"

CHAPTER TWENTY-FIVE

Brooklyn Sloane
December 2022
Monday — 6:37pm

THE LIGHT JAZZ MUSIC that drifted through the condo was interrupted by the repetitive chime of the phone. A text message had been received, but Brook was still standing in front of the full-length mirror of her bedroom. It was rare that she ever had the need to wear a formal dress, but this Tom Ford liquid sequin floor-length column dress had been in her closet for the past two years. She'd purchased it for an event that had been cancelled, but she'd never gotten around to wearing the dress, which had been discounted to an outrageous price.

The red fluid fabric skimmed her figure with a simple tank-style design where the fabric left both her arms bare. Her neck was highlighted with an elegant white gold ruby pendent, her right wrist was adorned with a 4.8-carat white gold diamond and ruby tennis bracelet, and her left wrist was where she wore her Rolex diamond platinum presidential watch. The shape of the dress was very flattering to her figure, and the slit halfway

CHAPTER TWENTY-FIVE

up the side made it comfortable for her to move around easily on matching three-inch red heels.

The only problem that she'd run into was where to keep her firearm. She'd opted to take her Berretta Px4 Storm in S&W .40 caliber out of her private safe. The weapon was compact enough to fit into the red clutch purse that had been shoved on the top shelf of her closet, alongside the heels that she'd bought to go along with the dress two years ago.

It didn't take her long to touch up the matching red lipstick and nail color. With her black hair and blue eyes, red complimented her physical features. She hadn't had time to wash her hair upon arriving home, so she'd opted to wear her hair up while allowing a couple of strands to frame either side of her face in order to soften her cheekbones.

Once she'd given herself self-approval, she walked across her bedroom to pick up her phone. She'd been expecting a text from Theo, who had promised her that he'd send her a message when he was headed down to the lobby. Having given the evening some thought over the last few hours, there was a chance that tonight wouldn't amount to much.

Even so, she found it best to immerse themselves into the world of those involved with the investigation. Reading body language and facial expressions sometimes offered more than hardcore evidence.

Brook quelled the small bit of bile that rose to the back of her throat. Leave it to Bit to be able to multitask like a professional. He'd sent her contact information on Scotty Nevin. She'd known that her brother's former friend had gone to a trade school after graduation. The last time that she'd spoken to him, she'd discovered that he'd ended up on an oil rig as a deep-sea qualified welder.

Scott had actually done quite well for himself, with the exception of his personal life. Divorced twice with four children by three different women.

Brook had already asked him an endless number of questions back when she'd first started her hunt for Jacob. There really wasn't anything left for them to cover, but she couldn't stop ruminating over the seed that Graham had planted regarding the summer of 1996.

Had something occurred at summer camp that she'd overlooked all those years ago?

She'd contacted each and every camp counselor, most of the attendees, and even some of the parents. They hadn't appreciated being questioned, especially by the sister of Jacob Walsh. The Walsh name had been tainted, and with good reason. Had the tables been turned, she wasn't so sure she'd be willing to speak with a sibling of a serial killer who'd terrorized her hometown.

As Brook had been staring at her screen, Theo's text had come through that he was heading down to the lobby from his condo. She didn't have time to make a call, so she decided to send an email to Scotty. She'd thought long and hard about how to craft her inquiry, so it shouldn't take her too long.

Brook picked up her red clutch purse, which weighed a bit more than intended with her compact firearm tucked safely inside. She'd already taken her license, her carry permit, one of her credit cards, and a hundred dollars in twenty-dollar bills out of her everyday wallet and tucked them inside the cell phone pocket that she'd bought last month. Her red lipstick had slid in perfectly underneath her weapon for when she needed to freshen up in the restroom throughout the evening.

Five minutes and one email later, Brook stepped out of the elevator and into the lobby. She'd opted for a long black cloak overtop of her red dress instead of a coat. It complemented her formal attire while keeping the cold at bay.

Theo's appreciative whistle drifted through the air before she caught sight of him near the front desk. Lou was the doorman

CHAPTER TWENTY-FIVE 211

this evening, and his infectious smile widened even more at the sight of her.

"You clean up pretty well yourself, Theo," Brook replied in kind as she closed the distance between them. He was wearing a black dress coat over a tuxedo, and based on the fit, one that was not a rental, either. "Lou, do I even want to ask about fantasy football?"

Lou's smile vanished, but there was no sign of anger. If anything, determination was written across his features. His white bushy brows practically touched in resolve as he shook a finger her way.

"Don't you go believing Charlie when he says he's got this year's season wrapped up," Lou warned. "I simply forgot to make a substitution last week, but I'm ready for this weekend. Plus, my wide receiver is better than his."

"We believe you, Lou." Theo gave the counter a tap of his hand before looking at his watch. "We better get going."

"You two enjoy your evening," Lou said with speculation in his wise gaze. "Whatever the two of you are working on, be careful. It never works out the way those James Bond 007 novels say it does."

Theo motioned for Brook to turn first, and then the two of them fell into step toward the exit. Being the gentleman that his parents raised him to be, he rested his hand on her lower back as he reached for the door.

"I didn't say a word to him that we were working a case tonight," Theo said, as if she didn't know any better. "I swear, Lou has got a reading on every single person's pulse in this place."

"I thought about hiring him when we started the firm," Brook said in jest as the bitter cold hit her face.

"That would have been an interesting hire," Theo said with a laugh as he gestured toward his Jeep. "I pulled it around when you said that you needed a few more minutes."

Brook decided that she would wait to tell the team that she had once again reached out to Scotty Nevin. There was no reason to even have such a conversation if nothing came of Scotty's recollection from so many years ago.

Once Theo had helped her into the passenger seat, it wasn't long after that he'd settled in behind the steering wheel. They made it to the venue with little traffic to contend with due to the timing of the event. Rush hour traffic had faded, and Monday night tended to be rather quiet.

"I've got to hand it to Bit," Theo said as they passed the black 2022 Mercedes Sprinter technical van. He'd parked it across from the valet, and it blended in with the dark of night. "He did an exceptional job in outfitting that vehicle. There isn't an antenna to be seen. He's been talking about acquiring state of the art earpieces, so that we can communicate in real time."

"It's only a matter of time before the NSA or CIA tries to steal him," Brook muttered as she picked up her red clutch that she'd nestled beside her in the seat. It was their turn in the valet line, and the attendant was already reaching for her door handle. "Ready?"

"Does my eyepatch match my tux?"

Brook refrained from rolling her eyes as she braced herself for the cold. She hadn't needed to do so in light of the portable heaters and clear plastic panels positioned on both sides of the entryway. It was a nice touch for the attendees, and she exhaled in comfort as her red high heels hit the pavement.

Theo made it around the Jeep in record time, taking over for the valet attendant. She rested her hand on his arm as they advanced in unison toward the door that was currently being opened just for them. Theo murmured his appreciation as they walked through the entry. Before too long, his dress coat and her cloak had been handed off to the attendant at the coat check.

Theo tucked the small ticket into his pocket.

CHAPTER TWENTY-FIVE 213

"According to Bit, the only ones to have arrived at this point are Dr. Lance Heinsel, his date, and also his brother." Theo held out his arm for Brook to take as he escorted her into the main room. "So, this is how the other half lives."

Theo hadn't exaggerated, either.

The large room was elegant in an understated way with what seemed like an abundance of high-top tables that lined each side of the room. This was not a dinner event, but the tables had been provided for those who preferred someplace to set their drinks while engaging in conversation. The high-top tables were covered with white tablecloths, and each had a white lantern-style centerpiece to complement the sophisticated atmosphere. Those in attendance had gone all out with their apparel, wearing their most beautiful gowns and tailored tuxedos.

In the back right corner was a grand Christmas tree that stood at least twenty-feet tall. It had been decorated with the color scheme of the hospital in mind, so the blue and gold trimming matched the hospital logo that was front and center behind the stage.

The hospital's fundraiser should do well tonight.

Brook could sense the vibrations of her cell phone, but she hadn't needed to look at the display that was discreetly tucked against her clutch purse. With her compact firearm tucked inside, there was little room left for her phone.

"Bit has definitely decided that he's ordering earpieces so that we can communicate in real-time."

"That doesn't surprise me in the least," Brook murmured as she reached for a glass of champagne that one of the servers had presented to them on a tray. Theo declined as he continued to scan the occupants in the room. "Two o'clock."

Theo's gaze swung in that direction.

"Dr. Heinsel and his date seem to be engaged in a deep conversation," Brook said quietly right before she took a sip of her champagne. The sweet bubbly tingled her tongue and the back of her throat. "No sign of the brother."

Theo gestured toward a high-top table to their right. Such a place gave them a perfect view of those entering, while also keeping an eye on those gathered in the center of the room. Holiday music was drifting through the speakers on stage, as well as the overhead speakers. There was no escaping it.

"You know, I thought this was going to be a complete waste of the evening." Theo rested his right elbow on the table as he kept an eye on the entrance. "Then I realized you didn't want to attend this gala to talk to those involved in the investigation. You want to read their body language. You're still having trouble with the profile, aren't you?"

"I wouldn't go that far." Brook finally located Gary Heinsel. He didn't wear his tuxedo as well as his brother. As a matter of fact, the way the jacket laid on the man's shoulders, it was a safe bet that it was a rental. "There are a few key factors that I'm waiting to add. It would help to have a cause of death on the other three victims."

"I was thinking about our missing vehicles," Theo said before abruptly changing the topic. "Incoming."

Millie Gwinn entered the room on the arm of a male subject.

"Isn't that interesting?" Brook hadn't expected Kyle Paulson to be Millie's plus one. It must have been last minute plans. Otherwise, Alex or the protective detail would have included tonight's plans in their afternoon update. "I guess it's not too much of a surprise."

"I'm honestly shocked that she's agreed to keep her protective detail," Theo said as he monitored the couple's progression. Mille looked stunning in a black dress with matching heels. "Once the focus of the investigation switched to Cranston, she was immediately moved back into the ICU. All of the previous prerequisites had been forgotten."

CHAPTER TWENTY-FIVE 215

"Which is what the hospital board is hoping that she does about the situation," Brook surmised, noticing that Kyle was the one who stopped to talk to group of people. He was right in his element, with the exception of his tuxedo being a rental. Again, she could tell from the way the jacket didn't quite form to his shoulders. She was beginning to think that her initial assumption at him being frugal was right on target. "According to the protective detail, there hasn't been anything out of the ordinary in her daily life these past few weeks."

"Maybe we should cut back and save the money." Theo turned his attention to her. "We are doing this pro-bono."

"I'd rather err on the side of caution."

The two individuals assigned to Millie hung back, but they were close enough to keep an eye on their charge. Brook had to hand it to the duo. They were dressed appropriately, and upon first glance, no one would suspect them of anything other than being guests. Of course, their jackets weren't buttoned nor was the fabric tight in the chest to make room for their shoulder holsters.

"You were saying?" Brook prompted Theo about the previous direction of topic. "You had a thought about the missing vehicles?"

"Before I left the office, I asked Bit to look into the make and model of those missing cars. Depending on the year, he might be able to trace their last known location based on their built-in navigation systems." Theo shrugged when she glanced at him for the results. "I'm guessing they didn't have newer models since I didn't get confirmation from Bit. I'll be meeting Detective Raines first thing in the morning as we hit a few more lakes since we've widened the search area."

Brook and Theo remained at the high-top table for another half hour, keeping tabs on the Heinsels and Millie. More people had joined the fundraiser, and the crowd had thickened, though not to the point that they couldn't see the entrance.

Theo had only left briefly to collect a rum and coke from the one of several bars positioned around the large room. He'd also gotten her another glass of champagne, which she'd been in the middle of enjoying when a round of applause broke out around the room.

"That's quite the entrance," Brook said as the Kolsby family paused just inside the double doors. She and Theo had known from Bit's text that they had arrived, though in different vehicles. The only one not in attendance was Nolan. "He's like royalty."

Dr. Kolsby raised an appreciative hand and motioned for the crowd to go about enjoying their evening. Catherine and Stephen were on one side, while Brett and a blonde woman stood on the other. Brook didn't recognize the woman, but her name would almost certainly be supplied within the next few moments. Bit had been feeding them information through their cell phones on the guests as the evening wore on.

"Renee London, twenty-nine years of age, and in pharmaceutical sales," Theo replied after reading Bit's text. "As for Nolan, his phone is pinging from the family estate. He's been there since this afternoon."

Brook noticed right away that Dr. Kolsby avoided Millie and Kyle. As a matter of fact, the doctor had purposefully walked straight forward into the crowd as if he hadn't known that she was standing with a group of employees off to the side. While the hospital board might have seen the benefit of treading carefully where Millie was concerned, it was evident that Dr. Kolsby didn't feel the same.

"It looks as if this is where we part ways," Brook murmured, picking up her glass of champagne as Theo lifted his drink in salute.

It wasn't long until they both blended in with the crowd.

Chapter Twenty-Six

Bit Nowacki
December 2022
Monday — 8:42pm

The interior of the Mercedes Sprinter van was something to behold, and Bit had never thought he'd be in such a position to put together something so grand.

He'd outfitted the inside with a three-hundred-and-sixty-degree HD day/night nine camera video surveillance of the area that surrounded the van. It even contained a 3-240mm zoom, a Keysight N9423C Radio Frequency spectrum analyzer, a precision GPS tracking beacon/transponder, a digital twenty-four channel video/audio recorder, and a full server suite with 1GB mobile internet uplink 550MB downlink back to S&E Investigations.

The others would never understand his excitement over the state-of-the-art equipment. They also wouldn't comprehend why he still needed to improve the van's audio communications with the team. He truly believed that the team members required a set of micro-earwig wireless full duplex team communication devices. Of course, the earpieces would have to be small enough not to be noticed, yet still capable of full duplex hands free wireless, multi-channel networked comms up to three miles from the van.

Brook had taught him how essential it was to do things right.

He had also made sure to include two rolling stools that could be locked into place when needed, along with a small refrigerator that fit perfectly underneath the long counter that held three HD twenty-seven-inch monitors. Given the weather, the small portable space heater kept the inside at a comfortable temperature for the occupants. There wasn't a need for coats or gloves, which would have only been uncomfortable to wear for an entire evening.

"Brook and Theo just left their table," Sylvie advised as she pointed to the screen. He'd been able to connect to the security cameras positioned throughout the venue. Given the number of feeds, he had four cameras split on one monitor so that they had multiple vantage points besides the views caught by the van's passive-infrared cameras monitoring the front entrance of the venue. "It looks as if they are covering more ground by splitting up."

On the monitor, a two-meter round circle in red marked the GPS location of each of the team members' electronic tags that Bit had given to each of them to carry somewhere on their bodies. By using another application, he was able to overlay and track the location of each of the principal targets that they were also monitoring throughout the evening. Team members were represented as blue dots, and the surveillance targets were red dots while superimposed on a blueprint of the building.

Of course, the system only worked if each of the participants kept their cell phones with them.

"I don't get why we're doing this," Bit said as he took a bite of a Twizzler stick. "I mean, I'm not complaining. I love being out here in the field and watching from afar, but it's not like

CHAPTER TWENTY-SIX

the killer is going to strike tonight. We've already established that the women were killed within days after an event like this one, and we aren't even sure the fundraisers aren't entirely a coincidence."

"Brook likes to read a situation, as well as the subjects, in person." Sylvie shook her head when Bit offered her a Twizzler. "Did you see the way that Dr. Kolsby walked past Millie as if she wasn't there? That means it wasn't his decision to stop alienating her. In poker parlance, that is what we call a tell."

Bit held the Twizzler in between his teeth as he quickly typed out a message for Brook and Theo. He'd wanted them to know that Devin Cranston's mobile signal indicated that he was on the move. While he and his father had basically been disinvited to the fundraiser, it was still a good idea to keep tabs on them both throughout the evening. All the phones listed on the warrant had their GPS tags activated remotely to keep track of each user's location.

Devin leaving his apartment wasn't as odd as Nolan's phone being stationary at the family estate. Nolan lived alone in a high-rise that was paid for by his father. Why stay at his dad's house when no one else was there?

"So, you're saying that Millie could still be in danger." Bit had a messaging app up on the monitor, which allowed him to leave his own cell phone tucked into his pocket. He continued to monitor the other targets on the second display. According to the cell phone's GPS data, Dr. Cranston was still at his residence. "I can't believe that she brought that stuffed shirt along. I don't like him."

"You don't like anyone who works across the hall," Sylvie countered as she pulled a chip out of the numerous snack bags that he'd made sure was in the basket off to the side. The crunch was loud, but he found it cute, not that he would ever say that aloud. "Kyle and Chet aren't bad guys. Chet just isn't ready to settle down with anyone. I know next to nothing about Kyle, but he seems nice enough."

Chet Johnson had taken Sylvie out to dinner a few times. Bit might have initiated an in-depth background on the man. Before Bit had to use the information that he'd gathered, Sylvie had thankfully moved on. He wasn't sure if she was dating anyone specific right now, but she hadn't mentioned anyone recently.

"Trust me," Bit muttered as he tried to concentrate on the screen in front of him. "You're better off without a guy like that."

Sylvie sat up a little straighter and rolled her chair closer to the monitor.

"That's weird," she said over the crinkling of the chip bag. She'd folded the top down and then tossed the bag next to one of the keyboards instead of the basket. He winced at the clutter in his workspace. "I didn't see his name on the list."

Sylvie quickly picked up one of the tablets that he'd made sure was on the counter for moments like this one. She had accessed the guest list from their files. Another quick glance at the monitor confirmed whose name she was searching for among the invitees.

"Josh Perisot," Sylvie murmured with interest as Bit went ahead and quickly typed out the new intel. "He's not on the guest list, and that most definitely isn't his wife. Their wedding picture had been on the wall near the front door."

The woman who Josh was now escorting through the entrance was not someone who Bit recognized, so he quickly and efficiently stopped the footage, scanned her face, and then uploaded her photo to his facial recognition software that he might or might not have tapped into the federal database.

He'd learned quickly that being vague was in everyone's best interest.

"Nora Mallor," Bit said as he then typed her name into another program that would provide them with basic details until

CHAPTER TWENTY-SIX   221

a more thorough background check could be conducted using the proper channels. "Forty-seven years old, divorced, and a neurosurgeon."

"Well, well, well," Sylvie said as she continued to monitor the couple. "I wonder if his wife knows that he's out for a night on the town. See? We can learn some things from these types of events."

Bit and Sylvie settled back and continued to monitor the cameras for anything that looked out of place. It wasn't long before she once again had the bag of chips in her hands, eating them one at a time. She'd brought with her a travel mug of hot tea, but she'd finished that hours ago. He'd made sure that there were bottles of water, soda, and even some juice bottles in the mini-fridge. The three side panels of the appliance held his energy drinks.

"Are you..."

"I'm watching, Little T," Bit said as he rolled his chair closer with interest. He was going to have to buy rolling stools with backrests. He and Sylvie kept having to shift backwards so that they were resting against the other side of the van. "Devin Cranston is currently a mile away from our location. Do you think that he's driving here?"

Bit had pulled up the text messaging app so that it was positioned in the corner of the monitor. He wanted to be able to send Brook and Theo an alert should Devin decide to crash the event.

"There's a chance that he isn't happy with how the hospital board has handled the situation with his father," Sylvie said as she continued to watch the red dot on another screen inch closer to their location. "Think about it. When Millie accused Dr. Kolsby of murdering someone, the hospital board's answer was to transfer her out of ICU and basically accuse her of being under too much stress. Dr. Cranston parks near a burial site, and the hospital board cancels his surgeries until such time that it's determined the police have cleared him of any charges, which hasn't happened yet. Considering both men hold prominent positions, my guess is that Dr. Kolsby bills more hours with his patients. With his clientele, he's got to be raking in the money."

"I'm sure all the press coverage regarding Dr. Kolsby talking that jumper down off the hospital's roof helped their public image," Bit said as he relaxed somewhat after monitoring Devin's position on the screen pass their location. "Kolsby is practically a celebrity."

Sylvie crunched on another chip.

They would keep observing the locations of everyone to ensure that nothing was missed in the coming hours. As for what was transpiring at the fundraiser, Theo was now speaking with Millie and Kyle, while Brook was engaged in conversation with an older gentleman. She wisely had Dr. Kolsby in her line of sight.

"Did you notice that Gary Heinsel has been watching every move that Brook makes?" Sylvie asked skeptically, if not even with unsettling concern. "It's downright creepy. It's obvious that he knows who she is, but why such an odd amount of interest?"

Bit didn't have to respond to Sylvie's question, because they both understood the attraction, especially if Heinsel was guilty of murdering a woman. Something had crossed Bit's mind that he hadn't brought up in their daily debriefing this morning.

"Hey, Little T?"

"Yeah?" Sylvie finally tossed the empty bag into the small trash bin that he'd secured to the wall of the van next to the refrigerator. She turned to meet his gaze. "Uh-oh. I know that look. Plus, you pushed your hat back. What's going on in that head of yours, Bit?"

"Have you noticed that Boss hasn't given us an entire profile?"

"Yes," Sylvie said, drawing out her answer. "It's tough. I mean, she was given a suspect before finding the bodies. And we still

CHAPTER TWENTY-SIX

don't know how three of the victims died, which is a major part of how Brook drafts her profile."

"What if Heinsel is working with Kolsby? I mean, what if that's why Boss is having such a hard time?" Bit proposed hesitantly, accepting that his mind had definitely been warped since working in the private sector of law enforcement. "I've said it before, but what if there *are* two killers?"

Chapter Twenty-Seven

Brooklyn Sloane
December 2022
Monday — 9:11pm

"As I said, I believe that we handled the situation appropriately given the circumstances," Raymond Bonvoy stated matter-of-factly.

The board member had intentionally sought Brook out after hearing that she'd obtained an invitation. After all, he'd handpicked the attendees this evening either based on the balance of their portfolio or what their presence could convey to the media come tomorrow morning. Millie clearly fit in the last category, evident in Dr. Kolsby's advancement toward the stage. He was still carrying himself rather gingerly from his previous surgery.

"I think you'll see with David's upcoming speech that all has been forgiven," Raymond advised with a tight smile. "Those skeletal remains discovered have nothing to do with our most prominent psychiatrist."

"Unfortunately, the same can't be said for the hospital's top cardiothoracic surgeon," Brook pointed out, not willing to give

CHAPTER TWENTY-SEVEN

this man an inch. She didn't care for the way that he'd cornered her, and she certainly didn't appreciate his condescending tone. "I don't believe that Dr. Cranston is here tonight. I'm sure that the hospital board didn't intentionally revoke any of his privileges or tonight's invitation given that a person is innocent until proven guilty under the laws of our country. Right, Mr. Bonvoy?"

Brook had raised her voice only slightly, but he'd received her message loud and clear. Raymond was prevented from responding when there was a loud tap of the mic that echoed throughout the room. Everyone's attention was now focused on Dr. Kolsby, who stood on stage as another round of applause erupted in the room. He even took a slight bow before flashing the crowd a smile, encouraging them for more praise. It was the perfect opportunity for her to step away from Raymond Bonvoy so that she could continue monitoring the body language of the other subjects.

Gary Heinsel met her gaze without apology, even lifting the side of his mouth in a condescending smirk. She'd read over his files twice, and there was no doubt that he'd murdered his brother's lover. The motive was unclear, but there was no refuting the evidence from the crime scene.

Unfortunately, a technicality in the arrest had gotten the case thrown out, though not before Heinsel had attempted to jump from the roof of the hospital. It was evident that he was aware of who she was and why she was here.

Another interesting note was how Dr. Lance Heinsel was keeping his brother on a short leash. Such a protective nature for someone his age had her believing there was more to the story than maybe an argument gone too far.

Had Lance Heinsel convinced his brother to do something heinous that he couldn't do himself? Brook couldn't concern herself with a detour tonight, and she didn't believe Gary Heinsel had anything to do with the four victims at the burial site.

While she hadn't rounded out her profile, she was confident about certain aspects that she'd ascertained from the crime scene. The timeline also came into question. Heinsel wouldn't just change his MO in the middle of a killing spree. Serial killers refined their methods over time. They didn't just completely change their plan.

Gary Heinsel had been a patient of Dr. Kolsby. Could his involvement with their investigation be that simple? Had Dr. Kolsby been referring to his patient's crime while being awakened from a medically induced coma? Had an innocent statement led them to a much bigger crime?

There was no mistaking the fact that Millie Gwinn and Donna Laurel shared the same physical features. Laurel had been stabbed to death in a fit of rage while in her apartment, left to take her last breath in a pool of her own blood. There had been no attempt to draw her away from her apartment, no effort to remove her body from the scene, and her vehicle had still been parked in the lot next to her building.

Brook's phone vibrated, so she quickly pulled the display away from the fabric of her clutch.

Josh Perisot was a last-minute addition to the guest list. Award being given later this evening.

Those two sentences had been sent by Sylvie to let Theo and Brook know that they did not have to question the motive of his presence tonight.

"Thank you, everyone," Dr. Kolsby said in greeting to the crowd. "Thank you."

Brook shook her head at a server who had offered her another glass of champagne. She'd already had two flutes to blend in with the crowd, but there was no need to keep up appearances since all the guests' attention was currently on the man standing on stage. She quickly sought out Brett Kolsby, who was standing next to his date. His gaze wasn't on his father, though.

CHAPTER TWENTY-SEVEN

Brook followed the man's line of vision to Theo, who stood out among the crowd with his black eyepatch. However, the accessory wasn't the reason for Brett's interest. It was the fact that Theo was standing next to Millie. Though she did have her protective detail close at hand, Theo had engaged in conversation with her about ten minutes ago.

As for Catherine, she had taken the opportunity to have a discussion with her fiancé. She had a smile pasted on her face, but it didn't quite meet her eyes. She was definitely upset, and Stephen didn't seem inclined to appease her. As a matter of fact, he pulled his arm away when she attempted to place her hand on his forearm.

"As most of you know, I was in a multi-car pileup a month ago. During my recovery, a dedicated ICU nurse had some concerns about an utterance I may have made that she took to her supervisor." Dr. Kolsby paused while everyone's attention focused on Millie, whose gaze darted with unease around the room. "While Millie might have misunderstood the situation, I give her credit for standing up and doing the right thing. We don't see enough heroics in day-to-day life, do we?"

A round of applause broke out once again, though this time for Millie.

"I know you all have questions about how my subsequent situation led to the remains of four young women, but I pride myself on my work ethic." Dr. Kolsby paused to let the weight of his words settle over the crowd. "I would not and will not break patient confidentiality. I will not betray my colleagues nor my practice in that manner."

Brook met Theo's gaze, both of them astounded by the man's audacity. He was spinning his involvement and clearly pointing a finger at Dr. Cranston. This evening had been a complete setup, and the hospital board had gone along with it. Millie seemed a bit confused, but it didn't take her long to comprehend why Dr. Cranston wasn't in attendance.

Speaking of absences, Brook began to peruse the people standing near Millie. Theo was to her right, and a woman was standing to Millie's left. The protective detail was close by, but Kyle Paulson was no longer in sight.

Had Kyle gone to one of the bar stations or restrooms?

"One of the reasons that I wanted to address you this evening was to tell you myself that I will begin stepping back from my role at the hospital and my personal practice," Dr. Kolsby announced before his words were greeted with a few gasps of surprise. Brook had to hand it to the man. He certainly could play to the crowd. "I'm not here to acquire your sympathy, but instead to be a spokesperson advocating for your annual physical. You see, I was recently diagnosed with..."

Brook tuned out Dr. Kolsby's grandstanding as she continued to survey the spectators. She was pleased by the information that she'd gathered throughout the evening. The only thing that had struck her as odd was that Nolan Kolsby wasn't in attendance. From her understanding, the Kolsbys usually attended these functions as a family.

On the other hand, Nolan wasn't happy that his family had brought him into the middle of the investigation as a possible suspect. Brook didn't necessarily believe that their actions had anything to do with him. The Kolsbys had gone to great lengths to push all the attention onto the Cranstons.

Still, Bit had sent a message that stated Nolan was currently at the family estate. There was only one way to get the answer as to the reason why.

"I'm so sorry to hear about your father's diagnosis," Brook murmured to Brett as she finally made her way to his location. She'd noticed that her change in position had garnered Stephen and Catherine's attention. "I wanted you to know that Nolan has been cleared of any wrongdoing in the case involving the four remains that were found last week."

"Cleared?"

CHAPTER TWENTY-SEVEN

Brook certainly had the man's attention now.

"The only reason that my father had me and Catherine stop by your office with stipulations was for you to leave Nolan out of the investigation," Brett said testily, turning his back to his date. He held a drink in his hand, and his knuckles had turned white with agitation. "We told you the truth about Nolan's previous trouble with the law. He was young and immature. Besides, it's my understanding that the police are looking into the Cranstons. Why would you continue to look into Nolan's past?"

"The Cranstons," Brook repeated with a tilt of her head, purposefully ignoring his question. "Family friends, correct? I'm surprised you aren't more concerned about them, Mr. Kolsby. Devin was one of your best friends growing up, wasn't he?"

"Devin is the reason that my brother got into so much trouble back then. We don't really talk anymore."

"You must be referring to when the two of them bought drugs off a nurse who was stealing them from the hospital? The same nurse who went missing, and whose remains were among the four bodies found last week?" Brook tsked her tongue, which further irritated Brett. "Like I said, Nolan was cleared when we discovered that he was in rehab at the time of Andrea Firth's murder. Odd, considering that he'd attended a fundraiser the day prior."

Brook had made a conscious decision to push the boundaries that had been inadvertently set. The Kolsbys weren't usually the family who received pushback, but she wasn't someone who sat on the sidelines. Such isolated barriers had been slated for demolition, and she was now prepared for the fallout. S&E Investigations had taken Millie's case pro bono a couple of weeks ago. In that time, a lot had been discovered...except for concrete answers.

It was time to change the narrative.

"What are you insinuating, Ms. Sloane?" Brett asked as his father continued to talk about his future plans. "You have your answers. The Cranstons clearly having something to do with those remains, and you just said yourself that my brother couldn't have been involved in the murders. What is it that you're trying to prove?"

"...like to thank my children, who have been nothing short of amazing throughout my recovery," Dr. Kolsby said into the microphone. "Brett? Catherine? Please join me."

Brett had been caught unaware, but Brook still had time to illicit one more reaction.

"It's too bad that Nolan remained at the family estate this evening," Brook murmured as Brett took a step in the direction of the stage. "I'm sure he would have wanted to be included in such recognition."

"How the hell do you—"

"Brett?" Catherine called out, cutting off whatever Brett had been going to say. "Shall we?"

Brook could connect the dots, though.

Brett was well aware that Nolan was at the family estate, which begged the question—what exactly was Nolan doing at his father's residence?

Chapter Twenty-Eight

Brooklyn Sloane
December 2022
Tuesday — 6:17am

Brook had known that caffeine would be her closest ally today. While she usually only managed four hours of sleep on any given night, last night's event had her staring at her laptop until after three o'clock in the morning.

She'd fallen asleep on the couch, only to wake up to a text from Graham. He was going to try and fly back into town before the storm hit on Thursday. They hadn't really talked since their dinner last Wednesday, and she had been relieved when he hadn't pressed the issue.

She'd already picked up her large caramel macchiato from the café, walked the remaining distance to the office building, and changed out of her winter apparel for her usual office attire. Today was going to be extremely busy as they ran the leads that they had obtained from last night's gala.

Dr. Kolsby and the hospital board had used last night's fundraiser as a way to appease their benefactors. They had done that in spades, using Millie's presence to their advantage. She'd known what they had planned, and Brook understood the woman's need for normalcy after the past few weeks.

As for Brett Kolsby, he'd pretty much ignored his date the entire evening. There was no denying that he had knowledge of Nolan's presence at the family estate last night.

Catherine and her husband had some tension between the two of them, while Dr. Kolsby seemed to be very comfortable in his element. As a matter of fact, he'd ignored Brook and Theo the entire night. Dr. Kolsby always made sure that he was not in speaking distance of her. Truthfully, it was quite the turnaround after their previous discussions.

While Dr. Lance Heinsel and his brother warranted further investigation, Brook hadn't seen the doctor speak with Dr. Kolsby at all. Not once. Had that been by design or did the two of them really not run in the same circles?

Gary Heinsel was another matter altogether.

The man had posed for pictures with Dr. Kolsby and engaged in conversation for a good twenty minutes before parting ways. Brook had made a note on her daily planner to reach out to the prosecuting attorney who hadn't been able to take the man's case to trial.

There was a possibility that she could offer her advice and cull a favor or two out of the DA. The key to the investigation was Lance Heinsel. He was the reason that Donna Laurel had been killed, and that angle needed to be pursued by the investigating officers.

Brook had been in the middle of powering up her computer when she caught movement in her peripheral vision. Kyle Paulson had been in the process of reaching for the buzzer outside the double glass doors, but he didn't have to compete the motion. She used the notification on her tablet to access the application and unlock the entrance.

CHAPTER TWENTY-EIGHT

Pushing back the chair, Brook made sure to pick up her morning beverage. There were only a few sips left, but she preferred to have something to hold onto while listening to what was bothering Kyle. His movements weren't as smooth as they usually were, and she highly doubted that his agitation had anything to do with a client. He'd left the fundraiser early, and it was evident that she was about to find out the reason why.

"Good morning, Kyle. Is there something that I can help you with?"

Even with calling it an early evening, Kyle didn't appear as if he'd gotten a restful night's sleep. In fact, she doubted that he'd gone to bed at all from the exhaustion written underneath his eyes.

"How well do you know Millie Gwinn?"

Kyle's question was surprising, not that Brook allowed her emotions to be on display. She gestured toward the seating area, and he didn't hesitate to sit down on the couch. He set his briefcase on the floor, not bothering to remove his dress coat.

"I don't," Brook replied honestly as she claimed her usual seat facing the glass pane that separated her office from the waiting room. It was hard not to notice the gifts piling up on the tree skirt. "Millie is a client. Why do you ask?"

"Is it possible that she killed those women?"

There was a deep anguish in Kyle's voice, and she had the sense that it had taken everything in him to walk through her doors and lay such an accusation at her feet. While he'd worded it as a question, there was no doubt that he'd already made up his mind concerning Millie's involvement.

Brook had immersed herself with every statistic regarding serial murderers after she'd discovered her best friend's body in a cornfield. People tended to believe what they heard on television or read online without verifying the facts. They didn't know that most serial killers were social and able to navigate through daily life without anyone being the wiser. Serial murderers weren't always Caucasian males or motivated by sex. While the percentage of female serial killers were relatively low compared to that of male serial killers, there were many active cases that the Bureau had open involving the possibilities of a female killer.

Had Brook considered such a theory in this particular investigation?

Of course.

It was one of the reasons that she hadn't completed her profile.

There was still too much information that they didn't have in order to put the pieces of the investigation together. A burial site usually indicated a male serial killer. Many females lacked the physical strength to dig an improvised grave in compacted soil strewn with tree roots. Such an undertaking would be a long, arduous process while being exposed to discovery at any given moment.

Their unsub had a preference in race, age, and physical appearance.

Eighty percent of Brook's profile pointed toward a male serial killer, although she wouldn't fill out the rest of her profile until she had all the facts presented to her from the forensic anthropologist. Considering the location of the burial site from the nearest access point, the depth of which the graves had been dug, as well as the overall location...well, all three denoted a male serial killer.

"Why would you ask me that question, Mr. Paulson?" Brook asked as she crossed her legs in a casual pose. She kept things formal since neither of them had ever offered to address each other by their first names. She basically saw him in passing, and vice versa. "Did something happen last night when you were with Millie?"

"Did you know that Millie was the one who suggested Andrea Firth apply for a position at the hospital?"

CHAPTER TWENTY-EIGHT 235

Brook hadn't known that small detail, but she wouldn't go jumping the gun quite yet.

"I wasn't aware that the two knew each other," Brook replied honestly as she turned the cup in her hand. "Were they close?"

"Well, no," Kyle replied with a frown. He was sitting on the edge of the leather cushion as if he was going to stand up at any second. "She mentioned something about running into Andrea at a club downtown years ago. Millie suggested the hospital when she discovered that Andrea had been let go at an outpatient lab of some sort when the place decided to close down."

Brook made a mental note to see if Andrea Firth had been let go from the outpatient lab due to something else, like stealing supplies. Andrea had been fired from the hospital due to stealing pain medicine, so it stood to reason that such behavior had carried over to her new place of employment. No charges had been filed against her by any previous employer, but the hospital's legal department had been in the process of doing so before being told that Andrea had gone missing.

The most interesting factor in Kyle's disclosure was that Brook had specifically inquired about the names of the victims to Millie. She, in turn, had said the only name that sounded familiar was that of Laura Keery.

At no time had Millie indicated that she'd been acquainted with Andrea Firth.

"Do you have reason not to believe Millie's statement?"

"That's the thing," Kyle said as he somehow managed to lean forward even more. Brook couldn't help but glance down at his worn shoes. "An hour after we arrived at the fundraiser last night, someone brought up a woman by the name of Laura Keery. I guess she was one of the victims found at the burial site."

"And what was discussed about Ms. Keery that seemed odd to you?"

It was clear that Kyle was omitting some pertinent facts, and Brook would not handhold him into disclosing something that he believed was relevant to the case. If he had something to say, then he should come right out and be upfront with whatever details that he could provide her.

"Well, that was pretty much it, but it was the man who I overheard while I was waiting at one of the bar stations that were positioned around the room." Kyle inhaled deeply, as if he needed additional courage to share some hideous secret. "He was talking to someone and saying that maybe the police should steer clear of the upstanding doctors at the hospital and focus on Millie. That she'd had issues with all the victims. He'd heard through the grapevine that she'd said things to the police that only the killer could have known, but that she'd somehow convinced them and your firm that Dr. Kolsby was the killer. And when that didn't pan out, she then set up some cardiothoracic surgeon to take the fall."

Brook mulled over what Kyle had just shared with her, but nothing about his story added up. Bit would have his work cut out for him, because she was going to ask that he scour the footage from the main ballroom last night. She wanted a list of people who had been standing within ten feet of Kyle Paulson. She had no reason to believe that he'd lie, but she also couldn't take his word at face value.

"Is that why you left early?" Brook asked, purposefully not giving her opinion on the matter quite yet. "Were you uncomfortable staying with Millie? Do you believe that she could murder four women, carry their bodies to the trunk of her car, drive them out to the country, dig multiple five-foot deep graves, dump their bodies inside, and then fill up those graves with dirt all by herself?"

Brook could see that Kyle was doing the calculations in his head. Millie had a slight frame. She was maybe five feet and three inches tall. That wasn't to say that she couldn't have

CHAPTER TWENTY-EIGHT 237

figured out a way to carry out such a progression of acts, but again, female serial killers usually didn't take their victims to a burial site.

"I never thought through the situation like that," Kyle shared reluctantly as the tension began to ease from his shoulders.

"Did you recognize the man who said these things?" Brook asked, more interested in the male subject than her client. Everything else could be explained away easily. "Did you get a good look at him?"

"I was so shocked to hear what was being said about Millie that I didn't want to turn around and be caught listening," Kyle explained with a shake of his head. "I'm sorry, but by the time that I got my drink, Millie had joined me. I have no idea if the man was still standing behind me or if he'd left when he caught sight of her."

"Kyle, are you saying that you left the fundraiser last night because you thought there might be truth to what this man said about Millie?" Brook didn't mean to offend his sense of pride. Well, that technically wasn't true. She just really needed to understand the situation. "Did you even explain to her what you overheard? Maybe give her an opportunity to defend herself?"

"No offense, but I didn't sign on to get involved with someone who could potentially be a serial killer," Kyle said as he straightened his back in defense of his actions. "Millie and I haven't seen each other in quite a while, and I thought that last night was a way for us to reconnect."

Not to mention that such an event could have been a financial windfall for the hedge fund, but Brook didn't bother to add her two cents on the subject. Her previous statement had given her opinion of his choices loud and clear.

"I appreciate you letting me know what happened last night," Brook said as she softened her tone. She had to remind herself that it wasn't her place to judge. What she could do was figure out who had been talking loud enough for Millie's date to overhear and cause him to leave in the middle of their date. "I'll look into the situation."

Kyle seemed to want to say more on the subject, but he eventually reached for his briefcase and stood from the couch.

Brook realized that he could have gone to the police with this information. Such allegations would have made headlines. Instead, the media coverage had been playing clips of Dr. Kolsby's retirement speech and the picture that was taken of him and Gary Heinsel. The grey cloud over the hospital these last few weeks seemed to have dissipated with a simple fundraiser. It was amazing how such views could be altered with the right spin campaign.

"Kyle?"

He'd made it to the doorway of her office before she stood from the chair. She waited until he turned around to ensure that their next run-in wouldn't be an uncomfortable one.

"Thank you for informing me about last night. For what it's worth, you made the right decision to distance yourself from the situation."

"Millie had two men watching over her last night. In hindsight, that protective detail meant that no one in her presence was in any danger. I didn't even take a minute to think about that," Kyle said with regret as he slipped his right hand into the pocket of his dress coat. He pulled out a set of keys that would no doubt unlock the main doors of his office. "I don't have a high opinion of myself right now."

She could only monitor his departure with a tinge of regret.

She hadn't handled the situation as well as she could have, either. Unfortunately, she couldn't rewind the clock. What she could do was figure out who had wanted to plant such seeds of doubt in Kyle's mind about his date. What purpose was there to be gained by spinning the focus back onto Millie?

Brook had been right about today.

CHAPTER TWENTY-EIGHT

The team had their work cut out for them, and caffeine would be her closest ally next to the manpower represented by her team.

Chapter Twenty-Nine

Brooklyn Sloane
December 2022
Tuesday — 1:42pm

"Millie Gwinn was just taken down to the station for questioning. Her protective detail was shown the door shortly after the police took her into their custody. The uniform officers weren't too keen on having two armed men at the scene, either."

Brook had just collected a bottle of water to offset the amount of coffee that she'd consumed throughout the day. She slowly closed the refrigerator door as she digested Alex DeSilva's statement. It was easy to connect the dots on why Detective Soerig had pulled such a stunt, especially given that she'd only been promoted to detective last week. Her inexperience was now on full display.

Considering Soerig's initial opinion on Millie and the investigation, Brook had to assume that the detective was getting pressured by her superiors.

CHAPTER TWENTY-NINE

"Was Millie at the hospital when this happened?" Brook asked, turning on her high heels and making her way out of the kitchen. "Or at her apartment?"

"Apartment," Alex replied, sitting back in his chair if the faint squeak was anything to go by. She'd known exactly where he'd called her from, because she'd heard the annoying sound every time that he'd adjusted his lean frame during their previous meeting. "I'm not sure what has changed in the investigation, but I figured you would have let me know if you'd dropped her as a client. I already called a lawyer. He should be at the station before she even arrives with the uniformed squad."

"I appreciate you front-running the situation." Brook pulled the phone away from her ear when she stuck her head into Sylvie's office. "I need you to go down to the police station. Soerig is bringing Millie in for questioning."

"How does Soerig even know what happened last night?" Sylvie asked as she quickly pushed her chair away from her desk. She didn't waste any time collecting her dress coat. "Do you think that Kyle called the police?"

"No. Soerig was probably at one of the lakes with Theo and Raines this morning. I instructed Theo to keep them in the loop. Soerig probably shared the intel with her superior." At least, Brook was hoping that was the case. "Alex called one of their lawyers, but since this is a joint operation, I want you there for any questioning that Soerig somehow manages to conduct. I suspect any lawyer worth their money isn't going to allow their client to be questioned based on a hearsay statement made by an anonymous source."

Brook raised the phone back to her ear as she retraced her steps.

Instead of the kitchen, she entered Bit's tech room.

"Alex, I've got to do some damage control." Brook set her bottle of water down near the Charlie Brown Christmas tree. "I appreciate the heads up."

Brook disconnected the call.

She pulled a chair up beside Bit, who had turned down the holiday music coming from the sound bar.

"What's up, Boss?"

"Millie Gwinn was just taken in for questioning," Brook shared as she made herself comfortable. "What have you found on the footage from last night? Were you able to isolate Kyle at one of the bar stations?"

"I think our neighbor across the hallway has a drinking problem." Bit quickly and efficiently split the screen so that there were six feeds. "He had five drinks in the span of under three hours. It wasn't long after his fifth drink that he left, so I concentrated on that five-minute span. No one connected to the case was standing nearby, and there was no notable shift in Kyle's body language."

Brook was proud of how much Bit had learned in the past year. Granted, he'd already had street smarts and a sense for when a situation was about to go awry, but searching footage like he'd been doing today was a bit different. He'd taken what he'd learned from the team and had applied it to how he gauged people in any given situation.

"Did Kyle say he left the fundraiser immediately after overhearing some guy talk about Millie?"

"No." Brook took her time and viewed the six different footages that were all running at the same time. "You said that Kyle had five drinks in the span of less than three hours. What is this sixth frame?"

"Oh, there are more than six," Bit revealed as he motioned to a second monitor. He'd pulled up four more clips that showed Kyle from a different angle. "These cameras caught him near one of the bar stations that was positioned near the stage. In two of these, Gary Heinsel was close enough to be overheard, but so was Josh Perisot. In this frame, Brett Kolsby was nearby, but

CHAPTER TWENTY-NINE 243

he seemed to be listening more to his date than he was talking himself."

"I need to go speak with Kyle to find out what time of the evening this so-called conversation was overheard," Brook said as she pushed back her chair. "Good work, Bit. I'll be back shortly."

Sylvie wasn't in her office, which meant that she'd already left to drive to the station. The investigation seemed to have kicked up a notch, but Brook didn't like the sense that they had lost the initiative.

"Kate, I won't be long," Brook advised as she crossed the foyer. "I'm just going across the hall to—"

Brook's phone rang before she could finish her statement. She opened the glass door before looking at the lighted display. She slowed her steps as she took the call.

"Theo, I already have Sylvie on the way to the police station."

"Why?"

Brook came to a complete stop in front of the elevator bank. She'd thought that Theo had been contacting her regarding Detective Soerig taking the lead and not consulting anyone of her plans, but Brook had clearly been wrong in her assumption.

"Detective Soerig decided to bring Millie Gwinn in for questioning," Brook divulged as she took a couple of steps toward the entrance of the hedge fund. "Alex just notified me. If you weren't calling me about Millie, I take it that you found the vehicles?"

"I was actually calling you to tell you the opposite," Theo countered after a long pause. His tone had dropped a level, which usually happened when he was bothered by something. He hadn't shared anything with her regarding Hadley, and Brook hadn't seen the detective inside the building since that first morning. It could have simply been a one-night stand, but it didn't matter in the end. Brook could sense that Theo was hurt by the woman's actions. "We thought we might have something, but it turned out to be a sunken boat. The unsub had to have taken the cars somewhere else. We can expand—"

"If Detective Raines wants to expand the search perimeter, let him. I'd rather have you here. Bit has been combing over last night's footage ever since he got in this morning. A fresh set of eyes wouldn't hurt." Brook figured Theo could use a break, especially if it meant keeping the peace between the two detectives and S&E Investigations. "There's a bowl of chili in the kitchen for you from the deli. Kate hasn't put it in the fridge yet."

"I need some of those heated gloves that I keep seeing on television," Theo muttered, his bad mood coming across the line loud and clear. "I'll be back soon. Tell Kate that I'll bring her a hot chocolate from the café."

"What if Kate wasn't the one who ordered you a bowl of chili? It could have been me," Brook countered, hoping that he would take the hint. She was almost certain that her question had garnered a silent laugh. "I'll take a—"

"I've got you covered. See you soon."

She had no doubt that Theo would be reaching out to Hadley, but that situation was between them. Brook wouldn't interfere unless their choices started to compromise the case. All Hadley had done was her job, in a roundabout way. She still had a lot to learn when it came to working with other agencies. There was a good chance that her orders had been dictated to her from above, but Hadley still should have notified Theo and Detective Raines.

Brook viewed the detour of the case as nothing more than a mere distraction, which wasn't necessarily a bad thing. Whoever had attempted to turn the tables back on Millie had done so with purpose. While Hadley was otherwise preoccupied, the unsub might feel a sense of relief that the focus had been taken off the Kolsbys and Cranstons.

CHAPTER TWENTY-NINE

Brook wouldn't waste an opportunity that had been handed to her on a silver platter. She needed to find a thread somewhere that would ultimately lead to more.

She'd never been inside the offices of the hedge fund before, but there was a desk to the right of the entrance. It wasn't surprising to find that the layout was much like the offices of S&E Investigations, only without the modern décor.

"Would you please let Kyle Paulson know that I would like to speak with him?" Brook asked the receptionist who she'd seen numerous times over the past year. "Brook Sloane from next door."

"Of course, Ms. Sloane." The young woman stood from her chair and came around the large counter. "My name is Lizzy. Please, follow me. Can I get you a cup of coffee? Water? A soda, perhaps?"

Brook politely turned down the offer.

It was rather odd that Lizzy hadn't given Kyle notification before leading a guest back to his office. The receptionist walked past several offices before Brook changed her mind regarding the layout. Several office walls had been left out of the design. In its place was a very long and wide trading desk with three individuals spread out so they had room to work. While their monitors couldn't rival the ones in Bit's domain, she was quite impressed with their modern technical equipment.

"Kyle, Brook Sloane is here to see you," Lizzy announced as she entered an office on the lefthand side. Lizzy hadn't even bothered to knock. "Are you sure that I can't get you something to drink?"

"I'm sure, thank you," Brook murmured, stepping inside the doorway so that Lizzy could exit. She walked away, leaving Brook to her business. "Kyle, I'm sorry to drop in on you like this, but we've been looking through footage of last night's fundraiser. Did you leave right after you overheard what was being said about Millie?"

"No," Kyle replied as he leaned back in his chair. He pushed slightly away from his desk, where he'd been looking at several spreadsheets on the monitor. "I stayed for maybe another thirty minutes or so. Did you figure out who was behind me?"

"Not yet, but a timeline will definitely help us." Brook didn't want to waste his time any more than necessary. "I won't keep you. Thanks."

Before Kyle could say anything else, Brook retreated and began to walk down the hallway. She could sense the weight of everyone's stares. They were curious as to why she would visit Kyle during the day. It was only a matter of time before rumors began to swirl amongst this particular group.

"Ms. Sloane. Is everything alright?"

She stopped abruptly when Chet Johnson stepped out of his office directly in front of her. Considering firms like this one always gave different sized offices to their employees based on position and seniority, Chet was most likely at the lower end of the payroll.

"Hello, Chet." Brook figured that he thought she was here to discuss investing in their hedge fund, but that was far from the truth. While this past year had been a bit tenuous with financing a new firm, she was actually in the best position moneywise than she'd been in a very long time. Unfortunately, that figure wasn't what this firm would consider a high-net-worth individual. "Yes, everything is fine. Thank you for asking. I've got to get back to my office now. Have a good day."

Brook didn't waste any more time.

She had the information that the firm needed to narrow the search of the footage. While none of their current scope aided her in finishing the profile, she'd spent the morning attempting to take a step back from the various directions that the others were taking in the investigation.

Fortunately, Brook didn't have to use the biometric scanner to gain access to the office. Kate had caught sight of her and used the electronic buzzer. The lock disengaged, and Brook pulled on the door handle.

"You have a call on line one."

Brook didn't bother to go into her office. She walked up to Kate's desk and held out her hand for the receiver, waiting for the button to be pressed.

"Sloane."

"This is Murphy down at the medical examiner's office. I just notified Detective Raines. We've received the toxicology reports back from the lab, and we finally have a cause of death for the other three victims."

"And?" Brook asked as her phone vibrated in her hand. A quick glance at the display told her that Detective Raines was calling her with an update. "What have you ruled as cause of death?"

"Cyanide. My best guess? Someone used the old standby...rat poison."

Chapter Thirty

Brooklyn Sloane
December 2022
Tuesday — 6:02pm

"Is it Thursday yet?"

"It's probably not what you're after, but I keep a bottle of my favorite Moscato in the lower lefthand cabinet of the kitchen," Brook divulged to Sylvie, who seemed to seriously consider collecting the sparkling wine and pouring them both a glass. "It's been a hell of a day, hasn't it?"

Brook was sitting at the conference room table, her chair half-turned so that she could see both the wall and the 4k LED monitor. She'd almost completed her profile, but nothing fit the way that it should given what they knew of the case thus far.

Sylvie had spent the majority of the afternoon at the station with Millie. Detective Soerig had peppered their client with questions that she hadn't been able to answer. Upon the realization that the interview had garnered nothing with the exception of upsetting Raines and Theo, the detective had finally relented and eased up on the interrogation.

CHAPTER THIRTY

Brook had asked Sylvie of her opinion on Hadley's change of heart, and apparently the directive to push Millie *had* come from above. Former Senator Ponzio had been pushing for the upper brass to leave the Kolsbys and Cranstons alone.

It appeared that Dr. Cranston had just as many political connections as Dr. Kolsby.

"Did I miss something?" Sylvie asked with curiosity as she pulled out a chair. She had a cup of tea in her hand, which indicated that she didn't plan to leave the office anytime soon. Bit had gotten sidetracked with the autopsy report and instructions from Brook to see if he could locate any active serial killers in the area with that type of signature. "I don't think that I've ever seen Theo in such a bad mood. That's saying something considering we were all there for his previous eye surgery."

"You'd be in a bad mood too if you spent hours outside in this cold weather with no results to show for it." The least Brook could do for Theo was to have his back, just as she would if the situation had been the other way around and involved Sylvie. "I'm having Bit check the junkyards in the surrounding area. Theo made the calls when we first realized that the victims' vehicles were missing, but the records that the junkyards keep are rather lax. There's a chance that Bit can access their security feeds and narrow the timeline to the week after each victim went missing."

"I was going to say that we needed something to go our way, but..." Sylvie's gaze was focused on the 4k LED monitor. She'd leaned forward and wisely set her teacup on the table. "Brook, your profile states that the unsub could be a woman."

"*Could be* are the operative words, Sylvie." Brook sighed in frustration as she twirled the stylus in her hand. "Poison is usually preferred by women in most cases, but that still doesn't explain the burial site. There are more signs pointing to these murders being committed by a male unsub."

"Hey, Boss? I come bearing gifts!"

Bit had walked into the conference room, but he didn't stop until he was standing in front of the monitor. He could have used the remote that was near Sylvie, but he chose to use the touch screen feature. He quickly moved her profile to the side and brought up some of the footage that he'd been scanning on and off all day long.

Brook was pleased to note that he was no longer the hesitant and meek young man who had started at the firm a year ago. His confidence had grown, along with his maturity.

"Really?" Bit turned to look at them expectantly with his hands up in the air. "Santa Claus? I come bearing gifts? You don't get the—"

"We get the pun, Bit," Brook said wryly as pressed one end of the stylus to her forehead. Everyone had growing pains. "What have you got for us?"

"You have no jolly in your holly, do you?"

It took a moment for Bit's own words to register with him.

Of course, Sylvie spitting her tea everywhere might have had something to do with him replaying those words in his head. Brook had definitely been too hasty with her assumptions of maturity, but at least he was still the best of the best in his field.

"Oh, snap. Boss, I didn't mean—"

"Bit?" Brook interrupted, biting the inside of her cheek so that she didn't add to Sylvie's inability to breathe. "The footage?"

"Yeah, yeah," Bit murmured as he reached out and pressed the screen. "Um, I've been able to pinpoint three possible people who the stuffed shirt might have overheard at the fundraiser last night. Right here, Dr. Heinsel is talking to his date while Kyle is ordering a drink."

The footage played out, but Brook noticed that Dr. Heinsel's date laughed two times during their brief conversation. It was highly doubtful that they had been talking about Millie Gwinn killing four women and plotting to set up one or two respected doctors at the hospital.

CHAPTER THIRTY

"Next."

"Here." Bit quickly switched out the footage for another frame. "Brett and Catherine were standing at the end of the bar when Kyle ordered his fourth drink. I didn't notice them before due to the angle of the camera and an older couple standing in between the Kolsbys and the stuffed shirt."

"And the third possibility?" Brook asked, not really liking where her thoughts were taking her. "And do you really have to refer to Kyle as a stuffed shirt?"

"Stephen Averill." Bit didn't continue until he was able to press play on the last video. "And yes, Kyle Paulson is definitely a stuffed shirt. Anyway, I didn't know it was Averill standing behind the stuffed shirt due to the way that they were standing. Averill's back was to the security camera the entire time that the stuffed shirt was standing near the bar. As you can see here, the stuffed shirt walks away, and Averill stays for at least another five minutes before turning to speak with a woman."

Bit allowed the footage to play out, giving Brook and Sylvie the opportunity to witness the video themselves.

"Patience," Brook murmured as she leaned forward in her chair. "When choosing poison as a murder weapon, patience has to be ingrained into the unsub."

"The woman who Averill is speaking to is a brunette."

"Could be a coincidence," Brook countered, although she didn't have a strong opinion one way or the other. "The background check that we performed on Averill showed that he grew up in a loving home, had two doting parents, was the star quarterback for his high school football team, and he excelled in college. Not only that, but he was part of a fraternity. Nothing in his past suggests that he could be our unsub."

Brook couldn't stop her thoughts from steering to her own childhood. The same could have been said of Jacob, but what if she'd missed something? What if she'd overlooked something so minor to everyone else that she'd ignored the significance to Jacob?

"There's something else that I should mention," Bit said as he rested his hands on the back of a chair. By this time, Sylvie had used a napkin to clean up the droplets of tea that had landed on the table. She'd even thrown the napkin in the small trashcan underneath the thin table positioned next to the door. "Nolan is still at the family estate. He never went home last night."

"Given that we don't know the context of Nolan's relationship with his father outside of this current situation, it could be a normal thing for Nolan to spend some time with his dad," Brook said aloud more to benefit herself than the others. "For all we know, Nolan has made amends with his father after learning about his illness. Such a horrific diagnosis has a way of letting bygones be bygones."

Bit had stepped back in front of the large monitor to reset the screen to the way it was when he'd first entered the conference room. The way his hand stilled over the profile displayed his disbelief at the words typed out in the first paragraph regarding the unsub's gender.

"Do you think that the stuffed shirt was right about Millie?" Bit asked as he turned around to face them. He pushed at his grey knit cap the way he did when he processed information. "Are you suggesting that Millie Gwinn set all this up to deflect suspicion onto herself? Are you saying that *she* could be the serial killer?

Chapter Thirty-One

Brooklyn Sloane
December 2022
Tuesday — 6:41pm

"Older siblings are the most patient."

"My sister would agree with you," Bit said as he ate a sour patch candy. Saliva instantly pooled in Brook's mouth at watching him chew, and she had to switch her focus onto one of the monitors in front of them. "Can you believe that I once threw a steak knife at her?"

Sylvie's sour patch candy must have gotten caught in her throat. She was going to have to learn not to eat around Bit anymore.

"I wanted to be like those magicians who could throw knives and hit the apple on someone's head." Bit shrugged, as if every brother threw knives at their sisters. "The only reason that I wasn't arrested for murder was because Paula held up her hand just in time. She needed sixteen stitches. That sucker got stuck right in the middle of her palm."

Brook, Sylvie, and Bit had returned to his office so that they could pull up Millie Gwinn's hospital schedule for the past three years. Brook didn't believe for a second that their client was the unsub, and facts backed up her belief. Millie had been on a family vacation when Margo Urie had gone missing subsequent to her death.

"I think what Brook is saying is that she believes Catherine Kolsby might be our unsub," Sylvie clarified with her hand on her chest. She'd gotten her coughing fit under control and was ready to get down to business. "If Catherine is killing these women, then you might be right. Brett would be the one who transported the bodies, dug the graves, and buried the evidence."

Brook still held her stylus as she recalled Stephen Averill standing near Kyle at one of the bar stations. He'd also been seen talking to a young brunette before getting into an argument with Catherine as Dr. Kolsby was giving his speech at last night's fundraiser.

"Or her fiancé," Brook suggested as she began to clip the loose threads. "What if that is Catherine's motive? What if Stephen Averill has a roaming eye? What if he even went farther and had affairs with each of those women?"

"Catherine would have protected what was hers," Sylvie added as Bit rolled closer to his keyboard. He began to try and confirm the timeline using her schedule. "Stephen and Catherine live together, so maybe Stephen had sex with the victims at his house. Catherine found out, poisoned them, and her husband helped bury the bodies as a way to make amends for his poor behavior."

Brook had crafted the profile doing her best to focus only on the evidence provided at the crime scene and revolving around the victims. Still, it was like being thrown in the middle of a movie without knowing the characters, the setting, and the overall plot.

CHAPTER THIRTY-ONE

"The victims had no phone calls or texts from Averill," Bit said as he pulled up the phone records of the victims. "Not from Averill or any of the Kolsbys. Now that we know what we're looking for, let me pull up some footage of the other fundraisers and charity events. The ones attended by the victims were for the high-net-worth donors. A lot of the hospital personnel attended those, and..."

Brook left Bit and Sylvie to try and find some shred of evidence that Catherine or Stephen could be connected to the victims. Averill hadn't come across as someone who could easily be pulled into being an accessory to murder. It wasn't that he didn't love his fiancé, but transporting and burying the bodies for someone else took a lot of dedication.

Dedication usually reserved for siblings, not murderous spouses.

Brett Kolsby.

Could Brett and Catherine be working together?

Brook bypassed the conference room. By the time that she'd walked into her office, she'd formulated a plan. It didn't include the other police departments. Hadley had bowed under the pressure of former Senator Ponzio, and Detective Raines would want to follow the law down to the letter.

With what Brook had planned, there needed to be a bit of leeway.

She picked up her cell phone and accessed her speed dial list. Thankfully, Theo picked up on the first ring.

"Are you with Hadley right now?" Brook had been direct, but she wasn't oblivious to how Theo might have taken her inquiry. "I need you to do something, and I don't want her to know."

"I'm just leaving Devin Cranston's apartment. You mentioned earlier today that he'd driven over to Nolan's apartment last night. Given that Nolan was at his father's residence, I thought that it might benefit us to know what was going on."

"And?"

"Apparently, Devin was supposed to meet up with Nolan." Theo paused, but Brook couldn't get the sense of what he might be doing. "When I asked why they had agreed to meet, Devin said that Nolan had called him earlier yesterday to say that he might have figured out who killed Andrea Firth."

"Do I want to know why Devin shared this information with you?" Brook asked warily as she spotted Sylvie in the doorway. "He hasn't been very forthcoming thus far with the police."

"You have nothing to worry about," Theo assured her over what sounded like a scraping noise. He was also a little bit out of breath. "I think he's concerned, because Brett has been ignoring Devin's calls regarding Nolan's so-called disappearance. I didn't let on that we knew Nolan was at the family estate. Anyway, the two of them used to be close friends, and now Brett won't give him the time of day."

"I think I might know why," Brook said guardedly before going into more detail about the theories the rest of the team had been floating around the past hour. "I was hoping that you would stop by Catherine and Stephen's residence. Not without backup, of course. Sylvie will meet you there."

Sylvie nodded that she understood the assignment, but she didn't leave Brook's office to go and retrieve her coat. She motioned that she had something to add to the conversation.

"The two of you haven't been watching the weather, have you?" Theo asked through what sounded like a chatter. "The storm arrived a little earlier than expected, and there's already two inches on the ground."

"Hold on a second," Brook advised Theo, pulling the phone away from her chin to address Sylvie. "Go ahead."

"Bit just pulled up some old footage of the other fundraising events. Stephen Averill was seen talking with each of the victims. He's tied to each one of them. We might want Detective Soerig and Raines in on this."

CHAPTER THIRTY-ONE

Brook had a feeling that the two detectives would want to wait until morning, but she didn't like that Nolan's phone was still pinging from his father's residence. Add in that Brett wouldn't return Devin's phone call, and their previous theory began to grow legs.

Had Nolan figured out that Brett had been helping Catherine?

Had Brett done something to Nolan?

"Head out and meet up with Theo at a public place away from the residence," Brook instructed as she tossed the stylus down onto her desk. Her tablet was in the conference room, but she'd worry about that later. "I've changed my mind about involving Soerig and Raines. I'll call Raines to meet you there, and Soerig can meet me out at the Kolsby estate. Oh, and be careful. Theo said that the stormfront moved in sooner than expected."

"You know that Stephen and Catherine aren't going to speak with us without their lawyer," Theo said, his voice a bit more contained than it had been earlier. He must have gotten into his Jeep and was waiting for the engine to warm up. "What are you planning?"

"If we give them forewarning, you're right. They will lawyer up." Brook quickly shut down her computer and then walked over to where she'd left her winter boots underneath the coatrack. "That's why I'm driving out to the Kolsby residence. Nolan is there, and I want to speak with him."

"Do you really think Dr. Kolsby is going to allow that to happen?"

By this time, Brook had made her way over to the couch. She tossed her black high heels to the side and slipped both feet into her winter boots. She tucked her pants firmly inside so that the fabric wouldn't get wet when she walked in the snow.

"That's why I'm going to time my arrival five minutes after you and the others show up on Catherine and Stephen's doorstep," Brook explained before she stood from the couch. She'd come back to the office after driving out to Dr. Kolsby's residence. She'd collect her things then. "Dr. Kolsby will inevitably get a call from his daughter, and he'll no doubt head over to her residence. I'll then ring the doorbell after he leaves. Bit said that both Brett and Nolan were at the father's residence. There is a chance that Brett could accompany his father. Hopefully, Nolan will remain behind so that I can have a chat with him in private."

"Why not take Sylvie with you?"

"I'm taking Bit with me," Brook advised Theo as she grabbed her dress coat. She didn't even bother with her purse since she had her phone in hand. The case on the back still held her driver's license and her credit card from last night. "I'll drive the van. I walked into work this morning. Besides, Bit can keep an eye on everyone's location to let me know if I have a shot at talking with Nolan alone. He might be our only way of learning what is really taking place amongst that family as they implode. Like I said, the others will lawyer up if they realize that they are cornered."

Brook passed by Sylvie in the hallway on the way to Bit's office.

"I'll let you know when we're about to knock on Averill's door," Theo said before disconnecting their call.

"Bit, I'm taking the van."

"You're taking what?"

"The van," Brook said as she stood in the doorway. She'd already slipped her cell phone into her pocket. "Are you coming?"

Bit didn't hesitate. Instead, he hastily pushed against the clear mat underneath his chair. He had one arm shoved into the sleeve of his winter jacket in record time. She didn't move out of his way, so he was brought up short with half his jacket dangling to the side.

"You might need your firearm. Keys?"

Bit flashed her a crooked grin as he managed to find the other sleeve of his jacket. He dug into one of the pockets and produced a key fob. She snatched it out of his hand before turning on the heel of her boot. She made sure that he didn't see her smile at his astonishment as he walked over to a cabinet to unlock the drawer and collect his holstered weapon.

"That's right, Bit. I'm driving," Brook declared, figuring she'd let him know when they reached the van that he would be too busy keeping track of their targets' locations to be maneuvering through the snow. "Don't worry. I won't wreck your precious tech van."

"Famous last words," Bit muttered underneath his breath.

"What was that?"

"Nothing, Boss. Not a thing."

Chapter Thirty-Two

Brooklyn Sloane
December 2022
Tuesday — 7:32pm

"Watch the curb," Bit muttered in warning as he glanced up from the tablet in his lap. She could sense the weight of his stare when he checked to see if he'd upset her. "You know, just in case you didn't realize just how close the tires were to that last curb."

If he uttered one more advanced directive of their position to the curb, a noticeable slick spot, or a chunk of snow that had fallen off another vehicle, Brook wasn't going to be responsible for her actions. She inhaled deeply and counted to ten, just as her therapist had instructed her to do to ease the tension in her shoulders, which just so happened to be quite often lately.

Theo had texted the group maybe three minutes ago to say that they were about to knock on Averill's front door. According to the position of the couple's phones according to Bit's location application, both Stephen and Catherine were at their residence.

CHAPTER THIRTY-TWO

Brook had slowed down her speed, not that she'd been going too fast in the first place. The snow was currently coming down in large flakes the size of Texas and sticking to the ground instantly. Snowplows were out in force, but it shouldn't take long for Brook to speak with Nolan. Whatever information he divulged to the two of them could be acted upon tomorrow, unless he outright confessed that he had proof of his sister's misdeeds. Once the police had her in custody, it wouldn't be long afterward that she gave up whoever had helped her transport the bodies and dig the graves.

"Dr. Kolsby is leaving his residence," Bit said as he subconsciously rested his right hand against the dashboard. Brook had always prided herself on being a good driver, and Bit was testing her patience. "He's already at the intersection, so we should have a clear route to his estate by the time we make the next right."

"What about Nolan?"

"He's still at the residence, as well as Brett Kolsby." Bit paused, as if he was double checking his answer. His next statement had her counting to ten again. "Slick spot ahead. Did you see that car fishtail? I think he fishtailed."

"What about Devin Cranston?" Brook asked, not wanting to be blindsided when they walked into the house. If they were even invited inside the foyer, which wasn't a given. "What is his location?"

"It looks as if Devin is at his father's house."

Everything was falling into place, even the snow, which was something that they could have done without while executing such a high-stakes plan. She probably should have waited until Thursday or Friday to try and speak with Nolan, but there was something odd about him being at his father's house for the past two days without leaving for so much as a change of clothing. Plus, according to Devin, Nolan had missed a planned meeting at his apartment.

Was there a possibility that Brett and Stephen were innocent? Had they been kept in the dark about Catherine's jealousy? Were they not the ones who had been helping her dispose of the bodies after all these years?

It was reasonable for Brook to question her own work. She'd been crafting this profile backwards from the very beginning. While the older sibling held the traits of patience, loyalty, and the drive to protect those in their circle, the profile couldn't account for outside factors.

"Brett and Nolan are both here," Bit advised as Brook pulled around the circular drive until she was able to put the gear into park. She unfastened her seatbelt. Bit continued to monitor the screen on the tablet. "Dr. Kolsby is about five minutes from his daughter's residence."

Brook turned off the engine, not that Bit seemed to notice.

"Bit?"

"Yeah?"

"You're going inside with me."

Her statement had certainly garnered his attention.

"I am? I mean, I am. I'm going inside with you." Bit quickly turned off the tablet and set it down on top of the console. His seatbelt was still fastened. "Shouldn't we wait for Detective Soerig? She should be here any second."

"Bit, you're my backup."

Brook opened the driver's side door, doing her best to keep it open against the strong gusts of wind. By the time her boots hit the ground and she'd slammed the door shut, she'd counted to ten once again. The headlights of the van were directed at the section of the circular drive that broke off to take the homeowner around the back of the property.

"Bit, follow me," Brook instructed quietly after he'd finally joined her outside the van. The snow was falling harder now, but the outer lights coming from the residence gave them ample

CHAPTER THIRTY-TWO

illumination to follow the tire tracks. "How big of a garage do you think this property has off the main house?"

"It's an eight-car garage," Bit said as he lifted his grey scarf higher over his chin to protect himself from the cold. The material matched the knitted hat on top of his head. "Oh, you think..."

"It's a possibility."

They both fell into step to make the trek around the side of the house. Her grimace was both due to the falling snow and the fact that they were wasting precious time. Dr. Kolsby was most likely pulling up to his daughter's residence. Depending on how Theo, Sylvie, and Raines handled the situation, there was a good chance that Kolsby or their lawyers would send everyone packing within a few minutes.

Brook stood to lose her chance to speak with Nolan.

"Boss?"

Headlights swept across them before they'd even walked thirty feet. Brook breathed a sigh of relief and quickly turned back to the unmarked cruiser.

"Bit, take off your gloves before we enter the house," Brook advised as they came to a stop in between the van and Detective Soerig's car.

"Why?"

"So you have the ability to reach your firearm if the need arises. It's highly unlikely, but you never want to be caught off guard," Brook advised as Detective Soerig turned off the engine. She exited the car before closing the door as quietly as possible. Her frown spoke volumes, prompting Brook to give an explanation. "I'm well aware that this situation is unorthodox, but I believe—"

"That a woman is the perp. I know. I read your text," Hadley replied with disapproval. "If you believe that Catherine Kolsby is guilty, why are we even here?"

"Because Catherine didn't transport those bodies herself, and she certainly didn't dig four, five-feet deep graves in hard ground with a bunch of tree roots crisscrossing all over the place. She needed an accessory." Brook didn't like the resistance that she was getting from the newly minted detective. Had she not had a personal relationship with Theo, Brook would have requested Raines instead, but that's not how this evening had panned out. "I'd like for you to cover the back. While you're there, you might want to take a look inside the garage."

"We don't have a warrant."

"I'm not saying you should search an eight-car garage, Detective. I'm simply suggesting that you glance in one or two of the windows as you're walking past to cover the backdoor. You should know that looking through windows is covered by the plain view doctrine." Brook's cheeks were starting to lose sensation. She'd also made sure that her leather gloves had been left inside the van. She currently had her hands inside the pockets of her dress coat, much like Bit. His blue gaze was bouncing between her and Hadley as they continued to argue, which needed to stop if they were going to use their time wisely. "I'm well aware of what the general consensus of profiles is among homicide detectives. And yes, there are times when a profile can be completely off-base. That isn't the case here, Detective."

Brook and Hadley had originally come an understanding and a mutual respect. She hoped that was still the case.

"Nolan Kolsby hasn't been home to his apartment in two days. There's a reason for that, and I'd like to find out why."

Hadley had on a winter jacket with the same beanie that she'd worn as an officer. She hadn't made the full transition to detective, at least in her mindset. Brook had no doubt that the woman would excel in her field, but the shift to investigations was a complete one-eighty. It took time, and that was one thing that they didn't have on their side.

CHAPTER THIRTY-TWO

"Fine. I'll take the back."

"You have Bit's number, so please text if you happen to stumble over anything on your way around the house," Brook said, wanting to emphasize how important it was that the detective look in all the windows of the garage. "Bit, let me do most of the talking when we get inside the house."

At least, Brook hoped that they made it over the threshold.

"No worries, Boss. You lead, I follow."

They finally made it to the grand entrance where Brook rang the doorbell. A quick glance at Bit revealed that his nose and cheeks were red, and his eyes were glassy from the cold. Even standing, his leg jostled in nervous energy.

"What is it?" Brook asked as they waited for someone to answer the door. She'd gotten pretty good at reading the team, and Bit had something on his mind. "Spit it out, Bit. Now isn't the time to keep your thoughts to yourself."

"Vests."

"Vests?"

Brook was used to Bit's wayward thoughts, but he'd lost her on this one.

"Bullet proof vests with the ability to read our vitals. We need them, Boss. I'll order them tomorrow," Bit murmured, lowering his voice even more as the door began to slowly open. "If we live that long."

Chapter Thirty-Three

Brooklyn Sloane
December 2022
Tuesday — 7:53pm

"What the hell are you doing here?"

"I'd like to speak with Nolan, please," Brook stated, having already positioned herself in the doorway. Unless Brett literally shoved her back with the heavy door, she could successfully make it into the foyer. "He called me a few moments ago."

"He..." Brett let his words trail off as he glanced over his shoulder. "Peg, call my father. Now."

Thankfully, Bit didn't contradict her. He was directly on her heels with his cell phone in his right hand. He should have kept his dominate hand available, but such training wasn't inherent in him. She'd been easing him into field situations, and she realized that this could technically be called the deep end.

"Mr. Kolsby, I don't know what your problem is with Nolan calling me. I told him that I was in the area and could stop by," Brook fabricated as she took another step farther into the

CHAPTER THIRTY-THREE

foyer. Brett frowned as he unconsciously stepped back so that his personal space wasn't invaded by her. "Nolan is here, isn't he? I hope I didn't misunderstand the conversation."

"Brett, your father raised you better than to leave guests standing outside in that kind of weather," Peg admonished as she pushed him aside to open the door a bit wider. She had on her winter coat, scarf, and gloves with a set of keys in her hand. "I was just leaving for the evening, but please, come in. Don't mind Brett. A lot has happened this evening that maybe you can help us understand."

"You don't see what is going on here?" Brett asked with agitation. "It's obvious that they set this up. The police are at Catherine's house right now. Did you call Dad like I told you to? I'll call him. He can send one of his lawyers over here."

Peg sighed in exasperation as she motioned for Brook and Bit to enter the house before closing the door behind them.

"Again, I apologize for Brett's behavior." Peg set her keys down on the entryway table before reaching for the buttons on her coat. "I'll let Nolan know that you are here and make the two of you some hot cocoa. Unless you prefer coffee or tea. You'll need something to take the chill off."

"You don't need to do that, Peg. Really," Brook stressed as she motioned for Bit to keep his jacket on. "You were heading home, and we don't want to keep you. We won't be long. We just need to have a quick word with Nolan."

"Nonsense." Peg frowned and shook her head as Brett had managed to get ahold of his father. Brook could tell from the way he was speaking into the phone that she was running out of time. "I'll go get Nolan, Ms. Sloane. Please, make yourself comfortable in the den."

Brook led the way, not having to verify that Bit was right behind her. She could hear the squeak of his rubber boots with every step. Once she'd entered the den away from prying ears, she made sure that Bit was ready for any situation.

"Unzip your jacket," Brook advised quietly as she took a spot in front of the blazing fire facing the bulk of the room. It was apparent that Dr. Kolsby had been enjoying his evening before receiving a call from his daughter. "And hold your phone in your left hand. You'll have easier access to grab your weapon should you need it."

"But I won't need it, right?" Bit asked, his gaze darting from his phone to the thick double doors that they'd used to enter the den. "Right, Boss?"

"You two need to leave now," Brett exclaimed before Brook could address Bit's concern. "We aren't talking without our lawyer present."

"Nolan called me, though. He specifically stated that he wanted to speak with me in person," Brook said with a feigned frown of misunderstanding. She distanced herself from Bit slightly so that they weren't too close together should Brett decide to get physical when she pushed the issue. "Mr. Kolsby, have you even informed your brother that I'm here?"

Brett lifted his phone without taking his irritated gaze off Brook, purposefully pressing three digits in a way that couldn't be misunderstood.

"Feel free to initiate that call," Brook said as she tensed slightly. Though the residence was quite large, it would have been impossible for Nolan not to realize that someone was here or to have missed Brett's raised voice when he'd told Peg to call his father. "I'm simply here at the request of Nolan. I'm all for the police doing a welfare check on him."

Brook had baited the hook, and Brett Kolsby had swallowed it. He slowly lowered the phone, but he was prevented from answering when Peg entered the room.

"I have the milk warming on the stove," Peg said as she entered the room. "As you know, Dr. Kolsby isn't here at the moment, but..."

CHAPTER THIRTY-THREE

Peg came to a stop when she sensed the tension in the room. Her brows furrowed as she studied Brett, who was standing with his feet shoulder-width apart with the phone dangling at his side.

"Brett, please go and tell Nolan that his guests are here," Peg said sternly, clearly expecting him to follow her directive. "I'll see that our guests remain comfortable. There's no need to worry."

In that solitary statement, Brook realized her mistake.

While Catherine was probably involved with the murders, Brook was confident that the bulk of them had been committed by Peg. The profile came together seamlessly now that Brook could visualize it clearly. She wasn't clear on a few things, but she would be by the end of the evening.

"While Brett is fetching his brother, I'll go and take the milk off the stove." Peg never dropped the façade, and she even pasted on a welcoming smile just as she'd done earlier. "I won't be but a moment."

Peg quietly followed Brett out of the den as if this was any other ordinary evening. Brook quickly pulled her phone from her pocket and sent a text message to Detective Soerig before doing the same with Theo. Brook hoped to have the situation contained before Hadley decided to somehow enter the residence.

"Are you getting an M. Night Shyamalan vibe?" Bit whispered as he stared at Peg's retreating back. "Or is that just me?"

"Bit?"

"Yeah?"

"Don't drink the hot cocoa."

Chapter Thirty-Four

Brooklyn Sloane
December 2022
Tuesday — 8:11pm

"I THOUGHT STAYING IN the house in Northern Illinois was bad," Bit muttered underneath his breath. "I'll take creepy dolls over being poisoned any day."

Bit was holding up quite well under the circumstances. Brook hadn't counted on her visit turning in more than anything else but a simple interview with Nolan Kolsby. The only reason Brook was hesitating to show their hand right now was Nolan's notable absence.

Detective Soerig had sent them a text that she'd discovered the vehicles were not in the garage, but they had been parked behind the large structure partially covered by tarps. Brook had to assume that Dr. Kolsby had little to no idea what had been happening under his own roof. Then again, he had known certain details regarding a woman being stabbed. Had that been due to the knowledge that his daughter or Peg were murderers? Or had Millie reminded him of Donna Laurel?

CHAPTER THIRTY-FOUR

There were many questions that still needed to be addressed, but Brook's first priority was to ensure Nolan's safety. He was somewhere in the house, and she needed to locate him. There was a chance that he was in on covering up the murders, but Brook couldn't take the chance that his life wasn't in danger.

Brook made sure that she had easy access to her weapon, just as she had advised Bit. He'd lost the redness in his nose and cheeks now that reality had settled in, but she noticed that his he'd switched cell phone into his left hand. He was as ready for any situation as his mind would allow him to be, and she was proud that he'd smothered the latter choice of his fight or flight response.

"Here we are," Peg said as she walked into the den with a tray of mugs that had mounds of marshmallows on top. "While you two chase the chill away, I'll go see what is keeping Brett and Nolan."

"There's no need for that, Peg."

Peg stopped, and her movements stilled with her back to Brook. The older woman had heard the knowledge in Brook's tone. Seeing as she'd instructed Bit to stand near the desk, he almost certainly had a better view of the woman's face. He had also brought his right hand up and rested it on the butt of his weapon just inside his coat at the hip, causing the material to be tucked to the side.

"The police are on their way," Brook advised without raising her voice. There was no need to add a sense of panic to the situation. "I think it's best if you take a seat here in the den until they get here."

Peg didn't respond right away. By the time that she'd turned around to face Brook, she was studying her hands as if they had a life of their own. Somehow, the weathered lines on her face appeared to have deepened in the span of seconds.

"She was always my good one," Peg whispered with sadness. She sighed loudly before surprising both Brook and Bit as she made her way over to Dr. Kolsby's recliner. "My sweet, sweet Catherine."

"Peg, my advice is for you to wait for the police before giving your statement," Brook stated firmly, shooting Bit a warning glance when he clearly would have argued her stance. The investigation had become quite complicated with so many individuals involved in the process of the murders, and Brook didn't want S&E Investigations to be hung out to dry if any of the convictions failed based on their decisions in the final moments. "Again, they should be arriving shortly. What I need to know is if Nolan is okay. Is he hurt? Did he discover evidence implicating you? Catherine? Brett? I need to know where Nolan is right now, Peg."

Using Peg's first name would keep her in the present, because she appeared very determined to visit the past.

"Catherine didn't mean to hurt that poor girl. She was simply trying to save her relationship. Oh, how she had fallen hard for her Stephen," Peg said, settling back in the chair as if someone else's life wasn't at stake. Brook glanced at the doorway, but there was still no sign of Brett. "It was love at first sight, you know. It reminded me very much of my first impression of David. I realized early on that he didn't feel the same, but I still carried out the role of his wife as my own, taking care of the children over the years. I didn't want that kind of disappointment for Catherine, of course."

Brook grimaced when it was evident that Peg had simply given up. The older woman had known all along that it would end like this, and she was ready to face her punishment. Maybe Dr. Kolsby's recent diagnosis made it easier to accept her own ultimate ending.

"Uh, we are in the den," Bit whispered into the phone.

Brook had heard the vibrations of his cell phone, and he was most likely speaking with Hadley. She should be entering the house soon.

CHAPTER THIRTY-FOUR 273

"Tell Hadley to come through the front door," Brook advised him softly while still keeping an eye on the open double doors of the den. "Brett and Nolan are still unaccounted for somewhere in the house. Have her notify Theo and the others that we have a situation here."

Brook slowly pulled out her own phone and quickly hit the record button. There was no need for her to explain to Peg that she was about to recorded, because D.C. allowed for a one-party consent when recording. It had become painfully clear that Peg was in her own world.

"Catherine invited that poor girl into our home. I walked into the kitchen, and there she was...on the floor, surrounded by a pool of blood," Peg practically whispered as Brook motioned for Bit to remain in the den so that she could help Hadley search the rest of the house. He still had his cell pressed to his left ear, but he quickly lowered it to quickly shake his head in disagreement. "I had no choice but to call Brett. He always took care of his siblings. Such a kind and protective boy. We had no choice but to keep David in the dark. I don't know why he said what he said at the hospital. The three of us tried to figure it out, but we were so busy trying to find a way out. You see, David would look differently upon his children if the truth got out, and I couldn't allow for that to happen. I was the glue. Me. I held this family together through all its trials and tribulations."

"You'll be fine," Brook mouthed as she slowly took a few steps toward the double doors. She'd slowly withdrawn her firearm and motioned for him to do the same. Considering that Theo and the others had been roughly five to ten minutes away, discounting the weather, they should be arriving within minutes. She lowered her weapon to her side to show him how he should proceed. There was no need to escalate the situation, and Peg seemed very comfortable getting things off her chest. "Like this. You should already have a round in the chamber."

Bit did as he was instructed after he'd tucked his cell phone inside the pocket of his jacket. Brook had no idea if he'd disconnected the call with Hadley or just left her on the line.

"Months later, Catherine came home and was all upset that Stephen was speaking with another young woman at one of the fundraisers. I urged Catherine to invite her to the house, and that was when I showed her that there were less painful ways to get rid of one's problems." Peg seemed to have more remorse over a life that she'd desired and never obtained than the young lives that she'd taken. "Brett, that dear boy, cleaned up the mess each time. He'll make an excellent father one day, don't you think?"

Brook shook her head at Bit, who seemed inclined to answer...and one that Peg might not appreciate too much. He wisely kept his mouth shut as Brook quietly exited the den. She could have left her phone behind, but she'd recorded enough of Peg's confession for the police and prosecuting attorney. Brook had no idea if she'd need her phone, and she didn't want to be caught without it. She cautiously rounded the corner just in time to see Hadley opening the front door.

"You take the back, I'll take the upstairs," Brook whispered as she continued smoothly across the marble entryway.

Hadley simply nodded her understanding and began to clear the rest of the rooms on the main level.

Brook finally made it to the top of the stairs. She paused only long enough to try and catch the slightest of sounds that would indicate which direction Brett might have taken. While she wasn't sure of her conclusion, she had a sense that Nolan hadn't remained at the family estate of his own volition. If that did turn out to be the case, then he was in very real danger.

Since the house was quite large, Brook had wasted at least two minutes checking several bedrooms. It wasn't until she had a choice to make a right down a second hallway that she heard men's voices.

CHAPTER THIRTY-FOUR

"...wake up. Now."

Nolan's voice was inaudible, but Brett's was loud and clear.

"Nolan, wake up! Snap out of it. We're going to need you to say that Peg was the one who killed those women. All of them. Do you hear me?"

Brook silently continued down the hallway toward the open bedroom door on the righthand side. Brett had no idea that Peg was already downstairs in the study confessing to their crimes.

"Peg is keeping them busy while I get you out of the house. Come on, Nolan. Wake up! Think of Catherine."

Brook was close enough to hear that Brett's voice seemed a bit muffled. The distant pitch of his tone indicated that he was facing away from the door. She slowly peered around the frame to find Brett shaking Nolan's body, where he was lying on the bed.

"I'm going to need you to get on your knees, Brett," Brook said evenly as she slowly raised her firearm. "Fingers laced behind your head."

Movement to Brook's left showed that Detective Raines had joined the party and was moving slowly in her direction. Theo, Sylvie, and no doubt countless of other officers were now on the scene.

"We know that you transported and buried the bodies." Brook paused a moment to ensure that Brett was going to listen to reason. It didn't appear that he'd obtained a weapon in the short amount of time that he'd been out of her sight. "Your brother looks like he's having trouble waking up. Let us get him some help. Tell us what you gave him, and we'll see that he gets medical attention."

"Peg did this all on her own." By this point, Brett was facing Brook and was obviously trying to find a way out of his own self-made grave. "Peg drugged those women. She was the one who killed them. Not Catherine."

Brook could have attempted to get more information out of him, but it was pointless now that Peg had already basically given a detailed account of what had taken place over the last three years. Getting Brett on his knees so that Detective Raines could make the arrest was paramount.

"Brett, we can get everything sorted out down at the station. Detective Raines is going to enter the bedroom, place you in handcuffs, and then call for the EMTs to check on your brother," Brook explained as calmly as she could, hoping that Theo or Sylvie had found Bit and Peg in the den. An officer would need to detain her, as well. "Please, get on your knees and lace your hands behind your head."

Brook had advanced far enough into the bedroom that Detective Raines had been able to enter and assess the situation. She still couldn't spot any weapons, although Brett appeared ready to break down. He was rubbing his face in panic as he tried to come to terms with his situation.

"Nolan will back me up. He will. Peg was the one who killed those women. Catherine had nothing to do with any of it."

"Mr. Kolsby, you should do as Ms. Sloane instructed," Detective Raines advised cautiously as he took a step forward. Brook finally allowed her gaze to settle on Nolan, who was no longer conscious. Whatever Peg or Brett had drugged him with must have been potent. He had a grey pallor to him, and his chest wasn't rising and falling as steadily as it should have been. "My officers have Peg in custody, and we can all go down to the station and talk this through."

"I want my lawyer there. Do you hear me?" Brett seemed to have come to the conclusion that his lawyers could get him out of this dire situation, but that wasn't likely to happen. With Peg's testimony alone, the prosecuting attorney would have enough to take the case to trial. "I'm not saying another word without my lawyer."

CHAPTER THIRTY-FOUR

The next few moments passed without any further complications. Brook was able to reach Nolan's side and check his pulse, which seemed a bit erratic. An officer entered the room shortly thereafter and explained to her that the medics were enroute and that he would stay and ensure Nolan remained breathing on his own.

Brook holstered her weapon as she exited the room and made her way down the two hallways. She caught sight over the banister of Theo, Sylvie, and Bit standing in the foyer. It didn't take her long to reach the first level.

"You handled yourself like a true professional, Bit," Brook praised as she joined their small circle. She then focused on the other two team members. "What happened while you were at Stephen and Catherine's residence?"

"Once Dr. Kolsby got the call from Brett that you were at the house, it wasn't long before everyone started to connect the dots that we'd purposefully arranged for tonight's events to happen. Catherine brook down in tears, her fiancé didn't seem to understand what was taking place, and Dr. Kolsby then begged for his daughter to tell him what she'd done," Theo replied right as a medic entered the residence. A gust of cold wind entered first, causing the Christmas wreath on the door to swing back and forth. "It was almost as if he didn't know what his children had done. Odd, considering his confession was what cast suspicion on them in the first place."

"I'm sure Detective Soerig and Detective Raines will get to the truth," Brook said as she fastened her dress coat.

"If Catherine wasn't such a cold-blooded killer, I would have felt sorry for her," Sylvie murmured with a tinge of disgust. Her gaze trailed after the medics making their way up the stairs. "You should have seen her, Brook. She was begging for her fiancé to understand the depth of her love. She purposefully led all those women to their deaths. It was as if these family members were all corrupted by each other's sins."

"I would have traded you." Bit focused his attention on Brook. "No offense, but I'm going to have nightmares for weeks. I don't deal well with old people."

Theo lifted a hand to camouflage his grin. It quickly faded when Hadley walked into the house, followed closely by Detective Raines. The two had clearly been engaged in a dispute.

"...Kolsby is insisting that he didn't know about the murders, but that doesn't account for why he would know certain details as he was coming out from under anesthesia," Detective Raines said as he closed the door behind him. He wasn't wearing any gloves, and he immediately lifted both of his hands to his mouth to find some relief for his cold skin. "This entire family is fucked up beyond belief, in my not so humble opinion."

"You saw the youngest son upstairs," Hadley pointed out as she and Raines continued across the foyer toward the back of the house. They were obviously headed toward the kitchen. She met Theo's gaze. There was a promise lingering in her eyes, and Brook had a feeling that she would be seeing the newly minted detective in the foyer of their condo building quite often in the future. "I don't believe Nolan Kolsby had knowledge of the murders, but I certainly don't envy him right now. He clearly figured it out. You have to ask yourself how far Brett, Catherine, and Peg would have gone if they hadn't been able to get him to agree to be quiet. He looks half-dead already."

The two of them eventually disappeared from sight.

"I take it that Peg and Brett Kolsby are already on their way to the station?" Brook asked, wanting to know specific details so that she could inform their client. "From what Raines and Hadley just said, I'm going to assume that Catherine and Dr. Kolsby have also been detained?"

"Yes to both questions," Sylvie responded before pulling out her phone. "Would you like me to reach out to Alex? Millie shouldn't be needing a protective detail after this evening."

CHAPTER THIRTY-FOUR

"Yes, please. Theo, would you let Detective Raines know that he'll need to have his forensics team test the hot cocoa for poison?" Brook pulled her own cell phone out of her pocket. "I'll call our client and give her the news myself. Bit, go ahead and take the van back to the office before the roads get too bad. Sylvie can go with you. I'll ride back with Theo."

One of the benefits of being a private firm was that they didn't have to stay for the remainder of the evening while a forensics team scoured the residence and surrounding property for supporting evidence. Both Detective Raines and Hadley were in for a long night, and Brook didn't envy them. Millie had answered on the first ring, and her reaction was mostly relief that she was no longer in danger.

Technically, Millie most likely had never been in any danger. Unless, of course, Brett had decided to lash out to keep her from speaking out against them.

The team would have to wait for the official interview transcripts, but Brett had almost certainly used the location of Averill's sister to try and scare Millie out of continuing to back her own claims regarding Dr. Kolsby by breaking into the woman's apartment.

"Four deaths, and all because of one homicidal, insecure individual," Theo said as he joined Brook after her phone call. They both remained in the foyer as the medics brought Nolan down on a backboard. He still seemed to be in and out of consciousness. "Do you think he would have gone along with them?"

"No," Brook finally answered after she'd given Theo's question thoughtful consideration. "I'd like to believe that he would have done the right thing. Unfortunately, nothing will ever be the same for him after tonight. He has basically lost almost every family member overnight. Will you please make sure they reach out to his mother? Nolan will need all the mental health support that he can get in order to deal with the fallout of what his family has done. The hospital is going to have a hell of a time explaining away the highlight reel of their last very public spin campaign."

"I joined Hadley and Raines in the kitchen while you were speaking with our client. Hadley had an officer reach out to Nolan's mother already. She'll meet him at the hospital." Theo gave a small shrug when Brook shot him a look at the use of Detective Soerig's first name. He shrugged in acceptance and then held out his hand. "I won't tell if you don't tell."

Theo must have seen Graham leave the building the other night.

Brook reached across her middle and shook his hand in silence.

"What are your thoughts on Dr. Kolsby?" Theo asked as they walked toward the front door. He opened it, allowing another cold gust of wind to enter the foyer. Brook grimaced when she realized that she'd left her gloves in the van. She tucked her hands in her coat pockets as they began their trek to the Jeep parked behind Hadley's unmarked cruiser. "Do you think he knew all along?"

"I'd like to say that he didn't know, but we all sense when things aren't right with our lives...when we lose balance. He definitely knew something."

Brook thought back to that cold day when Sally had agreed to follow Jacob.

While Brook had never really said her fears about Jacob aloud, Sally had to have sensed the evil that surrounded him. The darkness that lived inside of him. While they hadn't continued to follow him that day off the highway outside of Peoria, there really hadn't been any need.

They'd *known*.

What they hadn't known back then was that knowledge was power.

Chapter Thirty-Five

Brooklyn Sloane
December 2022
Friday — 4:24pm

Colorful wrapping paper, shiny bows, and numerous strings of ribbon were strewn all over the sitting area in the foyer of S&E Investigations. Holiday music spilled from the sound bar on Kate's desk, and several glasses sat half-empty on the coffee table as voices carried down the hallway. Most of the team members were in one of the offices off the kitchen.

Brook had paid the building maintenance department to come in last night and remove one of the interior walls that separated two spare offices. That space would now be used as a common area for the team, which freed up space in the kitchen and kept them from having to crowd around one small table. There was a large, comfortable couch for Bit to use when pulling an all-nighter. She had to wonder how long it would be until he discovered that it was a pull-out. There was also a matching recliner on one side of the room while a massage chair that Sylvie never would have purchased for herself was on the other.

In addition, there was a workout area, of sorts. A small set of free weights, a treadmill, and a punching bag had been brought in and assembled on the other side of the room. The only thing that Brook had to worry about over the past few days was keeping the others from opening one of the two doors until it was time for the big reveal.

"You're not very good at this present thing, are you?" Graham asked wryly as he flicked open a large garbage bag.

"What do you mean?" Brook asked as she picked up some discarded wrapping paper. "I thought I killed it."

"How do you plan on topping those gifts next year?"

Graham smiled as he held open the garbage bag.

She crunched the paper into a ball and tossed it in.

"I will have you know that I listen to our employees," Brook reasoned as she went about collecting some more trash. "Sylvie has been going on and on about those massage chairs, Bit is always using Theo's couch to sleep on when working late, and Theo and Kate complain all the time about having to pay for gym memberships. I listened, gathered information, and bought presents based on their personal needs. I aced this whole gift-giving thing."

"I was in need of an office?" Graham asked skeptically as he had to swiftly move the garbage bag to the left in order to catch her next throw. "I will say that I like the black bookshelf with the leatherbound classics in alphabetical order. It does go with the modern décor we have going on here."

Graham's words brought her up short, because she hadn't even realized that his wife had done something similar right before she committed suicide. His good mood didn't indicate that he wasn't offended, and she hadn't decorated the spare office next to hers with that thought in mind, either.

CHAPTER THIRTY-FIVE

She'd simply needed something similar to what she'd bought the others so that they didn't know what she'd actually purchased for him. She was still debating on whether or not she should give it to him. As he'd already mentioned, she wasn't that good with the gift exchange thing.

"You need a place to work out of when you are in the city," Brook countered, attempting to keep their conversation light. She wasn't used to tiptoeing around such sensitive matters. Usually, it was other people who worried about what was said in front of her. "You own fifty percent of the business, so it only made sense."

It didn't take them long to tidy up the waiting area and take the gifts that she'd been given into her office. Graham had piled his on the couch near his suit jacket. As he walked beside her, he held up the coffee mug that Bit had given her with four capital letters on both sides—BOSS.

"Did you see his expression when he opened Sylvie's gift?" Brook asked as she set down the essential oil kit that Sylvie had given her. Each scent had something to do with relaxation, as if Sylvie was trying to hint at something. "I wouldn't be surprised if that antique doll wasn't the same one from that house in Northern Illinois."

"I don't think I've ever seen Theo laugh that hard. I do believe that he might have pulled a muscle," Graham said as he headed back out of her office.

She went ahead and set the rest of her gifts on her desk, smiling at the unique fingerless gloves that Theo had bought her. She had a feeling that he was secretly hoping for her to turn down her space heater so that it wasn't so hot in her office. That wasn't likely to happen, but she didn't mind him trying to change her mind. Not if she kept getting presents like the fingerless gloves.

"Here you go." Graham held out her glass of Moscato wine that she'd been nursing throughout the gift exchange. Speaking of her favorite wine, Kate had given her a handblown glass ornament in the shape of a wineglass, which Brook had immediately hung on the Christmas tree in the foyer. Brook hadn't had the heart to tell Kate that she didn't have a tree at home. "To another closed case."

Brook touched her wineglass to his preferred whiskey glass with a light clink. His glass had his military title etched into it, which had been a gift from Bit. In Graham's other hand was a small, gift-wrapped box with a gold bow stuck perfectly on top.

She slowly raised her gaze to his.

"You already got me a gift," Brook said softly, not taking the proffered present. All that kept registering in her mind was that it was small. As in...small enough to resemble a ring box. "See?"

Brook was pretty sure that a fruitcake couldn't fit into such a tiny box.

She purposefully reached behind her to hold up a pen that resembled the one she'd lost earlier this year. She'd spent months looking for it, still hoping that it had slipped behind a piece of furniture or had gotten stuck in the back of a desk drawer. Her bid to reach for the case that the pen was still in gave her time to sort through her thoughts for what could possibly be inside the box that was currently in his left hand.

"Brook? Open your other gift," Graham said softly with encouragement. "Please."

Brook slowly reached behind her to set the case with her pen back down on her desk. She quickly came to a decision and held up a finger as she walked around her desk to open the lower drawer.

Truthfully, she was a bit relieved that he'd gotten her an additional gift. It shouldn't have mattered, but it made her feel slightly relieved that she wouldn't appear as if she'd gone above and beyond what was expected of her.

"Well," Brook said after she cleared her throat a couple of times. She held up a small square package that she'd had wrapped at the frame shop. "Would you look at that? I'm not so bad with this gift exchange thing as you thought, am I?"

Brook was afraid that she was about to discover what she'd known all along—that she *was* really, really bad at exchanging gifts. She might have just crossed the same line that she'd been the one to draw into the sand between their personal and professional lives.

Who was she kidding?

She hadn't just crossed it.

She'd hurled herself over it without thinking about the consequences.

"On second thought, we've had a wonderful get-together with the team already, don't you think?" Brook remained behind her desk, needing the physical barrier between them. "We don't want to overdo it or anything."

What had she been thinking to contact the base that Graham's daughter had last been stationed? It was if someone else had taken over her body for those few moments it had taken to ask one of the commanding officers to check around for any type of sketch, drawing, or painting that Kelsey Elliott may have created on a whim while she'd been stationed there.

The likelihood had been almost nonexistent.

Besides, his daughter was off limits. Brook had no right to go diving into Graham's past, let alone precious memories that involved his family. Yet a package had arrived at the office yesterday with her name on it. Tucked safely inside had been a napkin with what appeared to be a coffee stain on the edge. In the middle and with lines drawn in blue ink had been a beautiful eagle with its wings spread wide as it was flying high above the ground. The accompanying note had signified the drawing had been tacked to a bulletin board. Someone had thought enough of Kelsey's drawing to save it, and the small hole in the opposite corner of the coffee stain was evidence of such action.

What had happened to the non-emotional and no-nonsense woman that Brook had been merely a year ago? She wanted that woman back with a vengeance.

"Breathe."

She hadn't realized that Graham had walked around the desk or that he'd taken the wineglass out of her hand. While his voice was barely a murmur, he respected her personal space given their location and the possibility that someone could walk down the hall at any time.

"I can't lose myself," Brook whispered as she tried to lay blame on the holidays. Everyone in the office had been so cheerful, mindful, and giving these past few days leading into Christmas. She blamed them, too. "I can't lose myself, Graham."

"It's a good thing that I'm an excellent tracker then, isn't it?" Graham shifted so that he was leaning against her desk. The rich, woodsy scent of his cologne should have had her taking a step back, but there was something so reassuring about the fragrance. He held up the small gift in the palm of his hand. "Your harness, just in case you're ever feeling lost."

"My..."

Brook frowned at him in displeasure.

He had made her curious as to what was in the box.

Clearly, that had been his intention.

"I was trying to be thoughtful," Brook said quietly as they slowly exchanged their gifts. It would be wise to micromanage any emotions that her gift might invoke, so she continued to do just that. "If I've overstepped, I—"

"You are so bad at this present thing," Graham said with a laugh. A real laugh. One where he'd thrown his head back and his eyes crinkled in the corners. "Brooklyn, open your present."

Brook picked at the tape on the side of the wrapping paper all the while giving herself a pep talk about how tomorrow would bring about a new day. Everyone else had a three-day weekend, and she would be back in her element. She would be at home, at her dining room table, in front of her dining room wall that she'd made into a murder board. She'd hunt down clues as to what her brother was planning to do next, and she wouldn't need to stress about her personal life.

Just visualizing herself in that scenario had the tension easing from her shoulders. She tossed the torn wrapping paper onto her desk and opened the small box.

"It's..." Brook had never seen anything like it before. "It's beautiful."

"It's what they call a worry ring," Graham said as he tucked his own gift underneath his arm and pulled out the intricate silver band that had undoubtedly been handcrafted with care. He took her right hand and slipped the wide band on her ring finger. She wasn't going to ask how he'd known her ring size since she hardly ever wore jewelry. "The outer layer spins around the main band, giving you the ability to rotate it when you think. You do that back-and-forth thing with a pen or stylus in between your fingers all the time. It's part of your thought process. So, I figured this ring can be your harness."

"My harness," Brook repeated as she turned her hand over. She placed her thumb on the outer ring and turned the intricate silver pattern in a circle. The motion instantly gave her a sense of calm. "Graham, thank you."

"See?" Graham flashed her a smile. "Gift exchanges can be good."

He then took his own present and tore the paper off faster than she'd anticipated, his quick movements causing her to go still. He didn't say a word as he stared down at the framed napkin, which she'd placed in a black frame to match the décor of his new office. Considering that Kelsey had put her initials in the bottom righthand corner, the drawing couldn't be mistaken as belonging to another artist.

Graham cleared his throat.

He'd been wrong.

Gift exchanges weren't always good, and she'd clearly overstepped her bounds.

Her gaze swung to the open door of her office when Theo's voice wasn't as muffled as before. He was talking to Sylvie and the others as they vacated the new common area near the kitchen. It would be mere seconds before they were back in the foyer and enjoying another round of drinks.

"I take back what I said earlier." Graham rubbed his thumb over the edge of the frame, his voice thick with emotion. "You are really good at giving presents."

Graham pushed off the desk and held the frame close as he met her gaze.

"Thank you, Brooklyn."

He was already halfway across her office before Theo came into sight, quickly followed by Sylvie, Bit, and Kate. They were all laughing and talking as they included Graham in on the conversation. He told them that he'd only be a minute, disappearing into the office next to hers.

"Brook, are you joining us?" Theo called out as he picked up his bottle of beer. "We have a few ideas about this New Year get-together that we're going to have with the other firms."

"Coming," Brook called out before glancing down at her ring.

Her worry ring.

Her harness.

Was it wrong of her to think that a ring was safer than a fruitcake?

"What a hell of a year."

Brook had whispered those words to herself as she shook off an emotion that she wasn't quite sure she recognized anymore. Picking up her wineglass, she took a healthy drink to process her thoughts. She'd only taken a few steps when she heard the chime of her cellphone. She came close to letting the call go to her voicemail, but she decided against it at the last second. Raines was still dealing with a few loose ends, and she didn't

CHAPTER THIRTY-FIVE   289

want to be the one responsible for holding up the case being handed over to the prosecutor.

"Sloane."

"Brook? This is Scott. Scotty Nevin."

She would have recognized his voice anywhere.

"Scotty, I didn't expect for you to call," Brook said as she carefully set her wineglass back down on her desk. She made sure that her back was facing the windowpane, not wanting the others to see her reaction. "I know we've been over this already. You could have simply emailed me back."

Brook couldn't help but visualize Scotty's shaggy, black hair and crooked grin. He'd been the outgoing one of the group, and the one who always led the boys into trouble.

At least, he was until Jacob had cut ties with the others.

"Your question was a bit different this time, Brook," Scotty said from a place that had to be surrounded by water. She could swear she'd picked up the sound of seagulls in the background. "I mean, my answer is the same, but your inquiry reminded me of when George got lost in the woods. Do you remember that?"

"Yes, I do." Brook wanted to smile at the memory of George Rickers taking the wrong path to the waterfall one morning, but something in Scotty's voice struck a chord. Everyone had banded together into small groups to search for him. They had located him in under four hours, though. "George was fine. Embarrassed, if I recall, but physically fine. The camp counselors didn't even inform his parents. It was a non-issue, Scotty."

"You asked me years ago if I could recall anything that happened to Jacob during those years, and I said no. I stick by my answer, but your email asked if anything happened that *didn't* include Jacob. That would be George."

"I don't understand," Brook said quietly as she rounded her desk and slowly sat down in her chair. Graham had joined the others, though every now and then one of them would glance her way to see what the holdup was that prevented her from joining them. When she looked back down at her hand, she caught herself subconsciously spinning her worry ring. Something told her that she was going to need her newfound harness for the rest of this call. "Scotty, why would George taking a wrong path to a waterfall have anything to do with Jacob?"

"We were all assigned search groups. You were with the younger kids, so you might not remember. Jacob was supposed to be with me and Daryl, but he said that he had to go back to the cabin for something. He told us that he'd catch up."

Another cry of a seagull cut through the line. The sound was quite ominous in contrast to the Christmas lights blinking on the tree in the corner of the foyer.

"Jacob never caught up with us, Brook. Once George was found, we all returned to the campground. The activities carried on as if George had never been missing in the first place. I don't recall exactly when Jacob rejoined the group, but I do remember that he was with us by the time the counselors let us have a bonfire that night."

"Four hours," Brook murmured more to herself than Scotty. Four hours was how long George had been missing. "You never asked Jacob why he didn't catch up with you that day?"

"No. I'm telling you, Brook. Jacob was fine by the time everyone showed up for the bonfire."

Scotty could continue to pull the wool over his eyes, but that was the summer when everything had changed. Brook had spoken to everyone she could from back then, and she'd always focused on situations or events that had happened *to* Jacob. George being lost in the woods for four hours had never even entered into the equation.

"That's the thing, Scotty. Jacob wasn't fine after that summer." Brook experienced a stirring in her stomach that hadn't been there since her brother had left the city. She'd just been given another present. "Something happened to my brother during those four hours. Something that will give me the answers that I've been searching for my entire life."

Chapter Thirty-Six

Jacob Walsh
December 2022
Saturday — 8:57pm

CHRISTMAS EVE. Not his favorite time of year, but tomorrow seemed very appropriate for him to finally be given a gift.

One that would cleanse his soul...for a time.

Jacob stood on the sidewalk across from a modest two-story home. A string of white Christmas lights had been strung across the eaves of the rooftop and wrapped around every beam of the porch. The steady lights couldn't hold a candle to the twinkling, colorful lights that had been draped around two pine trees in the front yard. To top off the holiday scene before him, the family's Christmas tree had been placed front and center of a living room window for all to see from afar.

The setting gave off the allure of a perfect family.

One that was nothing but a façade.

That didn't mean he couldn't appreciate the stillness of the evening. It was almost palpable, and the way the snow fell from

CHAPTER THIRTY-SIX

the overcast sky above was quite serene. The tranquil scene reminded him of the snow globe that his sister always insisted be set in the middle of the coffee table during the holiday season. He came to understand later in life why that snow globe had captured Brook's attention. The small illusion had held all her hopes and dreams that had never come to fruition...would never come to fruition.

The family who owned the house that he had been monitoring closely for the past few days belonged to a U.S. marshal. He was nothing more than a name among many that Jacob had ascertained from when he'd been in North Dakota.

Duluth, Minnesota wasn't much different when it came to the cold weather. He didn't care much one way or the other where his search took him, as long as it resulted in his coming face to face with Sarah Evanston once more.

They had unfinished business.

Movement in the window caught his attention.

A little girl had bumped into the tree as she clearly attempted to hide from her parents. She couldn't have been more than four years old. The pink pajamas and the high ponytail gave away her parents' intention, but she was obviously very stubborn. Santa Claus was coming to town, and she didn't want to miss his grand entrance as he made his way down the chimney.

Jacob recalled having to keep up the Santa Claus ruse with Brook during those few years after he'd figured out the truth until she'd come to learn that there was nothing magical about life. He'd thought of life the same way until that summer.

The summer that had put everything into the proper perspective.

There had been times throughout his life when he wished that he'd joined his friends in the search party. The one formed to find George Rickers when he'd gotten lost one day at camp. Then Jacob could have carried on and pretended life was grand as everyone else believed, but then he wouldn't have discovered the truth.

He would never have had the precious gift of being touched by evil.

The little girl in the window reminded him of Brook. He was surprised when she turned to stare out at the snow. She'd pressed her hands against the cold glass as she looked out over her front yard. He could sense the second that she'd caught sight of his large, dark form standing underneath the streetlamp. Her body movements had stilled, and she'd tilted her head to the side as she studied him.

The little girl showed no sign of fear.

Whether it was the excitement of Santa's arrival or her stubbornness at not wanting to go to bed, she wasn't at all frightened of his presence. She even removed her hand from the window and moved it side to side as she smiled brightly out into the cold night.

Jacob was slow to respond, because it hadn't been his intention to engage with anyone this evening. He'd simply been conducting his nightly walk, tamping down his eagerness for when the marshal began his usual cycle of meeting with those assigned underneath his care.

Wherever the man's travels took him, Jacob would be one step behind. If the marshal turned out not to be Sarah Evanston's handler, that was fine. Jacob would simply turn his attention to the next name on the list.

The little girl waved a bit more eagerly when it was clear that she was about to be found by her mother. Who was he to steal Christmas from a little girl who reminded him so much of his baby sister?

Jacob waved back before he disappeared into the cold darkness.

~ The End ~

CHAPTER THIRTY-SIX

From obsession to death, this pulse-pounding thriller within the Touch of Evil Series by USA Today Bestselling Author Kennedy Layne will leave you looking over your shoulder...

Click HERE

Former FBI consultant Brooklyn Sloane is about to walk into her favorite café wanting nothing more than her usual morning caramel macchiato when she notices a bloody handprint on the window. Anyone else would have instructed the barista to call the police, picked up her favorite beverage off the counter, and then walked the rest of the way to the office.

Brook isn't just anyone, though. She recognizes the signature of a serial killer who used to haunt the city over three years ago before abruptly disappearing into the restless wind. He had been known to stalk his victims for weeks before abducting and killing them. Their bodies had never been found, but he'd made sure that their loved ones knew of their demise with a single, bloody handprint...at the very place that they had gone missing.

Brook has one objective—draft a profile to find the killer before he strikes again. But as the team dives deeper into the case and into the lives of the previous victims, a twist in the investigation finally reveals itself. The killer has been dead ever since the previous killings had stopped. Are they chasing a copycat killer or something far worse?

OTHER BOOKS BY KENNEDY LAYNE

Touch of Evil Series

Thirst for Sin
Longing for Sin
Awakening Sin
Possessed by Sin
Corrupted by Sin
Fleeing from Sin

The Widow Taker Trilogy

OTHER BOOKS BY KENNEDY LAYNE

The Forgotten Widow
The Isolated Widow
The Reclusive Widow

Hex on Me Mysteries

If the Curse Fits
Cursing up the Wrong Tree
The Squeaky Ghost Gets the Curse
The Curse that Bites
Curse Me Under the Mistletoe
Gone Cursing

Paramour Bay Mysteries

Magical Blend
Bewitching Blend
Enchanting Blend
Haunting Blend
Charming Blend
Spellbinding Blend

Cryptic Blend
Broomstick Blend
Spirited Blend
Yuletide Blend
Baffling Blend
Phantom Blend
Batty Blend
Pumpkin Blend
Frosty Blend
Stony Blend
Cocoa Blend
Shamrock Blend
Campfire Blend
Stormy Blend
Sparkling Blend
Hallow Blend
Dandelion Blend

Office Roulette Series

Means
Motive
Opportunity

Keys to Love Series

Unlocking Fear
Unlocking Secrets
Unlocking Lies
Unlocking Shadows
Unlocking Darkness

Surviving Ashes Series

Essential Beginnings
Hidden Flames
Buried Flames
Endless Flames
Rising Flames

CSA Case Files Series

Captured Innocence
Sinful Resurrection
Renewed Faith

Campaign of Desire
Internal Temptation
Radiant Surrender
Redeem My Heart
A Mission of Love

Red Starr Series

Starr's Awakening
Hearths of Fire
Targets Entangled
Igniting Passion
Untold Devotion
Fulfilling Promises
Fated Identity
Red's Salvation

The Safeguard Series

Brutal Obsession
Faithful Addiction
Distant Illusions

OTHER BOOKS BY KENNEDY LAYNE

Casual Impressions
Honest Intentions
Deadly Premonitions

About the Author

Kennedy Layne is a USA Today bestselling author. She draws inspiration for her romantic thrillers in part from her not-so-secret second life as a wife of a retired Marine Master Sergeant. He doubles as her critique partner, beta reader, and military consultant. Kennedy also has a deep love for cozy mysteries, thrillers, and basically any book that can keep her guessing until the very end. They live in the Midwest with their menagerie of pets. The loyal dogs and mischievous cats appreciate her writing days as much as she does, usually curled up in front of the fireplace.

ABOUT THE AUTHOR

Email:

kennedylayneauthor@gmail.com

Facebook:

facebook.com/kennedy.layne.94

Twitter:

twitter.com/KennedyL_Author

Website:

www.kennedylayne.com

Newsletter:

www.kennedy-layne.com/meet-kennedy.html